THE
pool boy

A NASHVILLE NEIGHBORHOOD BOOK

NIKKI SLOANE

Beach Ball Edition

ISBN 978-1-949409-08-6

For Nick

ONE

Erika

When Clark's phone rang, his gaze flicked to mine. It was loud in the trendy restaurant, and his phone was on silent, but it rested face down on the table, so I could feel the vibration of it through my elbows planted on the tabletop.

He flipped it over and glanced at the screen, and he didn't have to say anything for me to know who was calling. His hesitant expression announced it was his boss, Derrick, and the software upgrade his company was rolling out was not going well.

I pressed my lips together to hold in my disappointment. We'd known for weeks going out tonight would be risky. Clark had been a programmer for Hale Banking and Holding Company long before we'd met and gotten married, and never once had an upgrade gone off without a hitch.

"It's okay," I said, pushing out a smile. "At least we made it through most of dinner."

He shot me an apologetic look as he stood and snatched up his phone. It was too loud in here, so he'd take the call outside. "Maybe they just have a question."

I quirked my eyebrow and tilted my head to let him know I thought he was dreaming. It seemed like the Nashville branch of HBHC couldn't run without him. I'd joked more than once that Derrick was his work husband and saw Clark far more often than I did. Processing servers were always going down, or a single error in a line of code would cause a massive issue, requiring him at all hours of the day.

Even on special nights like this one.

He wasn't outside long, and when he came back to the table, he didn't sit. "They, uh . . . need me to come in."

Of course they do, I wanted to snap.

My husband was an attractive man. He worked out three times a week with a trainer, had a handsome face, and took pride in his appearance. But I couldn't look at him, too frustrated with the situation. Instead, I stared at the remainder of the steak I'd ordered for dinner.

"Hopefully it won't take long," he added. "But I'm really sorry."

"It's okay," I lied, and forced brightness into my voice. "I'll take an Uber and see you at home. Good luck with the system."

"Thanks." He leaned down and dropped a quick kiss on my forehead. "Happy birthday, Erika."

That was what he left me with. No *I love you* or a kiss containing a speck of passion. I shouldn't have been surprised. My husband had never been affectionate, and over the last few years, his sex drive had faded to nothing—right as mine had ramped up to the max. Once the desire for me had gone, it seemed unlikely it'd ever come back.

Not unless I did something drastic.

I stared across the long, narrow dining room, wrapped with exposed brick, and considered my options. It meant I was deep in thought when the waiter appeared at the table-side and gestured to Clark's plate.

"Do you know if he's finished? Should I get these plates out of the way?"

"Yes, he's done," I said. "He had to go."

The man slowed as he collected the dish. "Oh. The gentleman said it was your birthday and ordered dessert. We were going to sing." He delivered an amused smile. "You still want that? Our voices aren't great, but our chocolate cake is."

I shook my head. "Oh, no, thank you."

He gathered the silverware and stacked it on the plates, resting in the crook of his arm. "You sure? You only turn twenty-one once."

When he winked, it was playful and harmless, and I couldn't help but chuckle. "Oh? And what about forty-two?"

He blinked in surprise, then looked at me dubiously. "No way." He shook his head. "Wow. No lie. I would have guessed early thirties at the most."

Warmth bloomed inside me. It was nice to hear, and he'd seemed genuine. "Thank you."

I'd been blessed with both good genes and a mother who believed her children weren't allowed to see the sun until she'd applied sunscreen to every inch of them. I looked young. My boss, Ardy, referred to me as "kid," even though he was just ten years older than I was.

But he also called nearly everyone "kid."

It also helped that over the last year, I'd gotten in the best shape of my life. I'd been focused to hit my goal by my next birthday, and this morning in the gym, I'd stepped up to the pullup bar and knocked out ten chin-ups without assistance.

So, tonight wasn't about turning a year older so much as it was a celebration of a year of hard work and determination.

The waiter brought me the chocolate cake anyway, but he was smart enough to put it in a take-home box. "In case you change your mind. Happy birthday."

I hadn't had sweets in forever, and as I stared at the white box, I was suddenly grateful. Clark probably wouldn't be home until the middle of the night, and a slice of cake would be a nice consolation prize.

It was around eleven o'clock that night when I got the idea. I'd been sitting on the covered back patio, holding a glass of cabernet sauvignon, and staring at my pool. It was lit by the underwater lamp in the deep end, and the shimmering water was enticing.

My first thought was to go for a swim. It was hot out, even by August's standards. I could leave my swimsuit in the house and skinny dip. It was something I'd never done before, partly because I'd spent a lot of my adult life not feeling comfortable with how I looked. Our backyard backed up to a forest and was large, putting distance between my neighbors on both sides. But it sloped down toward Dr. Lowe's house, meaning it was possible he could see over the top of our shared fence.

He didn't let it bother him.

A smile teased my lips. I'd never actually seen them because his hot tub was up against the house and hidden from view, but I'd heard Dr. Lowe and his girlfriend *enjoying* each other. The girl was half his age and quite vocal.

It'd given me a dull pang of jealousy. Not over Dr. Lowe, but young Cassidy Shepard. Apparently, she'd been lucky enough to find a partner whose sexual appetite matched the one inside me, and from the sound of it . . . the good doctor could keep her satisfied.

I stared at the pool, watching the pretty pattern of the pool liner bend and distort as the subtle ripples caused by the pump moved through the water. Dr. Lowe wasn't home right now. His house was dark, and I'd seen his car leaving the subdivision when the Uber brought me home a few hours ago.

If I went for a swim, perhaps Clark would come home, find me naked in the pool, and the sight of my bare, wet skin would be enough to entice him into joining me.

But it was also likely he'd be trapped at the office for hours, and by the time he walked through the door, I'd be pruney and cold, and he'd be cranky and tired. I had no control over when he'd be done.

I picked up the takeout container and carried both it and my wine glass inside the house, depositing them in the kitchen, before moving into my bedroom. My birthday present—the one I'd bought myself—was still in the box it'd been delivered in and tucked away in the back of my closet.

The deep red mesh and lace bodysuit cost more than I typically paid for an outfit, and this was something only Clark and I would ever see. If I were honest with myself, it was more for me than him. Sure, I wanted him to take one look at me packaged in the sexy lingerie and hopefully he'd remember I was a sexual being. That he'd used to find me attractive and now I looked better than ever.

But it was also a frivolous present to celebrate my success.

I stripped off my clothes and pulled the delicate fabric up over my curves, hooking the clasp in the back closed, then stood in front of the mirror to evaluate. My long, straight hair was a light auburn. The hue was so warm, I could pass as a redhead some days. I had blue eyes and fair skin, and last week at a launch party, a guy told me I reminded him of Amy Adams. He was drunk and maybe nearsighted, but I took the compliment anyway.

For the first time in forever, a pleased thrill shot down through me as I stared at my reflection. The crimson band belted across my natural waist was tight, but not unflattering. My arms had tone to them, and my thighs were proportional to the rest of me. I looked . . .

Hot.

Unexpected tears pricked my eyes, and I rapidly blinked them back, while sucking in a deep breath. I wasn't about to start crying over my excitement at how I looked. I mean, how fucking narcissistic would that be? And it wasn't even excitement, it was more like relief.

I set a hand on my hip and shifted on my black heels, tilting my head. For being so expensive, the lingerie wasn't exactly comfortable. The seams were kind of itchy. I slipped a hand into one of the cups and lifted my breast up, trying to fill the fabric better. The worst part about the weight loss was I'd lost a full cup-size in my bra. I'd never had big breasts, but now they were tiny.

Maybe I'd give myself another birthday present and get my boobs done. I'd been thinking about it a lot recently. Between my job at Warbler Talent and Clark's at HBHC, we could easily afford what we wanted. It also helped that we were debt-free.

I raked my hand through my hair, shaking a tangle loose, and pressed my lips together. The red bodysuit concealed my nipples and the cleft between my legs, but it didn't leave much to the imagination. God, it made me feel sexy. I wanted to be a smoldering temptress Clark couldn't refuse.

The makeup I'd worn to dinner was too subtle for what I had in mind now. As I leaned over the sink to get closer to the mirror, applying the darkest eyeshadow I had in my palette, I plotted my idea. I still had Clark's passcode to get into the building from last week, when I'd run dinner over to him.

It was ridiculous to wear my trench coat in August, but the lingerie was empowering, and the coat was part of the fantasy. I'd strut into Clark's office, drop it from my shoulders, and then have my way with him right there. It'd be almost midnight by the time I got into the building, and it was likely to be just him and Derrick still working on the problem. They were usually the last to leave after a crisis.

Plus, it was my birthday.

Clark was close friends with Derrick, and he probably wouldn't blink an eye when I showed up and asked to borrow my husband for a few minutes. Really, it was the least the company could do. Clark basically gave them all his nights and weekends. They could give me twenty minutes.

My bare thighs squeezed together beneath my coat as I drove to the HBHC office and parked in the parking garage beside the building. My sex-starved body tingled with excitement. It quickened my steps on my heels as I darted to the elevator and hurried to press the button.

Like me, Clark had been transforming over the last year. He'd always been attractive, but when I made my commitment to the gym, he matched it. He'd lost inches in his waist and gained them in his chest, filling out the sleeves of his dress shirts. I certainly wasn't going to complain about how he looked.

Maybe just how sore and tired he always was.

I had not missed the way a woman gazed at him tonight when we'd first come into the restaurant for dinner. She'd glanced up with a lifted eyebrow and parted lips, like he'd taken her breath. Six months ago, it might have filled me with pride that my husband caused strangers to lust after him. I would have grinned to myself that I was the one he chose to be with.

But . . . it didn't feel true anymore. Clark and I shared a bed most nights, but he hadn't shared himself with me in ages.

I rode the stifling, dingy elevator car down to the ground floor and was determined to change that. He wouldn't refuse me tonight, and once we reconnected, I'd get us back on course.

It was a short stroll down the sidewalk to the lobby doors, and once I was in the dark atrium, I went to the elevator bank and typed in Clark's code. The dull chime rang out, and the doors slid back to reveal a brightly lit and, thankfully, empty elevator car.

His office was near the top of the building, and the floor was shrouded in shadows. Out the windows, the city winked back at me. Most of the surrounding buildings were dark on the inside, but their roofs were lit, sketching the Nashville skyline.

I stood in the receptionist area and tweaked my head, listening for signs of life, but the floor was utterly silent. If the rest of Clark's team were still here, they must all be gathered in the server room several floors down.

My coat swished softly as my anxious hands tightened the sash at my waist. I was technically more covered than I'd been at dinner, but I felt naked anyway. The seams of my lingerie brushed and shifted against my skin, sensitizing me. I swallowed thickly as I approached Clark's closed office door, fighting back the urge to hurry. No one was around or going to catch me as I—

"Oh, *fuck*," a deep male voice groaned softly from behind the door.

I paused, my hand on the doorknob. Maybe if I hadn't been caught off guard, I might have been able to identify the speaker. Or, perhaps if I'd heard the sound of pleasure in my husband's voice sometime within the last four months, I would have known it was his.

But it was unrecognizable tonight.

Quiet gasps and sighs seeped from beneath the door, coupled with steady, rhythmic thumping, and it made my heart race inside my chest. My breathing went so shallow, thoughts stopped processing in my brain.

On some level, I knew what I was going to find, and although I didn't want to see it, my hand moved anyway. It turned the doorknob and pushed the door open, forcing me to look inside the office. My muscles tensed so fiercely; I couldn't move.

Clark's pants and boxers were pooled around his ankles, exposing his toned legs, and his shirt was hitched up out of the way. I stared at him in confusion, unable to understand the pair of hands latched onto his hips.

For a long moment, I struggled to interpret anything, but mostly, why my husband was bent over his desk, and why his boss Derrick was behind him, his pants also puddled at his feet.

TWO

- TEN MONTHS LATER -

Erika

Sweat trickled down my back, making my sleeveless silk blouse stick to my skin. Okay, this was getting ridiculous. The air conditioning at the office had never been great, and it had barely been working this morning, but now? It wasn't at all.

The once historic house had been converted into a commercial office back in the eighties, and the June heatwave gripping the city right now was too much for its ancient air system. The antique blue building was full of southern charm and had a great location beside Music Row, but the house came with drawbacks. The last hour at my desk, after I'd come back from lunch, had been unbearable.

If it were this hot on the main floor, I could only imagine how bad it was upstairs in the recording studio. I couldn't get any work done today. I was too busy melting. I picked up my phone and thumbed out a text to the owner of the agency.

> Me: It's 85 degrees in here and still climbing.

> Ardy: You're in the office?

I blinked. It was three o'clock on a Tuesday.

> Me: Am I supposed to be somewhere else?

Ardy: The air is broken. Maintenance said the earliest they can fix it is tomorrow. I thought Charlotte told you.

Since he couldn't see me, I made a face. I loved Ardy, but I tolerated his daughter, Charlotte. She was nineteen and supposed to be the office manager, but I was as hazy as she was on what her job responsibilities were. There were a lot of days she came and went as she pleased, or never materialized at all.

Her daddy was the boss, and she was the apple of his eye, and so she could solve any issue he had with her by flashing a simple smile.

Me: No, she didn't tell me.

Ardy: Sorry about that. Cut out early and lock up. I've got a meeting with Stella's team.

Me: You got it.

He was referring to Stella Mills, who was such a huge star, she was his only client. Like Taylor Swift, Stella had started in country music before crossing over to pop, and now, she had two Grammys tucked beneath her rhinestone belt. Ardy rarely came into the office and never when she was in town. He was focused only on her.

I stood, rolled my chair into my desk, and grabbed my purse. I didn't have any work I couldn't do outside the office and was relieved to get out of the sweltering space.

It felt like everything was going my way on the drive home. By leaving work early, I beat the traffic, and my commute took half the time it usually did. The demos I listened to on the drive weren't half bad either. Most didn't have a sound I was looking for, but at least none of them had me racing to skip to the next recording on my phone.

But my good luck ran out after I'd parked in my garage and then strolled down the driveway to grab the mail. There was a thick envelope waiting for me and the return address was my divorce attorney's letterhead.

"What now?" I groaned, collecting the mail and slamming the box closed.

During the divorce, Clark had fought me on everything. I gazed up at the house as I walked toward it and ground my teeth. At least I'd gotten to keep my home. It was one of only two things I really wanted anyway. He'd argued it was too much house just for me, but I countered that I'd been alone in that house for nearly a year before we separated because he was never home.

He'd been having an affair with Derrick all that time.

It'd been ten months since I'd walked into my husband's office and found him getting fucked by his boss, but I remembered the scene like it had happened an hour ago. How Clark was bent over, his hands splayed out on the desktop. How Derrick loomed behind him, his pelvis fitted tightly against Clark's bare ass. How their faces were flushed and shiny with sweat, and both of their mouths hung open in pleasure.

But most of all, I remembered the idiotic thought that struck me in that moment. It wasn't shock, or anger, or really even hurt . . . although those emotions came later. The first thing to leap into my mind when confronted with the image of these two men together, was that my husband's dick swinging between his legs was hard. Harder than I'd ever seen it in my life.

All the years we'd been together, and I hadn't known he was capable.

My sharp gasp yanked the men's attention to me, and then they both issued their own horrified gasps. They couldn't move fast enough, tripping over the pants wadded at their ankles as they hurried to separate and cover themselves.

"Erika," Clark blurted out, as he jerked up his pants. "What are you doing here?"

I back pedaled, unable to speak or rip my gaze away. As soon as Derrick had his pants up, he raced to zip his fly, and my gaze zeroed in on his wedding band. I'd met his wife a few times at the annual holiday party.

My mind was disconnected, but my body activated on the desire to flee, to try to outrun the emotional pain that would arrive any moment.

"Oh, fuck. Wait," Clark pleaded.

I didn't. I reeled around blindly, dashing for the elevators.

If I'd been able to register the desperation in his voice, it might have been heartbreaking. "*Please*, Erika. I'm so sorry."

He caught up to me right after I'd slapped the down button, forcing me to wait to finish my escape. I couldn't look at him. Instead, I focused on the carpet at the edge of the elevator doors and listened for the chime to announce its arrival.

By the time I boarded the car, he was crying. The first time I'd ever seen him do it. The story spilled from him in a mess of words as we rode together down to the lobby, him trying to explain how he wasn't bisexual or gay. He claimed he didn't like men, and neither did Derrick. That they'd become friends and bonded when they worked out together. They'd tried to fight off this thing between them, but their connection was too powerful.

He sobbed that they hadn't wanted to fall in love with each other.

"Love?" I repeated in horror. "How can you be in love when you're married to other people?"

It was the stupidest question.

Wasn't I already aware marriage didn't mean a thing to some people? Like my father. He'd had at least two affairs that my mother knew about, before leaving her for my stepmother. He'd probably had more. My father had always suffered from a wandering eye. Even now, I doubted he was staying faithful.

Clark hadn't been anything like that. He never looked at another woman once we were together. I'd thought we were rock solid in that department.

I sank my teeth into my bottom lip and let my eyes fill with tears as he begged for forgiveness. Didn't he know it was way, *way* too soon for that? I stood motionless and numb as he planted his face in my chest and shook with emotion. His fists curled around the edges of my coat, holding me to him, before he stilled. He drew back just enough, so I could see the puzzled look on his face.

He was wondering what the hell I was wearing.

I swallowed down my embarrassment. I'd come here tonight with a plan of seduction, completely unaware my husband was in love with someone else. He'd made me an oblivious fool.

A tiny voice cried out in my head that he'd done this to me on my birthday.

My voice was empty because I'd become a husk. "I loved you."

"I know," he whispered. "I loved you too. I'm sorry. I didn't mean to hurt you."

It wasn't the first lie he'd ever told me, and it certainly wouldn't be the last either.

I trudged toward the house, carrying the thick envelope along with my thoughts about the fallout that ensued. I'd done my best to stay civil, at first. We agreed via a short exchange of texts that he'd find somewhere else to stay for a few days, and I'd contact him when I was ready to talk.

But Clark couldn't even give me that.

I'd come home the morning after my birthday from my best friend Jenna's house to discover him packing his things in boxes, and the Fender American Standard Stratocaster guitar leaning against them.

"What the fuck are you doing?" I was too emotionally exhausted to control myself. "You don't even know how to play."

But I did. When we'd met in college, I'd been pursuing my dream of becoming a singer-songwriter. Clark had proposed to me onstage one night after my weekly set, saying my music had captured his heart, and he wanted to spend the rest of his life listening to me.

Clark straightened stiffly, and when his hand flexed possessively around the neck of the beautiful instrument

I'd used to create my favorite songs, I felt his fingers on my throat choking me.

His tone was sharp and definitive. "This was a gift from *my* parents."

"Yeah," I snapped. "A wedding gift to us."

I'd found his parents' present both romantic and encouraging. Ultimately, I'd failed in my dream, but his parents had been more supportive of my journey than my own family had been.

The guitar was just the beginning.

I could forgive Clark for falling out of love with me. Even his confusion over his feelings developing for someone else . . . especially a man. It was obvious he was struggling with it.

But the year of cheating? And the fact he had no desire to ever come clean about it? Not to mention the way he treated me after he'd been caught . . . that was fucking unforgivable.

Once he'd proven he was a liar, I realized I couldn't trust anything he said, including that he'd been safe with Derrick, and that he'd had no other partners over the last year. Clark and I hadn't had sex in months, but there'd been overlap, and if he'd caught an STD, I was now exposed.

He was *livid* when I tracked down Derrick's wife and confessed what I'd caught our husbands doing. I'd battled heavily with the decision to tell her. Clark had begged me not to tell our friends and family why we were getting divorced. Neither he nor Derrick were ready to be outed, and I didn't have any desire to do that.

But his wife had a right to know her husband wasn't

faithful, and I wouldn't have hesitated if I'd caught him with another woman. I was a firm believer that once a cheater, always a cheater, and if it were me—I'd want to know. Better to deal with the hurt now than waste years with a partner who lied and didn't love you.

Clark said I'd done it solely to punish him and Derrick, and there was no convincing him otherwise. He turned cold and mean and left rude messages on my voicemail when I wouldn't answer his calls. Each one of them tore my heart to shreds. I didn't recognize this man anymore. He wasn't even a shadow of the person I'd fallen in love with twenty years ago.

The same afternoon I'd had my first meeting with my attorney, I also had my consult with a plastic surgeon. Jenna drove me home after the surgery and stayed with me as my new size D breasts ached beneath their bindings.

It was one of the best decisions I'd ever made. I didn't care what anyone else thought, because I loved the way I looked now. Feminine and youthful and proportional. I had worked so hard to get healthy and fit, and my reward only motivated me to keep going with it.

The air conditioning in my kitchen did little to cool me down as I dropped the mail on the counter with a thud, followed by my purse. I glared at the letter, then sighed and slipped my finger beneath the flap, tearing it open.

The tension slipped from my shoulders as I read the cover letter from my divorce attorney, and then paged through the signed papers that followed.

It was official.

My marriage was dissolved.

My relief was so overwhelming, I gripped the edge of the counter with both hands to keep me upright. One long chapter of my life was finally closed.

I could hear Jenna's voice in my head, urging me to start a new one. She'd been on me for the last two months to start putting myself out there, but it felt wrong to do that before my marriage was legally over.

There was nothing stopping me now.

Nothing except my crushing fear.

I'd been so oblivious to my relationship falling apart with Clark, how could I trust myself with someone new? I'd buried the sexy red bodysuit deep in my closet because it was too expensive to throw out, but it was stupid. I hadn't been on a date in nearly two decades. By the time I found someone to wear it for, it probably wouldn't fit anymore.

I closed my eyes and drew in a deep breath, cleansing the thought from my mind. It was a good day today. I was off work in the middle of the afternoon with no obligations. This called for a celebratory margarita. And when I opened my eyes and stared out the window at the backyard, my bright blue pool glistened back at me.

Even better.

I'd have my drink beside the pool and enjoy the fabulous weather while I finished listening to the demos. I had a brand-new peach-colored bikini I'd bought last month on sale in preparation for the summer. Today was the perfect day to wear it.

Once I'd changed and fixed my drink, I stepped out on

the covered back patio and surveyed my options. There were chairs gathered around the table beneath an umbrella, or there was a set of lounge chairs next to the deep end of the pool shaded by the nearby pool house.

When Clark and I had moved in years ago, we'd had grand plans to turn it into a guest house, but those never materialized. The small house had electricity and plumbing, including a bathroom inside and an outdoor shower, but the floors were concrete, and the interior walls were just studs.

It meant the building was an oversized storage shed where we kept all the pool supplies and Christmas decorations. For a brief time after Clark had moved out, I'd considered turning it into a studio, but it didn't make financial sense. Eventually, I would realize the house *was* too big for me, and if I were going to invest in it, a guest house was more practical.

My flip-flops slapped against the concrete patio as I carried my margarita, my phone, and a towel tucked under my arm toward the loungers. It didn't take me long to spread out the towel and get situated on it, and then I was sipping my drink and slipping in my earbuds.

It'd been a hard ten months, but my broken heart and wounded pride had slowly healed as I'd settled into my new normal. In fact, other than the holidays, my life hadn't changed all that much. Clark had begun fading from my life before I'd realized it. Now that it was done, perhaps the most shocking part was just how quickly he'd discarded two decades with me and moved on.

You should do the same, Jenna would tell me.

I adjusted my sunglasses, settled back in the chair, and tapped the 'play' icon on the screen of my phone.

I finished listening to the demos around the same time I finished my margarita, and after I fetched a refill, there were emails to be answered. I managed bookings for several of the artists at our agency and did everything from scheduling and negotiating payment, to writing up artists' preferences and making sure those riders were provided to the events.

As I worked, the shade from the pool house began to recede. It was late enough in the day I hadn't bothered with sunscreen anywhere other than on my face, so maybe I'd get a little color.

My phone rang, and Ardy's name flashed on the screen.

"Hi," I said, suddenly feeling guilty that I was day drinking. I was by no means drunk, but the tequila made me feel loose and smiley.

"Hey," he responded. "We're working up an idea, and I need you to hit the ground running with it."

"Yeah?" I sat up and pressed my lips together. *Don't sound buzzed, Erika.*

"For Stella's final show of the tour, she wants to do something special. She got her start here in Nashville, so she wants to pay it forward. She's hoping to audition some locals and pick one to be her opening act that night. Johnny from her promo team was thinking we could shoot the talent scouting as a web series and have her fans help her choose the winner."

Not that Ardy could see me, but I nodded along with the idea. But, abruptly, I stopped. "Wait, she's already on tour. She's got—what? Fourteen shows left?"

"Eighteen, yeah." Ardy sighed. "Which is why I need you and everyone else at Warbler to run with this. We've got less than two months to pull it off."

My brain churned with prospects. "What are the requirements?"

"Obviously, we're looking for talent who's going to appeal to her audience, but no other constraints. Male or female, band or solo artist, it doesn't matter to her. You got someone in mind?"

"I have a few ideas, yeah."

"Great." I could hear the relief in his voice. "Get me a bunch more by Friday, and we'll pitch Stella before she leaves for Atlanta."

When our discussion was over, I immediately went to the Dropbox folder with all my clients' work and took a listen with an ear toward Stella's sound.

The sun was hot, and I wondered what kind of tan lines this swimsuit was going to give me if I wasn't careful. It was a halter top, and that wouldn't be flattering.

You can't get tan lines if you're not wearing anything.

It had to be the liquor that caused the thought. But . . . Dr. Lowe wasn't in his backyard, and I was obscured from his view anyway by the pool house. I grinned shyly to myself. There was something so freeing about the idea of topless sunbathing. Empowering. Like my desire to go skinny dipping last year, the thought excited me.

Maybe someday I'd even be comfortable enough to go to a nude beach.

Baby steps, the practical side of my mind scolded.

I glanced around, even as I knew no one could see me, and undid the hook behind my neck. The straps tumbled free, exposing my breasts, then I undid the second hook behind my back, before dropping my bikini top over the side of my chair.

I was so happy with the results of my surgery. My breasts were fuller, but still looked natural. My incisions had healed, the scars had already faded to a soft pink, and by this time next year, they'd likely be invisible. Even if I was the only person to ever see my new chest, it was worth it.

But hopefully, that wasn't true.

I had a considerable collection of vibrators that got the job done, but no amount of silicone and mechanics could truly replace the real thing. God, I was so fucking horny.

I reclined back on the lounger, streamed some music I wanted to listen to, and closed my eyes behind my sunglasses to think.

The best fit in my deck of artists was Lauren Kinsell. She was young, had a great look, and we could probably tone down her heavy country sound to broaden her appeal for a single show. Stella's target audience skewed heavily female, playing best to the 14 to 30-year-old age range.

I hadn't seen Lauren's set in several months. She had a regular gig on Thursday nights at a honky-tonk on Broadway Street, and I'd need to go this week to refresh my memory. While I loved her sound, last time I'd watched her perform, her stage presence hadn't been overly energetic or charismatic. She'd need a lot more for a Stella concert.

Hopefully, it'd just been an off night for her. Plus, she'd

likely improved since then. Either way, I was confident I could get her to where she needed to be for the audition. This was such a huge opportunity to come her way.

I believed in my artists with all my heart, and it was my job to get as many doors open for them as possible. Helping them walk through them and into their dreams was immensely satisfying.

Plan of attack plotted out, I raised my arms up over my head and arched my back, stretching contently in the sun like a cat. The warmth felt amazing on my—

A noise rang out as a metal pole clattered loudly against the concrete.

It made my heart stop. I pulled out one of my earbuds, lifted my head, and opened my eyes, only to find the pool boy looking at me with a shocked expression painted across his face.

THREE

Troy

I was sticky with sweat, which meant I was also covered in dust. It was a billion fucking degrees outside, and my stepfather, Bill, was huffing like he couldn't find any air.

I loved him like he was my biological dad. He was a good guy and made my mom happy. But he was also a lot older than her and in total denial about what kind of physical shape he was in. For example, he was carrying two boxes of tiles into the house, and I was carrying six. They were heavy as fuck too, and I'd done upper body at the gym yesterday, so I was struggling.

But I didn't let the other guys on the job site know. Most of them saw me as Bill's punk stepson, and any amount of bitching, even if it were justified, would only make it worse. I hated this job. Didn't need a reason to hate it more.

"You leaving?" Bill didn't mask his irritation when he saw me heading for the door.

Was he kidding? I tried not to snap at it. "It's five after three."

He glanced at his watch like that couldn't be right. But sure enough, it was. "I thought it was barely two." His demeanor changed and softened, and I gritted my teeth. He had that look like he was going to ask for something. "Any chance I can talk you into staying another hour? We could really use the help."

I shook my head. "I've got an appointment."

It wasn't a lie. Tuesdays *were* my standing appointment to clean Ms. Graham's pool, but I didn't mention to Bill how the timing was flexible. She hadn't been home a single time I'd gone over there, so I doubted she cared when I did the service.

He looked disappointed, but I didn't stick around to watch. I walked out the door and down the lawn to my black Jeep Wrangler parked on the street. The leather wrapped steering wheel seared my hands as I drove home, the top open and the wind whipping through my hair.

I couldn't wait to take a shower.

Remodeling homes wasn't just dirty—it was fucking disgusting. Mold and termites and asbestos and mouse droppings . . . I didn't want to think about what I was subjecting my body to every time I helped Bill's company knock down a wall or tear out a bathtub.

As I turned down the street I lived on, a familiar car was parked to the side of my driveway. Preston was here?

My parents' house had a three-car garage, and after I'd parked in my spot, I went through the kitchen and out the back door. My work shoes clomped on the concrete apron surrounding the pool as I walked toward my place. The exterior of the one-story guest house was the same as the main one, making the guest house look like a miniaturized version of it.

It had a nice setup, with a kitchenette and full bath,

and a bedroom that was separate from the living area. My own apartment, really. If I wanted to, I could come and go through the gate in the fence and bypass the house entirely, which was probably what my friend had done today.

Not that it'd do much good for me to sneak around. The guest house had sensors on it, so my overbearing mother could check the timestamps if she wanted. Plus, we argued constantly about me turning off the location on my phone. I was twenty-four, not twelve. She was a chronic worrier, but she didn't need to know where I was every second of every day.

My house was decorated like an adult lived there because my mother was an interior designer, but the big screen TV and the loud sounds of gunfire currently coming from it now were more my style.

My friend sat on the couch, focused intently on the game of *Call of Duty* he was playing . . . while using my PlayStation. Without asking. If he was logged in to my profile, I was going to throw his rude ass out.

"Um . . . hey?" I said pointedly.

Preston barely glanced my direction before returning his attention to the game. "What's up? My PlayStation's acting weird." When he didn't get a response from me, his posture straightened and he paused the game. "Is it cool if I hang out and use yours until my shift starts at five?"

Most people would have sent a text to ask before showing up, but this was typical Preston. My friend was an only child, like me, and could be self-absorbed a lot of the time, but he was working on it. He was two years younger than I was and still had a lot of growing up to do.

And I almost never remembered to lock the door on the guest house, so . . . lesson learned.

I checked the screen to see he was playing on his own profile. "Yeah, it's fine. I gotta take a shower."

He nodded and restarted his game.

It didn't take me long to get clean, and when I was done, I dressed in board shorts and a t-shirt from my traveling baseball team when I was in high school. I'd cut the sleeves off a lot of my shirts because I'd been more dedicated to the gym my last year of college and the old shirts had grown snug around my biceps.

Preston was still on the couch when I came out of my bedroom.

"What's going on with your PlayStation?" I asked.

"It won't connect to the internet. I probably just need to reset the WiFi router."

I blinked slowly. "It was easier to come over here than do that?"

He paused the game, put down the controller, and ground the heel of his palm in his eye. "Yeah, well . . . my dad's planning Cassidy's birthday, and I kind of needed to get out of there."

"Oh."

It made a hell of a lot more sense why he'd shown up without warning. Preston hadn't had that hard of a life. He was healthy, decent looking, and came from money. He owned his own car and had just finished his sophomore year of college at Vanderbilt.

But his relationship with his dad had been tough, and

my friend had been filled with resentment when he'd first come to Nashville at sixteen, forced to move in with the father who'd basically been a stranger up to that point in his life.

And just when things were finally smoothing out for them, the Cassidy situation blew it all to hell.

Cassidy Shepard had been Preston's girlfriend for years, although the rest of us didn't really get it. Near the end, he'd been enough of a dick to her, most of my circle of friends avoided hanging out with him whenever possible. He was my boy and all, but he didn't deserve her.

I was glad for both of them when they broke up. She could do better, and he needed to date around to realize not every girl out there was willing to put up with his shit. He'd seemed better after he'd spent his summer with his mom.

Then he came home one night to find his dad fucking Cassidy on the couch. Apparently, they were hopelessly in love.

Fuck, it was some messy drama—and it sucked for everyone involved. It'd been hard for Preston to get past it, but somehow he'd found a way. For as immature as he could be, he'd handled it way better than I'd expected.

His tone was worried. "I think he's going to do something big, like propose, or ask her to move in with him."

"Seriously?" I made a face. "They've only been together, for what? A year?" Not to mention, Cassidy was only twenty-one. Wait—not yet twenty-one because Dr. Lowe was planning her birthday.

Preston shrugged. "He floated the idea recently, saying they don't get to see each other as much as they want. I think he was putting feelers out."

"Would you be okay with it? I mean, things are good between y'all, right?"

He considered my question, not sure how to answer. "Sometimes it's weird, and other times, it's no big deal. They're happy, so that's good, and if she moves in, I could probably deal. I'm not there much anyway." He frowned. "But Cassidy being my stepmom? Yeah, I'm *not* ready for that."

Truer words had never been spoken. "I get it."

"I don't think she'd say yes anyway if he proposed. Cassidy will want to get her degree first."

"Okay." I wasn't sure what else to say. They'd been best friends in high school, completely inseparable, and they'd made tremendous strides this past year, but their friendship could never be what it was.

Thankfully, Preston gave me an out when he picked up the game controller. It was a clear signal he wanted the conversation to be over.

"Hey, man," I said, "I need to take off. Feel free to stay as long as you want."

"Where're you going?"

"Actually, over by where you live. I've got to clean Ms. Graham's pool."

He hadn't restarted the game, so he was able to give me a knowing smile. "You took a shower . . . to go clean her pool?"

He wasn't wrong with what he was implying, but I had to defend myself. "I was fucking gross. Besides, she won't even be there."

I'd been pushing my start time later and later in hopes of

seeing her, but so far, no such luck.

"She's always had that 'Stacey's Mom' thing going on, but since she got her tits done?" My friend did a chef's kiss. "She's hot as fuck."

I was *well* aware. Ms. Graham had been my primary source of spank bank material whenever I was without internet, and sometimes, even when I had access to PornHub. My fantasies about her were numerous.

And *detailed.*

"She isn't married anymore," Preston teased. "Now's your chance, Troy."

"Shut up."

He laughed at himself, but then sobered. "Maybe that's what I need to do, get me an older woman." He did a terrible, dramatic impression of Liam Neeson. "One with a very particular set of skills that she's acquired over her long career."

I gave him a look to tell him I wasn't amused.

He let it roll right off him. "All I'm saying is I'd let Ms. Graham ride me until she broke my back."

"Great." I picked up my keys off the counter and stepped into my flip-flops. "Lock up when you leave."

What Preston had said bothered me the whole drive over to her place, mostly because it hit a little too close to home. I'd spent years trying not to think about her. She was older—not to mention married—and my mom's best friend. Pursuing her would be stupid.

Then again, I wasn't the smartest guy around, was I?

I parked my Jeep in the street, halfway between her mailbox and Preston's, so I wouldn't block her driveway if she came home early. The privacy fence surrounding her property looked like wood, but it was textured concrete slats, and the gate was heavy as I unlatched it and went through.

I needed to come up with a better plan for getting her to notice me because cleaning her pool once a week while she wasn't there wasn't working.

Her pool house had two doors, but the workshop where she stored her chemicals was on the far side, so I climbed the sloping lawn, went around the backside of the building, and pulled the workshop door open.

It was nasty hot inside the unfinished space, and I moved with purpose to get the netted leaf rake. It'd been windy the past few days, and my pool at home was full of cottonwood seeds, so Ms. Graham's was sure to be the same.

The sun was so bright I didn't see her at first when I stepped out of the pool house and started toward the deep end. When my vision adjusted, I saw her lying out on the lounge chair, but my brain was much slower to recognize she was wearing a bikini. A peach one that showed off her flat stomach and—

Holy. Fucking. Shit.

She wasn't wearing a top.

I couldn't stop my gaze from tracing every mouthwatering inch of her. The sight of her pale skin and dark pink nipples soaking up the sun wasn't something I was prepared for, and my hands clenched in response.

Except doing that made the long pole of the rake pop free from my grip. It fell, almost as if in slow motion, and clanged loudly against the ground.

Ms. Graham's head lifted at the same moment she pulled one of the earbuds out of her ear, and her focus snapped in my direction.

My goal had been to get her to notice me, so . . .

Mission fucking accomplished.

FOUR

Erika

Troy Osbourne came once a week to service both my pool and the freestanding spa. I'd hired him last year to handle closing and covering the pool for the winter, then reopening it for me last month, and his weekly visits that followed had kept the water crystal clear and the pH perfectly balanced.

My pool had never looked so good.

But Troy always came when I was at work and let himself in through the gate at the side of my fence, so I had completely forgotten his schedule. He must have gone behind the pool house and inside to fetch his supplies, and when he'd rounded the corner and discovered me topless, he'd dropped everything in his arms.

Including the long pole with the net on the end.

It was as if someone had put their foot down on the sustain pedal of a piano, only this piano played the music of time, and the moment suspended with my long, drawn out gasp.

I was topless, and he was frozen, and holy shit, he was my best friend's twenty-four-year-old son.

It burst from my lips in horror. "Oh, fuck!"

In my panic, I grasped at my towel to cover myself, only to struggle hopelessly since it was pinned beneath my body. I leapt to my feet and yanked the terrycloth up, pressing it over my naked chest.

Troy still hadn't moved. His lips were open, as if he'd planned to say something, but now he was frozen and unable to do anything. I couldn't see his eyes behind his mirrored Aviator sunglasses, but he didn't seem to be breathing.

So, I did what any reasonable woman would when a gorgeous, almost-stranger caught her naked.

I ran.

I abandoned my phone and my top and fled as fast as possible toward the main house, crushing the towel over my boobs. There was no thought in my mind, only the basic need to seek shelter. My face burned a million times hotter than the concrete on the soles of my bare feet, and it wasn't until I was in the house that I could catch my breath.

"Oh my God," I whispered in the darkness of my kitchen, only to realize it was because I was still wearing my sunglasses. I shoved them back on my head.

Nervous energy coursed through my body and propelled me through the living room and into the master suite. I dropped the towel as I sprinted into my closet and grabbed the first thing that made sense. The sun dress was a deep indigo, and I pulled it on, not bothering with a bra.

Having the dress on made me feel marginally better, and a voice inside my head patronizingly reminded me of my desire to one day visit a nude beach. Troy had gotten an eyeful, but only above the waist, and now I was hiding in my closet like a scared little girl. My confidence still had a long, long way to go.

Finally decent, I sucked in a breath and willed my

heartrate to slow down.

It wasn't like this was the first time Troy had ever seen a topless woman before. He was young and attractive and had plenty of girlfriends while he'd been in college. I knew because Jenna had whined about all of the ones he'd brought home. None of 'those girls' were good enough for her son, she'd said.

I didn't envy whomever he eventually got serious with. I loved my friend dearly, but she was difficult to please, and in my opinion, had always been a little too strict when it came to Troy. I tried not to judge. I didn't have children, so what the hell did I know?

Like a spy, I tiptoed cautiously back into the living room and inched up to the window, scanning the backyard for him. I was curious. What did he think about seeing me?

He stood at the edge of the pool and was currently gliding the net through the water, skimming out leaves and flower petals that the magnolia tree nearby had shed. His gaze was tipped down, watching the surface of the water, and that, plus his sunglasses, made it difficult to read his expression.

Difficult, but not impossible. He looked deep in thought and also—

Hot.

I frowned at myself. Sure, he looked good, wearing faded red shorts and a t-shirt with the sleeves cut off. The toned muscles in his bare arms flexed as he grasped the pole and swished the net through the water. If I were twenty years younger, I might have lost my mind looking at him. But lusting after Troy was way, *way* inappropriate.

It didn't stop me, though.

Fuck, he was cute. His light brown hair was short on the sides and messy on top, and his strong jawline was shadowed with a few days' worth of stubble. Not enough to call it an actual beard. More like he couldn't be bothered to shave, and that, paired with his dark tan, made him look like he was two months into a lazy summer and not two weeks.

Everything about him was *enticing*.

Maybe tonight when I was tucked in bed with one of my vibrating friends, I'd let myself indulge in a fantasy in the safety of my own mind. One where I seduced a younger man who happened to look a helluva lot like Troy Osbourne.

I sighed wistfully, then pressed my lips together and furrowed my brow. What was wrong with me?

I knew I should stop watching from my hiding spot in the window like a creeper, but I couldn't help myself. There was something about the way his steady, sure hands gripped the pole that made me long to know what they'd feel like if they were holding me. How the sinewy muscles moved in his biceps and forearms as he lifted the dripping net from the water and swung it over to empty it in the rock landscaping beyond the edge of the patio.

What would he look like naked?

He'd probably look amazing. I felt feverish and uncomfortably tight all over as the image glanced through my mind.

Troy's head lifted, as if he had somehow heard my wicked thought, and his focus abruptly veered toward me.

"Shit!"

I pivoted away from the window and crushed myself flat

against the wall, desperate not to be caught. Once again, my cheeks burned hot with embarrassment. Why was I acting so stupid and immature about this? I wasn't a teenager anymore.

He'd seen me topless, so what? This didn't have to be a thing. What I needed to do was stroll out there with a casual, unashamed attitude. If I laughed it off and didn't make it a big deal, it should put us both at ease.

I straightened from the wall and sucked in a deep, preparing breath.

Relax, Erika. He's probably more uncomfortable than you are.

I needed to apologize. It got me to move toward the door, but didn't help much with my wobbly legs.

By the time I worked up the courage to step outside, he had vanished. For a split second, I wondered if he'd already left, but there were still supplies left out by the pool. A vial of water sat on the table beneath the umbrella. One chamber was stained yellow and another blue, signaling he'd tested the water to maintain the right balance. He'd probably gone back into the pool house to get some chemicals.

I snatched up my phone that I'd abandoned on the lounger before marching across the stone pavers toward the pool house.

Since it wasn't a finished space, there wasn't air conditioning, and Troy had left the door open in a feeble attempt to keep the air circulating. It was sweltering inside anyway.

A single bulb hanging from one of the rafters in the ceiling lit the room, which had a small collection of pool floats on one side and a shelf on the other, where all the chemicals and supplies were typically stored. At the back, there was the door to the bathroom and a bare set of stairs leading up to the second story. That was where the folded pool cover was stored, along with boxes of Christmas decorations.

I'd expected Troy to be at the shelves, picking out what he needed, but he wasn't. He was across the room, lingering beside the stairs. His sunglasses were propped up on his head and he stared at the hooks on the wall with a displeased expression smeared on his face, as if they'd somehow pissed him off.

I blinked with confusion, and the longer I stood there, the more it became clear he hadn't seen me come in and wasn't aware of my presence.

A hand reached inside my body and tightened its fist as realization swept through me.

"Goddamnit," he muttered under his breath, and ran a palm down the front of his body.

Because the fly of his shorts was tented.

Like he'd done when he'd caught me topless, I froze in place. It was physically impossible to do anything other than drag hot, humid air into my lungs and watch as he repeated the action.

If his intent was to make his erection go away, the brush of his hand had the opposite effect. Tortured pleasure twisted on his face as he glared at the wall. I wondered if he was mentally trying to make the blood flow in any direction other than his dick, but then surrendered.

His large hand closed over the front of his shorts . . .

And *squeezed*.

When he shuddered with satisfaction, his pleasure reverberated through my body. It tingled across my skin like electricity and sent my heart racing.

I'd never witnessed a more erotic sight than watching this boy tease himself. I was fascinated and mesmerized at the slow rub of his palm over the bulge.

Was there a chance he was thinking about me right now?

I couldn't catch my breath, but then it became irrelevant. The wind outside gusted and sucked the door closed with a loud, abrupt slam, making his attention swing sharply in my direction.

He didn't say it out loud, but the phrase *'oh shit'* streamed across his expression. His eyes went wide with surprise, followed by panic, before finally landing on embarrassment.

His hand dropped from his crotch as he turned to face me, and his shoulders straightened awkwardly. When he'd caught me, I'd run away, but there was nowhere to escape for him. Instead, he lifted his chin, puffed out his chest, and set his hands on his waist.

He filled his voice with suspicion. "How long have you been standing there?"

There was no way I could answer. I had to lick my parched lips to keep from dying.

And it was unstoppable the way my gaze drifted slowly across his body, taking in the bead of sweat that coasted down his neck and disappeared beneath his shirt. My focus slipped all the way down until it traced the thick line of his cock trying to jut away from his body, trapped beneath fabric.

I swallowed hard as my gaze worked back up to meet

his and found him guarded. He was trying so hard to appear unaffected. To contain whatever it was he was thinking.

He said it like it wasn't his fault. "You were topless."

I blinked, and as his meaning hit me, I jolted so hard it was a miracle I didn't crack the screen of the phone in my hand. I whispered it with disbelief. "You're saying," I glanced at his erection, "I caused that?"

His guilty gaze darted away to stare at the hooks once more, and his lips mashed together.

I hated that I'd accidentally caused him shame, especially when the truth was his words had set me on fucking fire. I hadn't been able to arouse a man in years, so to do that now, and one as young and hot as this guy? It stole my breath.

My voice was uneven. "You *liked* what you saw?"

His focus shifted back, and he stared at me like I'd just announced I loved the musical stylings of Smashmouth.

"Yeah." Troy blinked, considering his words. He shrugged, giving into what he really wanted to say. "I always thought you were hot, but you're a smoke show now, Ms. Graham."

My heart stumbled over itself as my brain tried to process the words.

He drew in a breath and lifted a hand to wipe the sweat from his forehead. "I'm sorry about walking in on you and what you just saw. Can we, like, forget that happened?"

There was desperation in his eyes, but I wasn't in control anymore. Someone else took charge and spoke in my voice. "Show me," I pleaded. "I want to see it."

He went utterly still. "What?"

Blood rushed loudly in my ears, drowning out the panic

at what I was suggesting. "You saw me," I offered. "I . . . want to see you."

As soon as the words were spoken, the sauna-like room became a furnace.

Oh, my God. What had I just asked for? Anxiety was a drug weaving through my system, making me vibrate, and it worsened as Troy stared at me with doubt clouding his eyes. The air around us was so still, yet tension crackled in it like invisible lightning. We were closed off in this small, oppressive room, which smelled faintly of sawdust and chlorine, and I was so far outside of myself we could have been on a distant planet.

His voice was rich, but unsure. Like I'd made an offer too good to be believed. "You want to see me?"

I bit down on my lip and nodded slowly.

The corner of his mouth lifted in a hesitant smile, and he delivered a look that said *we shouldn't* but also *let's do it anyway*. It was playful and reckless. A deadly combination.

He pulled the sunglasses off his head and set them on the unfinished stairs before grasping the hem of his t-shirt and stretching it up over his head.

Because it was a million degrees in here.

And maybe because he wanted to show off.

"Holy fuck," I whispered.

His impish smile spread to a full grin as he dropped the t-shirt to the floor. The shorts were slung low on his hips, flaunting the sexy V shape flanking his abs, and above there was his flat, beautifully toned chest. He had a body like Zac Efron's during the height of his man-candy roles, and his golden tanned skin made my knees go weak.

I wasn't thinking about how he was Jenna's son, or that when I'd met him for the first time, it was during his high school graduation party. All those thoughts were wiped clean by the muscles rippling across his torso, and the way his hands went to the ties knotted at the top of his shorts.

My heart threatened to beat out of my chest with nervous excitement, and I suspected it was the same for him. Troy seemed to struggle to catch his breath as his fingers worked the strings loose.

I stood completely motionless, watching as his shorts were undone enough for him to slide a hand inside. His eyes hooded and he gave a low, pleasurable sigh. It was hypnotic how he deliberately moved up and down, teasing both me and himself.

When we locked eyes, he understood what I wanted, but also how much leverage he had over me.

"I'll show you mine," he said, both joking and entirely serious, "if you show me yours."

FIVE

Erika

A thrill burst in my bloodstream. This was naughty and sinful, and so wrong; how could I refuse? The lack of sex had voided out my ability to make good decisions, and if seeing me topless had this effect on Troy, I was more than willing to do it again.

"Okay," I said, and deposited my phone on the shelf nearby.

He quirked a sexy eyebrow in pleased surprise . . . and then urged his shorts over his hips. They descended his legs, revealing his fist wrapped around himself, and my breath cut off.

He.

Was.

Impressive.

I stared at him unabashedly while he stepped out of his shorts. I was in awe, watching as he stroked his hand down the length of his hard cock. Every muscle in me had tensed to prevent me from leaping forward and touching him. The desire to do so was partly because my lust had made me crazy, and partly to see if he was real and not a figment of my imagination.

God, he was gorgeous, all glistening with sweat as he

oh-so-slowly fucked his hand and studied me.

I fisted the sides of my dress and lifted. Our gaze was only broken for a moment when I pulled the garment off and let it fall from my hands.

The electricity flowed as a current between us, and it hummed deafeningly in my ears. It had been erotic watching the rhythmic glide of his fist over himself, but it was incendiary to see the desire rolling through his expression as he stared at me. Troy's eyes were liquid heat, and his chest rose and fell with his labored breath.

There was a rough, raw edge to his voice. "Your tits are fucking amazing."

It seemed to have come out of his mouth before he'd thought it through, and it must have set off warnings he'd crossed a line because his face abruptly went blank. Was he worried he'd offended me? Because all his compliment did was make me burn hotter.

"Aren't they?" I said.

My lust pressed down, molding me into a new person . . . one who wasn't shy or worried about her partner's reaction. I cupped the undersides of my full breasts and pushed them together, displaying them to him. Almost as an offer.

Troy's sound of satisfaction was like I'd punched it from his center. His free hand moved, rising for a moment, like he wanted to reach out and touch me, but then thought better of it. We weren't close enough for it anyway, but the action caused my heart to flutter with excitement.

We couldn't . . . could we? It'd make all of this too real, with real consequences.

His gaze stroked over my curves, just as his hand worked himself over, and each pass increased the intensity of the need pounding deep inside my body. It was hard to breathe, hard to stand still, as he twisted his grip and pleasured himself while his stare burned into me.

"What are you thinking about?" I whispered.

"Don't ask me that." It was part plea, part warning. Because whatever the answer was, it was very, *very* bad.

I was drunk, delirious, and out of control with lust. "Do you want to touch me?"

"Yes." The word burst from his lips with no hesitation, but then he looked stricken. "No. I shouldn't."

A sobering thought hit me like cold water. "You have a girlfriend."

"What?" He froze. "No, no." He let out a tight, embarrassed sigh. "If I touch you, shit's going to . . . escalate."

Relief washed through and disarmed me. His phrasing was almost amusing. "Escalate?"

His pointed look was stern and provocative. "Yeah, Ms. Graham." When he repeated the word, he drew it out, weighting each syllable. "*Escalate.*"

"It's Erika." It was too formal and impersonal for him to use my last name, given what we were doing. Plus, it was a bit too much like *The Graduate,* even if I had seduced him into doing this. "Are you worried I won't be able to handle you?"

"No." He was perfectly serious. "I'm worried I won't be able to handle you." His gaze dropped down to his dick clenched in his hand. "Look at me. I haven't fucking touched you, and I'm already close."

My excitement ratcheted up to a new level. "Are you go-ing to come?" I was breathless. "Right now, in front of me?"

He shuddered through the powerful effect my words had on him, and his dick jerked under his grip. "Do you want me to?"

I hadn't thought about it until this very moment, and suddenly, I was desperate for it. If we didn't touch, what we were doing felt "safe." We'd walk right up to the edge of dan-ger, but not cross over, and I hungered to see him lose con-trol in my presence.

Need choked my throat, making it hard to speak, so I nodded quickly.

This time, when his hand resumed moving, it was faster, and a determined, focused look settled in his eyes. Did he feel like he was on stage, performing for me? If so, he didn't seem uncomfortable.

Not even a little.

He put his free hand on one of the treads of the stairs, as if preparing and needing something to hold onto. When he pumped his fist, his hips moved in time. The subtle gyrations ripped me open and poured more heat inside me. I wanted him to move like that against me, in either my hand, or in my mouth, or inside my body. It was pornographic how he swayed and rolled. A private show for me that was so lewd I could barely blink, not wanting to miss any of it.

His grasp was firm and tight because the skin around his grip moved up and down with him, making the head of his cock disappear as he focused on the tip. Short, heavy breaths worked loose from his lungs, and it was difficult to tell which he enjoyed more: jerking himself off or looking at me.

He'd been using one hand this whole time, and maybe it'd gotten tired or strained, because he ringed himself at the base, and his other hand came off the stair step to take over.

Wait, no. He cupped his hand, then tipped his head forward, and I watched as a bead of saliva trailed from his lips down into his palm.

"Yes," I encouraged. "Get it wet."

Holy shit. How many margaritas had I had? I'd never said anything like that before, and the abrupt dirty talk from my lips was startling.

But Troy? He very much approved of it. He shuddered as his fresh, damp hand took over, and the fatigued one massaged lower. God, it was sensual the way he touched and rubbed himself, as if enjoying it as much as I did.

"*Fuck*," he groaned in satisfaction. "I want to see all of you."

His gaze dropped to the only thing left on my body, the peach bikini bottom, and air whooshed out of me. Wasn't it silly to be bashful about this? And a little unfair, since he was completely naked and had followed every order I'd given him?

He wasn't sure how to interpret my hesitation, so his voice went husky. "You want me to come over there and help you?"

"Yes," I breathed. "And no, because if you touch me . . . I don't know what will happen."

His sexy pace slowed a little and confusion pulled his eyebrows together.

It forced me to continue. "I haven't had sex in a long time. You don't want to get within striking distance of me."

God, his amused grin made my bones melt. "Like you're dangerous, Erika."

Hearing my name in his seductive voice made all the moisture in my body rush to the center of my legs. I meant for it to sound sultry, but I faltered. "Just thinking about what I want to do to you is dangerous."

He closed both hands around himself, and I couldn't tell if it was to give himself more pleasure or to hold it back. "Fuck. Tell me about it."

Instead, I sucked in a breath, slipped my fingertip beneath the sides of my bikini bottom, and began to inch it down.

His handsome face filled with eagerness, and his hands stroked faster as I let the swimsuit fall away. It revealed the carefully manicured strip just above the juncture of my legs, and his gaze zeroed in on it.

"Goddamn," he groaned. "You like this, huh? Watching me?"

He could see how turned on I was and warmth flooded across my cheeks. "I do."

The hurried sound of skin sliding against skin filled every inch of the room, and his rising tempo made anticipation mount inside me. The expanse of Troy's gorgeous chest heaved with labored breaths as he closed in on his orgasm, and the sexual charge of it raced in my bloodstream.

I tensed my jaw to hold back a moan.

His thirsty gaze swept over me from my forehead to the tips of my toes as I stepped out of my swimsuit bottoms, and when his gaze returned to meet mine, the longing in it was so acute, it locked us together. We both wanted him to touch me, and we each had only a fingertip's grip on our control to prevent that from happening.

We stood across from each other, stark fucking naked, breathing in the heat and the sex that filled the room, and it was like a fire raging only inches from a barrel of gasoline. If we came any closer, it'd trigger a powerful mistake.

It came from him in a desperate rush as he heaved his fists over his cock. "You could play with your pussy. I don't have to be the only one getting off."

He was right.

"You want to watch?" I asked.

It was like I'd asked him if I could give him a million dollars. "Fuck, yeah."

My hand drifted provocatively across my leg, slowly moving to its target, and when my fingertips landed on my clit, Troy's lips parted and released a moan. It was absolutely the hottest thing I'd ever heard. And it gave me the courage to *really* touch myself.

I'd masturbated plenty of times before with Clark in the room, but that was usually when I'd laid beside him in bed after sex, working to get my own orgasm. In the beginning, he'd tried to assist, but it was clear I was more efficient at doing it, so a few years into our marriage, he'd given up being involved. Most times, he'd fallen asleep before I'd finished.

Clark had never asked me to touch myself, and he'd never shown any interest in watching me do it either.

So, it made my head spin that Troy was into it.

He was *so* into it.

We were both panting as my fingers rubbed quick circles over my swollen clit, causing sparks of pleasure to spider-web across my skin. Oh, my God, it wasn't going to take me long, not when this gorgeous fucking man was putting on a show and staring at me with so much hunger he was downright ravenous.

His hips moved, making him slide through his clenched fingers, and I reached out with my other hand to support myself on the nearby shelf. It was getting difficult to stand as the orgasm built inside me. Tremors vibrated up my legs, and I hurried my fingers to match his furious pace.

"I want those," he said, between struggling breaths, "to be my fingers."

Lightning zipped through me, short-circuiting my brain. I nodded toward his waist. "And I wish those were my hands."

A long, deep exhale of satisfaction came from him, and something suspiciously like a growl rose from his throat. It was primal and animalistic, and the hardwired woman in me responded.

"*Oh,*" I gasped. "You're going to make me . . ."

He groaned with pleasure. "Watching you come," he said, "is going to make me come."

I tensed my grip on the shelf until my fingers ached, but I didn't slow my other hand down. I moved so quickly, it was probably a blur to Troy, but then again, he was the same. This beautiful boy, wrapped in muscle and freckled, tan skin, jerking himself off so hard and fast, would have stolen my breath if I had any left.

My vision narrowed in on him as my climax took me. It pulled me into a tight ball and then flung my pleasure out through my limbs, making me shake and flinch with each wave. I cried out, and it was the signal he needed, because then he was the one with the swelling moans and the loud groan as he came undone.

The movement of his hips was jerky and erratic. His hands clamped down over the tip of his dick, trapping his release, but it meant the rest of him was uncovered, and I watched in fascination as the rhythmic pulses throbbed through the length of him.

My hand dropped away from the center of my legs, my body still tingling from the bliss, and when I straightened away from the shelf, it creaked quietly. It took me longer to catch my breath than for him, but Troy remained like a statue with his hands cupped over himself.

I nearly smiled. Was he . . . trying to be polite? Worried about dripping semen on my unfinished floor?

"That was insane," he said abruptly.

My amusement died as a chill descended on me. Or perhaps it was reality. What we'd just done *was* insane, and guilt filled every cell in my body. He was Jenna's son, for Chrissake. I shifted my gaze away. "Yeah."

"I meant, insanely hot."

Relief sparked, and my attention flew back to him. "Oh."

His voice was rich, and his expression was stripped bare of bravado. It was honest and hopeful. "Wasn't it?"

"Yeah," I breathed.

He nodded as if he'd said the word "*good*" out loud,

and then swung his gaze from me toward the open door to the bathroom.

I didn't watch as he marched toward it and disappeared inside. Instead, I retrieved my swimsuit bottoms and yanked them on. The sound of water ran from the faucet in the bathroom while I grabbed my dress, and I tried not to think about why he was in there washing his hands.

With him out of sight, the sex dissipated from the room and cleared most of the fog from my mind.

Oh, God.

What had I done?

I tugged my dress on so quickly, threads ripped. It was just barely in place when the water stopped, and Troy emerged from the bathroom. Still naked and devastating, and it was even worse when he put his hands on his waist and shot me a mock disapproving look.

"You got dressed fast."

It was odd how he was so confident without a stitch of clothing on, but then again, he had nothing to be embarrassed about. If anything, he was probably proud. Besides his sculpted body, his impressive erection had flagged some, but remained. Even though he'd reached satisfaction, his dick was broadcasting it was up for an encore.

Holy shit, I had to get out of this room.

The window of me maintaining my self-control was rapidly closing, and I *could not* sleep with him. He was a guy, and in my experience, it wasn't hard to convince them to hop into bed. Every signal Troy had given me made me confident he'd say yes if I asked.

And while a huge part of me wanted a quick hookup, it wouldn't be "no strings" with him. There were very big, very personal strings attached to Troy. Jenna would never forgive me, and my friendship with her was worth more than a night of meaningless sex. It was incredibly likely I'd already damaged it beyond repair.

Only if you tell her what you did.

My heart sank into my stomach. I was a terrible friend.

He'd commented that I'd gotten dressed quickly, and my tone was urgent. "I did. You should probably too, because . . ."

I tried to assemble the right phrasing in my head, but nothing sounded right, and as time dragged on, Troy's posture began to stiffen.

"Because," he said flatly, "this was a mistake."

Hurt lurked in his eyes, but I only caught it for a moment because he bent, scooped up his shorts, and jammed a leg into them. I couldn't hold his gaze as he finished pulling them on and did up his fly. My shame was too powerful.

"It wasn't a mistake," I said quietly, "but I shouldn't have asked you to . . ." I took the cowardly way out and let him fill in the rest of the words I wasn't saying. "I wasn't thinking, and I'm sorry."

He shook his head. "Nothing to be sorry about."

That couldn't be true because I felt guilty as hell.

Silence hung awkwardly between us, growing more uncomfortable than the heat. He had his shorts on, but his t-shirt was still a heap on the floor, and sweat darted down his chest in erratic zigzags, each droplet enticing me to follow its descent.

But an electronic trill cut through the air. I was so disoriented, it took a second to realize it was my ringtone. I reached out to pick up my phone, but as the name flashed across the screen, I hesitated.

It rang again, but I didn't move.

"You need to answer that?" Troy sounded guarded, but curious.

I swallowed a breath. "It's my husband."

It was a habit that hadn't died yet, and my thoughtless comment set him on alert. His expression darkened. "I thought you were divorced."

It'd taken so long to sort out since Clark had been a jerk and he'd legally been my husband until he'd signed the papers. I'd opened the envelope this afternoon, seen the signature, but the totality of it sank in just now.

I was *finally* divorced.

"Ex-husband," I corrected. "Sorry, I'm fighting twenty years of habit." I grabbed my phone and tapped the screen, sending the call to voicemail. "And no, I don't need to answer it."

"Y'all were married for twenty years?" Was Troy thinking now about the enormous age difference between us? When I'd walked down the aisle, he'd been a toddler.

"Yeah," I said. "It's funny how, in the final few years, Clark never wanted to talk to me, not until I asked for the divorce. Now he calls me all the freaking time."

Why was I telling him this? I shook my head, trying to rattle the awkwardness away, and pulled my shoulders back to straighten my posture. I didn't feel confident, but I could pretend I did.

"Troy," I started, unsure of what to say next.

He thought he knew what was coming. "This is where you tell me I'm fired, right?"

"No," I said quickly. "No, you didn't do anything wrong. It's just . . . I took advantage of you. I'm sorry. That won't happen again."

He cocked an eyebrow. "You sure? Because I'm okay with it happening again."

Eagerness fluttered in my stomach, but I squashed it down. "Well, it can't." I frowned. "Besides everything else, I'm too old for you."

Goddamn that sexy smile that lurked on his lips and how his tone patronized. "If you say so, Ms. Graham."

I sighed my frustration. "It's Erika."

He was about to deliver a retort, but my phone rang again and interrupted him. When I glanced at the screen and didn't answer, he tilted his head. "Your ex again?"

"No." I swallowed painfully. "It's, uh . . . your mother."

SIX

Erika

Jenna Hanson never went without a manicure. Her nails were perfectly shaped and painted every other week, and she usually opted for neutrals, so it would go with anything. But tonight, her fingernails were a Tiffany blue, and they were hard to miss as she tapped them absentmindedly against her glass.

She'd fixed herself a Moscow mule with dinner and offered to make me one, but I'd poured myself a glass of sweet tea from her fridge instead. It was Thursday evening, and Lauren's set wasn't until ten, so after dinner I'd need to drive downtown. I'd ordered takeout for Jenna and I and brought it over to her place, hoping to use our 'girls' night' as an opportunity to come clean about what had happened with her son.

Troy and I hadn't talked about it. I'd ducked out of the sweltering pool house to take Jenna's call, which was awkward and ran longer than I wanted it to, and by the time I was finished—he'd vanished. The pool supplies had been put away, and the back gate closed.

It'd been two days since that afternoon, and it was clear he hadn't told her. If he had, I would have received an angry phone call or visit from my friend by now. Jenna's blood ran hot, and she had a quick temper, but it also meant she was quick to forgive, and I hoped it'd be true this evening.

It wasn't surprising he hadn't told her. After Troy finished college, he'd been unable to find a steady job and temporarily moved back in with his parents. Tensions had reached a breaking point in February.

They'd had a huge fight, their first ever, she'd told me. He was a good kid—smart, caring, and respectful. But he was still a kid to her, and he'd struggled with his independence while living under his mother and stepfather's roof.

Mostly, Jenna had confessed, it was because she was micromanaging him. Her husband, Bill, owned a construction company, and she'd been pressuring Troy to take a position there, which he did not want.

"Nobody likes their first job," she'd said to me, when she'd relayed the story.

He'd rebelled against the offer for months, worried that once he got into a job, he wouldn't be able to escape it.

But Jenna was nothing if not persuasive. The woman could sell you a recipe for ice, and you'd walk away feeling like you got a bargain. We'd met when Clark and I bought our house and hired Bill's company to remodel the kitchen. Jenna was an interior designer and had helped me come up with a better footprint for the space; plus, she talked me into all the upgrades and high-end finishes that had made the kitchen my favorite room of the house.

We'd become fast, loyal friends.

Maybe *loyal* wasn't the right word to use anymore.

I stared at my glass of sweet tea as she talked about a mix-up with an upholstery order that resulted in a client's chair being recovered in a flamingo pattern.

"It was wild, I tell you," she said. "I was speechless, and then the woman turns to me and says she likes how quirky it is." Jenna tossed her sandy blonde hair over a shoulder. "It's a statement piece," she muttered, "just not sure I liked what it was saying."

"But the customer was happy?"

"Oh, yeah. She fucking loved it." She rested her elbows on the table as she prepared to switch topics, peering at me with a hard look, and my stomach filled with dread. I'd seen this expression from her before. It meant all-business. "So, you're officially back on the market."

I picked up my drink and took a sip, using it as an excuse not to answer.

My friend wasn't deterred. "Before you leave tonight, we're putting you on Match.com."

Tea slid down my windpipe as I swallowed wrong, and I sputtered, "We are not."

I loved my friend. She'd been my rock throughout the divorce, but she had a bad habit of thinking she knew what was best for everyone, sometimes without even asking if it was what they wanted. Uh, oh. What if she'd started building my profile already?

Movement behind her stole my focus. Then, all the air went out of the room.

Every time I'd come over since Troy had moved back in with his parents, I'd never seen him at home. Their guest house was a full apartment and that was where he stayed.

Until now.

He stood in the doorway to the kitchen, as if an invisible force field prevented him from moving farther, a bowl full of cereal, complete with a spoon, in his hand. Our gazes locked, and he blinked rapidly, as if he couldn't process what he was seeing. Had I done the same thing? Because it was exactly how I felt.

Jenna, however, was unaware since he was behind her. "Maybe not Match," she laughed. "How about Tinder? You said you're horny all the time now."

Oh, no.

My mouth dropped open, and the horrified sound that came from my throat was inhuman. Troy's expression flooded with shock as his eyes widened, and his gaze shifted to stare at the back of his mother's head.

"Jenna," I choked out, but she was oblivious to my distress.

"Actually," she nodded to herself, "I think that's exactly what you need. Find some hot guy who'll bang your brains out. Doesn't matter if he's stupid or broke or crazy, as long as he's down to fuck. You can ghost him later."

A void opened inside my head, preventing me from functioning, and a similar void was likely consuming Troy as he heard his mother utter the phrase "*down to fuck.*"

"After Clark?" Jenna scowled. "You need to be with a man who's dying to get on you. Tell me I'm wrong."

My heart was galloping a million miles an hour, and I couldn't stop myself from looking at him. His simple gray t-shirt was stretched tight across his chest, flaunting his powerful frame. Jeans clung to his hips, and his brown hair was mussed, but not messy. He was casually styled and effortlessly sexy.

His expression caused me to unravel. Jenna had said I needed someone dying to have me, and for one long moment, he gazed back like he could be that man.

And I wanted that too.

Warnings triggered in my mind, but the loudest was that she'd asked me a question, and if I didn't answer soon, she might wonder what I was looking at. I ripped my gaze away from him and focused on her.

My voice was weighted with reluctant truth. "No, you're not wrong."

She beamed a smile. "Yes! And once you have your fling, you're going to tell me every dirty detail, so I can live vicariously through you." She leaned closer like she was going to whisper a secret, but the volume of her voice did not change. "Ever since Bill hurt his back, we can only do it if I'm on top. I'm desperate for some spice."

That was the limit Troy could take, because he suddenly propelled himself into the kitchen.

"Hey, Mom. I'm out of milk. Can I steal some of yours?" He forced casualness into his tone, like he hadn't heard any of the previous conversation, and then paused, for a fraction of a second, unsure. "Hey, Ms. Graham."

My throat was sticky. "Hey, Troy."

Thankfully, his mother didn't notice. She turned in her seat to glance at him, and her attention went to the bowl he was carrying. "You're eating cereal? For dinner?"

He shrugged and opened the fridge.

Jenna sighed as she turned back to face me. "I swear I

taught him how to cook, but I think that's all he eats."

"It's easy," he said from behind the door. "And fast. I'm heading out in a few minutes."

"To go hang out with your boys?"

"Yup." He shut the door, dug into the colorful cereal with his spoon, and crunched a bite. "It's Preston's birthday."

"Ah, to be twenty-four again," she said with fake wistfulness before turning her amused attention back to me. "Remember when we were young, and our nights started at ten p.m.?"

Technically, my evening *was* starting at ten. At least my working one, since that was when Lauren's set began.

"Don't stay out all night," she said to him. "Bill's going to need your help tomorrow. They're demoing the bathroom in the Glasgow home."

"Great." His dry expression said it was anything but.

His eyes flicked toward me, and he held my gaze for a single beat, filling it with all the things unspoken between us, before turning and shuffling off.

"But have fun!" his mom added, realizing she'd overstepped yet again.

I swallowed thickly, finding air now that he was gone. It was unreal the effect he had on me, and it was extra tense because his mother was right there. I understood his frustration with her. When I was his age, I'd felt smothered by my family, and even marriage hadn't helped me escape.

"He's going to be exhausted," she grumbled under her breath. "He stays out all night, and then Bill says he's the walking dead the next day."

I pressed my lips together and mentally told myself not to get involved. "He's a good kid." It'd been an offhanded comment, but boy, the word sliced through my ears like a snapped guitar string. *Kid.* I forced it away. "Maybe he's got a girlfriend."

She shot me a dubious look. "He hasn't said anything to me about a girl."

It came out before I could stop myself. "Would he?"

"What's that supposed to mean?"

"Nothing," I said quickly. "I don't know why I asked it."

Beneath her bangs, Jenna's eyes narrowed with doubt. "Troy and I don't keep secrets from each other."

Well, that I knew for a fact, wasn't true.

And now I was keeping them from her too.

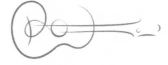

The stage at Blanche's wasn't big, and only as high as a barstool, but it was just tall enough that I could see Lauren's head and shoulders over the people standing on the floor in front of her. Her blonde hair was a sleek curtain draped on either side of her face, and the ends of it brushed against her sleeveless plaid crop top. It was tied in a knot above her flat stomach, of course, and she'd completed the outfit with cut-offs and cowboy boots.

Her country sound influenced her look, and she'd leaned into it hard for the tourists. It was paying off too. The white tip bucket with her name on it at the edge of the stage was nearly full. Although I had concerns those tips had less to do with her talent and more to do with her looks. The buttons down the front of her shirt were undone enough that the center of her pink bra was visible whenever she moved.

I didn't fault her for dressing like that. It fit her brand and a girl had to eat, after all. But I wished with all my heart the men in the crowd were seduced by her voice, rather than just her cleavage. She had stunning control and flawless pitch, and she was one of those singers who earned your trust in a single, pure note. As soon as she began, you felt confident you'd enjoy the song from start to finish.

The bar was crowded tonight, and I'd watched her set from several different areas around the room, evaluating her performance. I hadn't told her I was coming, and she hadn't spotted me either. It wasn't until she was finished and swiped her post-set bottle of Bud Light off the end of the bar that I made my approach.

Lauren had been both excited and nervous to see me, but her anxiety faded as we walked up the stairs to the second floor, where it was quieter, and I explained why I'd come. Eagerness warmed her face. She understood how huge this could be for her career.

"We have to find the right song for your audition," I told her. "I'm going to send you some ideas, and let's get together before your set next week."

Her thin eyebrows pulled together. "You didn't like any of the ones I did tonight?"

"For Stella's audience? No." This was business, and she

had a head for it, not to mention a thick skin. She wouldn't be offended by my honesty. "We need something crossover. Halsey has some stuff that might work for . . ."

I trailed off, cocking my head to the side as I listened to the sound filling the room. Blanche's was two stories, plus a rooftop bar, and although there was also a stage on this floor, it was empty tonight. The music from the band that had just started playing downstairs was piped through the sound system, and I stared at an advertisement for Jack Daniels as I evaluated the music.

The balance was off. The lead guitar was so loud, it overpowered the drums, and the moment it began, I'd written the performance off. A rookie mistake that didn't bode well for the group.

But then the vocals came in, and my thoughts derailed.

That tone.

The male voice was rich smoke and filled my body with heat.

The band was covering Chris Stapleton's *Midnight Train to Memphis*, and the singer mimicked the same bluesy gravel, but there were hints his range was much wider.

"You okay?" Lauren asked.

I motioned toward the speakers. "Who is this?"

I'd been in the business long enough I knew most of the acts around town, but this one I'd never heard before.

Her shoulders lifted in a shrug. "It was supposed to be Kicking Fences, but Kevin's got laryngitis. It's some new guy from the standby list with Kicking Fences' band backing him." She eyed me as she took a swig of her beer. "Why? You like him?"

I nodded. "I do."

In fact, I liked what I was hearing enough that when I finished with Lauren, I'd likely stay and watch the rest of the show.

We discussed a few more things and set up a time for me to call and check in with her late next week, but the entire time we talked, I had one ear focused on the sound coming from the main stage. The guy was too close to the mic and probably new, but there was so much talent there, it made up for it.

After we said goodbye, I hurried down the dark stairwell lined with photos of past acts that had gone on to make it big. I hoped the guy with the great vocals also had the 'it' factor. It was a good sign the crowd was into the performance because I could hear them shuffling along with the beat, plus the occasional catcall.

I turned the corner and blinked against the bright stage lights.

During Lauren's performance, the bargoers had been subdued, but now the floor was mostly full. People swayed to the rhythm and a few held up their beer bottles to pay respect to the band. Energy vibrated through the crowd, making the atmosphere as electric as the guitar the singer strummed.

It was a hot, dirty Nashville sound filling the space that was all sticky floors and neon beer signs.

I was thrilled the guy could sing *and* play decently, and for a moment, I was distracted by his practiced fingers on the fretboard. But awareness tingled the hairs at the back of my neck. Something was off. No, not off . . .

Familiar.

With his powerful, throaty voice, I'd expected to find a man in his forties or fifties with a flannel shirt, a beard hanging down to touch his belly, and a cowboy hat. And while he had on a blue plaid shirt, it was fitted snuggly to his tight frame, and the sleeves rolled back to the elbows to show off his forearms. A swath of leather cuffed his wrist. It gave him an edgy, youthful vibe, just a little too punk rock to be pure country.

Not that he needed help looking young—he was only twenty-four.

Sound faded from my ears, so the only thing that registered was the thump of the bass drum and the pounding of my heart. Each beat slammed into my chest as I stared up at Troy's handsome face.

SEVEN

Erika

It was as if someone had struck a match and lit a fuse inside me. Excitement buzzed through my bloodstream as I stared at the boy on stage while he cradled his Fender and leaned into the microphone to sing about barbed-wire fences. Either the lights or the pressure of performing had Troy already sweating. A thin gloss sheened his face.

But he didn't look uncomfortable.

Just like the intimate performance he'd given me, he had an easy swagger on the stage. He wasn't stiff or tight like most inexperienced performers could be. His shoulders were relaxed, and his stance solid, so he could both sing and play to the best of his ability.

It was the opposite for me. Every muscle inside my body was corded tightly with awe and excitement. He could *sing*. How the fuck did I not know this? Why had Jenna never mentioned it to me?

The manager and agent side of my mind was focused on the details. He had presence, but it could be packaged even better. It was difficult to see if he was enjoying himself because concentration lined his face. He was a man determined to hit each note perfectly, who hadn't yet learned to focus on the experience instead of his execution. As his manager, I could help him with that.

But the side of me that wasn't focused on her job, the one that was simply a woman, struggled to breathe. I'd seen him stark naked and thought he couldn't possibly have looked better, but seeing him bathed in the warm stage light with a guitar strap slung over a shoulder threatened to melt my insides. His music seeped into my body, making me smolder.

I was rooted to the floor, mesmerized by him, and it wasn't until the song was over that I could move again. I went to the darkest corner at the back of the bar, sat on a stool with a cracked vinyl top, and watched the remainder of his short show.

It'd been thrown together last minute, and they stuck to a setlist of tried-and-true favorites to keep the crowd engaged, all until the final number. The rest of the band exited as Troy switched out to an acoustic guitar and then settled at center stage.

I couldn't place the song after the first sets of chords, but when he belted out the first line of the lyrics, my mouth dropped open. It was U2's "Still Haven't Found What I'm Looking For," but he'd put a country spin on it, filling his voice with twang.

The song showed off his impressive vocal range. The high notes were packed with power, and the low notes soft and beautiful. It was up-tempo, but the audience was frozen. Like me, they were riveted in place. Troy had us all in the palm of his hand as he sang a stripped-down version of a song about elusive love.

I couldn't stop the sensation creeping along my nerve

endings or the thought from storming into my head.

I wanted to be what he was looking for.

His performance gripped me until the final chord, and it wasn't until the applause and cheers began to die off that I came out of my stupor. I lusted after him, both professionally and as a woman who was twenty years too old for him. And I was jealous of the younger girls in the audience who smiled up at this gorgeous singer and probably dreamed of going home with him.

Perhaps one of them would, but I hoped not.

There was a swallow's worth of beer left in the bottom of my glass, but I ignored it. Troy hopped down off the stage and had a brief chat with the band members there, and at the end of it, the drummer slapped a wad of cash into his hands. It had to be Troy's cut of the tips for the evening.

His Fender was retrieved from the bassist, and by the time he pushed through the side door, I was on my feet to hurry after him. A mixture of emotions swirled inside, including irritation. He was inexperienced, but still too good for this to have been his first-ever performance. Plus, I knew how Blanche's entertainment worked. He'd either auditioned or performed elsewhere to make it onto their standby list.

So, why the hell didn't I know how talented he was? The only thing that made sense was that it had been kept from me. But why?

Blanche's Honky Tonk had a cozy, dive-like atmosphere, but it was manufactured. The décor was fabricated to look aged and the seating worn, but it was actually new beneath. The building itself was old, but had been renovated recently, keeping its charm, while hiding the newer upgrades.

But not in the 'staff only' area of the bar. The hallway was grimy and ancient, with a light overhead that could barely illuminate my path as I wove around boxes of liquor and broken equipment. I'd been back here enough times and could find my way through. The guy who ran the place was a friend of Ardy's, and I'd helped schedule Lauren's standing gigs with him.

I loved this section of the building. It was *real*.

The white walls had been graffitied by past performers and staff. Cables for the sound systems ran in a jumbled mess along the wall and were strewn across the ceiling, leading toward a rack of electronics in the corner. Set lists had been tacked up to a cork board, along with employee shifts for the week.

Behind the manager's office and an employee break area was the green room. It wasn't big—only enough space for an old sofa, a mini fridge, and a desk perched in front of a lighted mirror. More than anything, it was a place for the talent to store their gear, tune, and mentally prepare for the stage. It was where Troy was, zipping his guitar up in its padded case on the couch as I stepped inside.

When I shut the door, he snapped upright in surprise. "Ms. Graham?"

I ignored the urge to correct him on my name, or the fact he looked both excited and nervous to see me. Instead, I demanded, "How long have you been doing this?"

He glanced quickly around the room, confused by what I was asking, and searched for the answer like it was written on the walls somewhere.

"How long," I clarified, "have you been performing?"

His gaze returned to me and the confusion dissipated. "Two years, I guess?" He let out a tight breath. "I started doing shows when I was in Chicago."

Meaning, when he was in college. It made a little more sense now why I hadn't seen him before. The last thing I had wanted to do during my long divorce was hang out in bars alone, on the off chance I'd scout some talent.

"What are you doing here?" he asked.

I wasn't sure if he meant in this room or the bar. "You know what I do, right?" Surely Jenna had told him I was an agent and manager, or at least in the business. "Lauren—the act before yours—she's one of my clients."

It wasn't news to him, that much was clear. His lips parted to say something, but nothing came out. I shifted my weight and put my hands on my hips.

"Why didn't your mom tell me you were performing? She knew I was going to be at Blanche's tonight."

He lifted a noncommittal shoulder. "Because she doesn't know I . . . Look, this is just something I do for fun." He jammed his hands in the back pockets of his jeans. "I'd appreciate if you, like, didn't tell her about it."

I blinked against the enormous information he'd just lobbed at me. He didn't do it for money, which wasn't surprising. At most, he'd made an extra hundred bucks tonight. But I liked how Troy had climbed on that stage because there'd been an opportunity, and he enjoyed performing.

Yet he wanted it kept a secret? "Why?"

"Because she'll tell me about all the people she knows who tried to make it and failed. That it's a pipe dream, and I need to finally get serious about my life."

My heart thudded painfully in my chest. I knew Jenna well enough that I heard the conversation they'd had with perfect clarity in my head. The hardest thing was I was likely the shining example of failure my friend had used when she'd talked to him. I'd struggled for five years before realizing my big break wasn't coming, and it was never going to happen for me.

I wondered if the thing I most exceled at was failure.

"I know she's right," he said softly. "That's why I only do it when they need someone to fill in."

"She's not right," I said automatically, before tempering myself.

Nothing was known in the entertainment business, and I wasn't going to stand in front of this kid and tell him I could make him a star. I didn't exaggerate or make promises I couldn't keep. But I'd seen something in him that was too strong to ignore, and the least I could offer him was the truth.

"You're talented, Troy. I see lots of potential." He gazed at me with deep skepticism, making me continue. "You think I'm joking? I'm not."

It was like he didn't want to believe me, but hope was a powerful thing. "Potential," he repeated.

"My boss represents Stella." I quirked an eyebrow at his surprised reaction. "Yes, *that* Stella. She's going to be holding auditions for the opening act of her final show here in town. I think you should try out with that U2 cover you just did."

He shifted back like the information had knocked him sideways. "What?" His gaze went unfocused, and his chest moved rapidly with his hurried breath. "I can't do that."

"Yes, you can, Troy. You *should*." I took a step toward him, forcing his gaze to sharpen on me. "She wants to find that diamond in the rough, an artist to pay it forward with. You are exactly what she's looking for."

He stared at me for a long moment, before breaking it off and glancing at his guitar. "Yeah, right."

"You liked playing tonight, and that was for maybe a hundred people. Imagine ten thousand. Don't you want that chance?"

"Sure. But it's never going to happen." He raked a hand through his hair, and I forced myself to focus on the line of buttons on his plaid shirt, instead of how sexy that action made him look.

I was too in the moment to think about consequences. Too blinded by how good he could be. "Maybe you don't believe me, but you don't have to. I can believe in you enough for both of us."

God, his eyes were stunning when they filled with surprise, and my statement unlocked whatever restraint had been holding him back. "If I try, then I'm going to want it."

"I get it." I understood what he meant with every fiber of my being. I allowed myself to be raw and exposed with him. "I used to be where you are, so I know how scary it can be to put yourself out there. To want something so bad and how it can crush you when it doesn't happen. But not trying? Not going for it? Shit, I promise you, Troy, that's so much worse."

My truth filled the space between us like a bridge, allowing me to reach him.

His voice was uneven. "When I fail—it'll prove her right."

I couldn't believe the words coming out of my mouth. "Then, you don't tell her." He jolted at my unexpected statement, but I kept going. "You're already keeping your performances separate from her, so this audition . . . could just be an extension of that."

His broad chest rose as he took in a deep breath and considered.

"It doesn't have to stay a secret," I added softly. "You can tell her after we land you that opening slot."

"You really think I have a chance?"

I delivered the most serious look I possessed. "Yes. I do."

"So," his voice thickened a single degree, but I felt the weight of it, "we're keeping this a secret too, then?"

My breath caught in my lungs, and my heart stumbled, but the rest of my body flooded with steam. "No, I was going to tell her about—"

Gone was the hopeful boy from a moment ago as he advanced toward me. My affirmation had replaced him with the confident man I'd seen before on the stage and in the sweltering heat of my pool house.

"Tell her what? That I saw you naked? That it got me so hot you caught me jerking off?" A faint smile teased his lips, and the air in the room abandoned us as he closed in. "And then we both got naked, and I came while I watched you play with your pussy?"

"Oh, my God," I whispered. The heat from the memory

caused a deep ache between my legs.

"You think she's going to be cool with that? Or us working together, once she finds out?"

No, she wouldn't be. Not in a million years. But he also brought up an excellent point. "What we did," I said between shallow breaths, "is not exactly how I like to start a professional relationship with a client."

"Hmm," he mocked in agreement, as he finished invading my space, moving so we were toe-to-toe. He was only a few inches taller than I was, but his presence was overwhelming. It derailed my thoughts on why it would be a good idea to put up boundaries. He was closer than we'd ever been, just inches from my lips. "You seemed to like it okay."

I stared up at his handsome face. He had long lashes feathered around his blue eyes, and as he blinked, I felt the sweep of his lust across my skin. It was powerful and addictive, promising to fulfill the craving I'd had for years.

"Troy," I whispered, although I had no idea if my plea was for him to stop or to act on the longing he'd created inside me.

"Isn't that what you came back here for?" He laced seduction into his words. "So I could give you a private performance?"

My shaky voice wouldn't even convince myself. "We can't."

"Sure, we can." And then he echoed back nearly the same phrase I'd given him. "We *should*."

Damn him and his fucking amazing voice. It was impossible to resist.

We hadn't touched when we'd been in the pool house together, but everything was different this time. He was far more in control than I was.

It was why I didn't move as he lifted a hand and cupped the back of my head, angling my face up so he could gaze down at me with hooded eyes. His warm breath wafted over my lips, threatening his kiss. I swallowed so hard he must have heard the click of my throat. It didn't stop him from his goal, though.

The strands of my long auburn hair shifted beneath his palm as he gently urged me forward, pulling me into him until his mouth closed over mine. The moment our lips touched, I went weightless. It was like leaping off a stage into the waiting hands of the crowd, yet never landing. Falling forever.

His mouth was the same as his singing voice. Gentle one second and full of commanding power the next. I softened beneath him, and I wasn't aware I'd moved until I found my fingers laced together behind his neck.

It didn't matter that it'd been a long time since I'd been kissed, because I'd *never* been kissed like this. Troy's lips moved against mine, urging me to mirror his angle and match his pressure. My pulse throbbed in my neck, banging like a furious drum as we tasted each other.

If he had a flavor, it was just like his music. Sinfully rich and hot.

My head spun, and I was grateful for the way he held me as he deepened the kiss. His tongue pressed at the seam of my lips, and although I shouldn't have, I opened my greedy mouth to let him in.

His tongue slid against mine, and I was hopelessly drowning in desire.

Fuck. It felt so good.

The way my heart fluttered over merely kissing a boy, it made me feel like I was eighteen and not forty-two.

He had one hand in my hair while the other gently grasped my waist, and his lush tongue filled my mouth. It was eager possession, and everything I'd wanted for so long. I went giddy with excitement. My body reveled in hands that actually wanted to touch and explore.

His mouth drifted from mine, planting kisses across my cheekbone, as he moved toward my ear. It made me shiver and melt when he discovered the tender spot on my neck, and then his lust-choked words filled my ear.

"Fuck Tinder," he uttered. "You don't need it. I'm right here."

To add to his sales pitch, he leaned in and pressed the hard length of his body against me, reminding me how male and ready he was. A sound of satisfaction escaped from my throat, and I pressed urgently against him.

My desire was so strong, it blurred the line between want and need.

But this could not happen. Tension twisted my insides, and when I solidified, Troy slowed.

"I don't get involved with my clients," I whispered, as his lips brushed across the curve of my neck.

He pulled back and stared at me with a hard, exacting look. The ends of the whiskers on his jaw glinted in the light, making them look a shade lighter than the rest of his brown hair. "I guess you can't be my manager then."

I blinked. "What?"

His kiss had been so distracting, I hadn't realized he'd worked the hand on my hip up under my shirt, so it could rest on the waistband of my jeans. The pad of his thumb traced the edge where the denim stopped and gave way to the bare skin of my stomach, and the connection was like a drug. Each gentle stroke of his fingertips made me weaker.

"Are you serious?" I asked.

His half-grin was devious. "Don't make me choose, Erika."

I thrilled at hearing my name on his lips, but my brain wouldn't be quiet. How was this even possible? "You'd give up an amazing opportunity—"

His mouth crushed against mine, silencing my words, and his searing kiss burned away all thought.

"I want this," he murmured into my mouth. "You told me to go for it."

"I meant the audition for Stella."

"You're saying you don't want this too?" His tongue flicked in my mouth, and a traitorous moan seeped out of my chest. He was just as talented at using his regular voice to persuade, as he was with his singing voice. "Why can't we help each other?"

"Are you," I gasped, "trying to extort me?"

"Of course not." He nipped at my lips. "Is it working?"

Fuck, it totally was, but I couldn't let him know. It didn't matter, though. He walked us backward until the edge of the desk hit me behind my legs, and then his hands clasped around my ribcage. His sure grip lifted and pushed me back, seating me on top of the desk with a loud thump.

I gaped up at him in shock, but he wasn't apologetic. If anything, he looked victorious. Lord, it was fucking hot. He moved to stand between my parted knees, and his mouth captured mine, driving me back against the cold mirror.

There wasn't a lock on the door. Anyone could walk into the green room right now and catch us. Honestly, what we were doing was incredibly tame by musician standards—I'd walked in on at least one orgy in the past with one of the bands I'd managed.

But if I was going to take him on as a client, this was beyond unprofessional. It was a line I wasn't going to cross.

Like you care. Didn't you cross a bunch already?

Troy's hands dove under the hem of my shirt and slid up, his fingers gliding up over my bare skin until his palms landed on my bra-covered breasts. His action sucked all the air from my lungs, and I slumped farther back against the mirror. Maybe I'd done it to give him more room, but I wasn't sure. I was halfway out of my mind for letting this happen, and I lost whatever sense I had left when his fingers hooked into the front of the cups of my bra and jerked them down.

My breasts tumbled free into his awaiting hands. As he palmed me, his mouth latched on to the side of my throat and sucked, sending sparks of pleasure skittering down my legs.

I wanted to wrap my thighs around his hips and lock my ankles behind his back. I wanted to ask him if he liked how my new tits felt and tell him the way he gripped me was so fucking perfect. Instead, I summed it all up in one word.

"*Fuck*," I gasped.

"Yeah." He was short of breath, and his voice went low and rough. "We should do that."

The image of us together sliced through my mind. I saw him tugging off my jeans, one leg at a time, while I struggled to undo his zipper over his massive erection. He'd pull a condom out of his pocket, tear it open, and by the time he had it on, I'd have stepped down off the desk and turned around.

He'd bend me over, and although he'd take me from behind, I'd get to watch through the mirror. I'd see his hands, which were rough with callouses from his guitar, clench on my hips as he drove into me. Satisfaction would twist on his sexy face.

It was the hottest fantasy I'd ever had, and I went cold with the realization that, that was all it could ever be—a fantasy. A sob of disappointment welled as a hard lump formed in my throat, but I swallowed it down.

I sat up so abruptly, I nearly knocked our heads together. "Wait, wait."

His hands froze, each one cupping a breast, and uncertainty tightened his expression. It grew into anxiety as I closed my hands over his and gently eased them down and away.

I hated the words, but knew I had to say them. "We can't."

There must have been enough seriousness this time in my expression because he retreated and straightened. He knew the answer but asked it anyway. "Why not?"

"Pick a reason," I said. "It's unprofessional. Inappropriate. I'm twice your age, and your mother's best friend."

"So? We're both adults." Was that desperation in his eyes? "She doesn't need to know."

I sighed and pushed off the desk to stand on my kiss-drunk legs. "Then, go with one of the other reasons."

"I'm serious." Troy's expression was firm. "I'd rather have a chance with you than the audition."

Everything went still.

I didn't ask it to be mean, because I was full of worry. "Are you insane?" There was no power in my voice. "This is a once in a lifetime opportunity."

"Yup."

He'd said it so simply, I couldn't help but wonder if he thought I was talking about me and not Stella's audition. No, that was ludicrous. Almost as ridiculous as this bluff he was making. He was a twenty-four-year old, self-assured guy used to getting his way.

"I don't believe you," I said. "Look, what we did cannot happen again, especially if we're going to be working together. So you need to put it out of your mind."

He laughed like he was amused, but it was tinted with bitterness. "Yeah, right. Forget it then. I'm not interested in auditioning."

What the actual fuck? "Because I won't sleep with you?" Anger flared inside my belly. "If you're too scared, man up to it. Don't try to use me as an excuse."

Oh, he didn't like that. His posture went stiff, and his eyes narrowed. "I'm not using you as an excuse." He dipped down to grab the strap of his guitar bag and jerked it up onto his shoulder, before shooting me a dark look. "I'm a lot younger and you were married, and it was wrong, but . . . shit. I wanted this for a long time. And then it happened, and it was even better than I thought it'd be."

It felt as if he'd picked me up and flipped me upside down. I didn't know where to look or what to do, but the weaker I became, the more he seemed to strengthen.

"And now," his tone was sour, "you're saying it can never happen again. I couldn't stop thinking about you before any of this, how the hell am I supposed to now? And work with you on top of it?"

It was like I was standing on ice. Any move I'd make would be precarious. I couldn't latch onto thoughts or process what he was saying. "What?"

"You can't be my manager," he said. "You don't know a thing about me."

I was too dumbstruck to do anything other than watch him stride to the door, yank it open, and walk through it without another word to me.

EIGHT

Troy

I parked my Jeep on the street in front of Erika's house and turned off the engine, but I couldn't make myself get out of the seat. Eventually the heat would get to me and force me out, but I need another minute to prepare. It was Tuesday, which meant I'd need to go inside her pool house.

Last time I had, it'd been one of my fantasies come to life. *Don't think about it.*

Because if I did I'd get hard, and I was frustrated enough already.

She'd sent me a text yesterday.

> Erika: Can we set up a meeting? I'd like to talk.

My answer was straight to the point.

> Me: No.

If I took a meeting with her, she'd fill my brain with ideas. I'd see record deals, and music videos, and thousands of fans screaming my name—when none of that was going to happen. I'd dreamed big once and failed so hard, I'd learned my lesson.

Hopefully.

Yeah, she'd said she'd believe in me enough for the both of us . . . but I was still gun-shy. And I figured, why risk getting burned again for nothing? At least with her, I had a chance. She'd opened the door, so I wasn't going to leave until she told me to. She wanted me to audition and I wanted *her*. That seemed pretty fucking simple to me.

I needed to get her to say yes.

The sun was baking me, so I shoved open my door, climbed out of the Jeep, and trudged toward her gate. When I climbed the hill of her backyard, I sensed I wasn't alone. She was already home?

Erika had been waiting for me, judging by the two glasses of iced tea that sat on the patio table. The ice inside them had melted, making the top half of the glasses look watery.

I pulled to a stop and was glad she couldn't see my eyes behind my sunglasses. It meant I could stare. I could take in every gorgeous inch of her. She was wearing white pants and a pretty blue top, looking like she'd just come from work.

"Troy," she said, her tone soft and warm. "Can we talk?"

I let out a breath as I considered her question. She'd told me I shouldn't get within striking distance of her because she was dangerous, and I was starting to think she may have been right.

She could be like Coach Parker all over again, promising me everything I wanted to hear. Telling me my dreams could come true, when it was all bullshit.

But I was smarter this time, or at least older. She wanted me bad enough to wait for me, so I could hear her out. I strode toward the table and grabbed a chair. "Yeah, sure."

She gestured toward the sweating glass in front of me. "You want some tea? I can get more ice."

"No, it's fine." My tone was guarded. "What do you want to talk about?"

"You," she said. "You told me I don't know a thing about you, and you're right. Can we fix that?"

My shoulders pulled back at her unexpected statement. "Uh . . . I guess."

"How long have you been playing?"

"I started about five years ago."

"Did you take lessons?"

I drew in a slow breath. "If YouTube counts, yeah. I watched a lot of tutorials on different songs I wanted to learn how to play."

It didn't seem to matter to her that I was self-taught. "Just guitar?"

"At first. I started trying the piano last year, but I'm pretty terrible at it."

"What about singing? Did you take vocal lessons or—"

I shook my head. "My mom made me sing in church, and I was in choir in high school, but that was mostly for the grade." I relaxed a little into my seat. "I, like, paid attention, though." I didn't want her thinking I didn't care. My voice was just as important to me as my music. "I watched videos about vocal exercises too."

"That's good," she said. "How'd you decide to start performing?"

A smile twitched on my lips. "My dorm had a talent show night."

Since she could hear the amusement in my words, she guessed the outcome. "You won."

I'd won easily. It hadn't even been close.

"Yeah," I said. "I discovered I like performing, so I found a couple of other guys to play with, and we got some gigs at the bars just off campus." I changed my mind on the tea and picked up the glass, swirling it to mix the water with the rest of the drink. "They paid us, and it was fun, but when I graduated, we had to go our separate ways."

I drank a long sip and didn't miss the way her gaze lingered on my throat as it bobbed in a swallow. She was trying so hard to stay professional, but it seemed to be a battle she was losing.

Good.

"Original songs?" she asked.

"Nah, just covers. I've tried writing my own stuff, but it's . . ." I frowned. "Everything I've come up with so far has been shit."

"Songwriting's not easy." Her voice was full of understanding, and it was a long moment before she spoke again. "What made you want to learn the guitar? Have you always wanted to perform?"

Oh, man. That was a question that could lead us into a whole *thing*. "No." My voice was uneven. "I did it because I wanted to impress someone."

Her posture straightened as if she suspected. "A girl?"

I took off my sunglasses and cast them down on the wrought iron tabletop with a clatter, giving her the full intensity of my stare. If this was as close as I was going to get with her, I might as well just do it.

"You could say that. She was married at the time."

Erika became a statue and it looked like chaos was scrambling the inside of her head. Was she doing the math? Five years ago, I'd been *nineteen*.

And she'd barely known I existed.

"Remember my mom's fortieth birthday party?" I leaned over the table, bringing us closer.

It had been a surprise party my stepdad had thrown for her at the country clubhouse. It'd been such a big deal, Bill put Erika in charge of handling the entertainment. While the band she'd hired had been great, they weren't the best performance of the night. My mom had asked if Erika could join the band on stage for a song near the end of the night.

It was the first time I'd ever seen her play. The first time I'd heard her sing.

"You were really fucking good," I said, even though it was an inadequate compliment. "I went to find you after that song, because I needed to say something. Like, tell you your voice was amazing, or that I couldn't take my eyes off you."

It wasn't that often I got shy, but with her?

I always struggled.

I shoved my awkwardness aside and continued. "I hadn't even thought of what I'd say or if it would be weird. I was younger. I did whatever stupid thing I wanted to back then." I still did now sometimes, didn't I? "All I knew was that listening to you felt—I dunno—*special*. I wanted you to know."

She was so stunned she could barely squeeze out the question. "Did we talk?" Her gaze dropped to the tabletop, and there was an ache in her voice. "That night was special for me too. It was the last time I ever performed."

"Oh." My tone matched her sadness. "No, we didn't talk. You were in the lounge with your husband. I didn't want to interrupt."

She sucked in a breath.

So . . . she remembered that. I'd discovered her and Mr. Graham hidden in the empty lounge beside the event room. It'd been late and nearly everyone at the party was drunk, and she'd tried to get her husband to fool around with her in a dark corner.

But he'd shut her down. Worse, really, because he'd acted offended by her suggestion. Like it wasn't incredibly hot, and she should have been ashamed of herself. The memory of it made me tighten my fist under the table.

"You saw us arguing," she guessed.

I gave a plain look. "What I saw was Mr. Graham being a fucking idiot. He turned you down when nearly every other guy in the place would have killed to be with you. You know that, right?"

It didn't look like she believed me, but it was the truth.

I made a face. "That shit pissed me off. How could he pass on you?" I crossed my arms. "I watched y'all together after that night, but it made it worse. He never touched you, didn't pay attention. Sometimes, I don't think he was aware you were even in the room."

The breeze blew, ruffling her hair, but she didn't move to push the strands back out of her face. The intensity between us had her locked in her chair.

"I always knew when you were around." My voice went soft. "So, I figured if he wasn't interested . . . I'd try to show you a guy who was."

She blinked, slowly processing all of it. "You're say-ing you learned to play the guitar, because you wanted to . . . fuck me?"

My chest expanded with a deep breath, and I rubbed the pads of my fingers against my forehead. "Okay, so it doesn't sound great when you say it like that."

It was encouraging that she didn't look like it sounded all that bad to her. Warmth colored her cheeks. "But we nev-er talked."

"I was working up to that." I quirked the corner of my mouth into a pained smile. "Your pool is the only one I work on."

She pressed her lips together. "Your master plan was to seduce me with clean skimmers and perfectly balanced pH?"

I laughed. "I told you, I was working on it." I didn't know how long she'd need after her divorce. She wasn't dating yet, according to my mom. "Look, maybe it's weird or it doesn't make sense to you—but it makes sense to me. You're hot. Us together? We'd be off the charts. And don't act like you're not interested." My dirty mouth hadn't shocked her before—in fact, she'd responded to it. I smirked as I went in for the kill. "Shit, you're looking at me right now like you want me to bend you over this table."

She straightened uncomfortably in her seat, which told me *everything* I needed to know. She was visualizing it right this second, me pulling her from her chair, getting her pants down, and bending her over until her tits were pressed against the wrought iron.

I loaded it with seduction. "You want me to?"

She tangled her fingers together in her lap, pinching her knees together. "It doesn't matter what I want, because you can't do that."

Was she kidding? "Yeah, I fucking can."

"No." She sighed. "I mean, we can't."

I flexed the muscles in my jaw with annoyance. "Why not?"

"Because if I slept with you, I might lose my job."

I . . . hadn't thought about that, but there was an easy solution. "We don't have to tell anyone," I offered. "I've already proven I can keep a secret."

Hadn't I? I wasn't talking about hiding what we'd done in the pool house from my mom or my performances at Blanche's either. I meant the years I'd gone secretly wanting her. Waiting to strike when the time was right.

Wasn't it now?

She sucked in a heavy breath and stared at me like she wanted to give in.

Just say yes, Erika.

"You're asking me," I said, "to take a chance on this audition. I think it's only fair you take a chance on me."

She gazed at me like she was standing on the edge of a cliff. "That's it? Your final offer?"

"Yeah." I was confident she was going to agree to it. How could she not?

The breeze stopped blowing, and the moment hung for an eternity. Much longer than I expected it to, and I searched her eyes for her answer.

She rose from her seat. "The pool's been cloudy the past

two days. Come see me when you're done."

What?

No.

It felt like I'd been punched in the chest. My mouth dropped open, and I sat in shock, watching as she strode quickly toward the house, abandoning me at the table with the two glasses of melted iced tea.

I'd fucking blown it and I didn't know where to go now or what to do next.

I'd been so sure she'd see this was a total win-win. But she didn't come back out of the house, and . . . I couldn't sit there all day like the idiot I was.

I took my time while cleaning her pool, trying to come up with a way to salvage the situation. I considered my options as I tested the water, skimmed its surface, and added the right chemicals in to balance the alkalinity.

When I put away the last of the supplies and made my way across the covered patio, Erika was waiting for me just inside her house. She slid open the back door and hovered, her hand still latched on the handle. I slowed my pace as I gazed at her, confusion wiping out the things I was going to say.

She'd changed clothes, which made sense, but why was she wearing a fluffy white bathrobe when it was eighty-five degrees outside?

I was only a few feet away when she shed the robe, shrugging it off her shoulders and letting it fall until it was a heap on the floor.

My mind went blank as I took in the sight of all the dark red lace wrapped around her magnificent body. Had

I died? Was I dreaming this? I traced every line and curve of the bodysuit like I was reading a secret message meant only for me.

She was so hot, I was going to damage my retinas just looking at her.

"Fuck," I whispered.

"Yes," she answered, her voice wavering. "We should do that."

NINE

Erika

It took Troy only a heartbeat to process what I'd said before he had his hands on my body. He rushed at me, clasping one arm behind my back and a hand clenched on my ass, and then his mouth crushed against mine.

His kiss numbed my mind, yet filled me with fire. My heart went into overdrive as he pushed his tongue past my lips and claimed my mouth, moving in as if he had every right. It pulled a groan of satisfaction from my chest.

The door was jerked shut and we stumbled deeper into the kitchen, me backpedaling, while he advanced. The eat-in counter jutted out from a wall and sectioned the space off from the dining area, and he guided us to it.

I didn't get a moment to catch my breath before he picked me up and plopped me down on the counter—but I gasped anyway. The stone was icy cold against my flushed, bare skin.

His mouth was needy. It moved against mine like he was starved for connection, and now that I'd finally allowed it, he was going to feast. In an instant, I was lightheaded and falling . . . only to realize he'd pushed me down onto my back. More cold stone kissed my skin, but then he was there, climbing up on the counter so he could follow me onto the peninsula.

I'd made this decision back when we'd been seated at the table, yet I'd second-guessed myself the entire time while I changed into the red lingerie I'd bought a year ago. I hadn't bought it for Clark, I'd reminded myself while tugging it into place. I'd bought it for myself. Plus, my ex-husband had never seen it.

While I'd only gotten a glimpse of Troy's reaction to the sexy bodysuit, it had been everything I'd hoped for and more. His eyes hazed and lips parted to take in a wild breath before he'd lunged at me.

My head was still spinning from what he'd confessed. Five years he'd wanted me, and now he'd become a man wild with lust.

It was wrong, but I couldn't help myself. I felt exactly the same way.

What we were doing was reckless. He was my best friend's son, and she'd never forgive this betrayal, but I was too desperate to stop. Troy and I were already past the point of no return, so I justified what was happening between us made no difference.

In for a penny, in for a pound.

The edges of his whiskers burned against the curve of my neck when he carved a steady path of kisses toward my breasts. Our hands were everywhere. Neither of us could get enough of touching the other. I wanted to explore more, and as soon as I fisted the back of his loose shirt, he was helping me pull it off.

I sighed contentedly when he lowered in and flattened

the warm, bare skin of his chest against me, but I only got to enjoy it for mere seconds. He planted a kiss in the hollow of my throat before his palms slid over my lace-covered breasts and cupped them, pushing them together. I arched and thrust upward to encourage his mouth to find my nipples trapped under the fabric.

Beneath him, I became wanton. I grabbed and clawed at his shoulders, squirming with satisfaction as he gave me my wish. God, his lips on my skin felt amazing, even through the whisper-thin mesh. There was a constant throb between my legs, pounding as a relentless beat of music that had the power to turn me into a slave.

"I fucking love your tits," he growled.

"*Oh*," I moaned. His teeth captured my nipple, delivering just enough force to bring pleasure but not pain. I'd forgotten how that could feel—the sharp tug it caused in my center—and how sexy it was to watch. His blue eyes studied mine while he toyed with my sensitive flesh, and I struggled to find air.

Part of me wondered if he was impatient and eager to get to the next phase of foreplay because he shifted over me, his skin squealing against the marble when he began his descent. Troy backed down off the counter as his hot mouth trailed along my body, leaving damp kisses across the mesh fabric in its wake.

My pulse sputtered. Anticipation caused goosebumps to lift on my skin. Was he . . . about to go down on me?

I gasped as he buried his face between my legs, and the sound I made was a perfect mixture of surprise and satisfaction. I bowed up off the stone. Just the heat of his mouth against me sent an acute shock of pleasure up my spine.

It'd been years since I'd had a man's tongue on me, and I quivered at the sight of Troy nestled between my thighs, his mouth closed over the snaps at the bottom of my bodysuit.

It was in his teeth, and my vision blurred until he was nearly indistinguishable. Fuck me, it was erotic.

Rather than undo the snaps, he hooked a finger under the crotch of the lingerie and jerked it aside. This time, when he set his mouth on me, nothing stood in his way. Not the fabric, nor a ring on my finger, nor the years spanning between us.

"*Yes,*" I cried, letting the word bubble up out of my chest.

His tongue was magic. It painted wide strokes of bliss, and I jolted from each one. Every delicious flick was so powerful, I instinctively gripped a handful of his soft hair, holding him to me.

I tried not to think about what we looked like. How I was spread out across the counter as this shirtless guy half my age fucked me with his incredible mouth, but the picture of it stormed into my mind and amplified the lust coursing through my veins.

His tongue abruptly ceased moving, and something suspiciously like concern tinted his voice. "You okay?"

I'd had my eyes closed to better enjoy, but they flew open and I lifted my head to peer down my body at him in confusion. What had I done that had him worried?

Troy sensed the question in my mind and delivered a soft smile. He smoothed his palm reassuringly up and down the inside of my thigh and his voice was as gentle as his touch. "You're shaking."

Warmth bloomed in my cheeks. "I haven't had anyone pay attention to me in a long time." I said it quickly before I thought better of it. "I feel like a virgin."

The deep noise of satisfaction he gave hit me like a wave. My head fell back to the counter with a loud bang, and then his mouth returned, nuzzling into me. He found my clit and closed his lips around it, and I moaned louder than I had in my entire life. Like all the pent-up sexual desire he'd filled me with released in that instant.

Each flick and flutter of his tongue made my legs shake harder and my heart pound faster. I had to drag air in and out of my lungs while I squirmed under the pleasure he gave.

"I like paying attention to you," he whispered, his lips moving against the most intimate part of me.

I was going to fly apart. Vibrate right off this countertop and burst into a million pieces. Since the surface was smooth beneath me, there wasn't anything to grab onto other than us, so I filled my hands with my breasts, massaging and teasing. Troy groaned his approval at what I was doing, his eyes hazing with lust. I'd never felt more sexually alive or powerful than I did in this moment.

Moans dripped from my lips as he coaxed them from me. He'd picked up speed and focused on my clit, and his palm against my thigh pinned me to the counter, holding me open for him. He swirled the tip of his tongue, causing electric shocks to fire across my nerves.

It was erotic and sensual.

Huge gulps of air from me were separated by needy whines. I was close—so fucking close—and the intensity of my approaching orgasm pressed down until it was all I could think about.

"Oh, oh, *oh* . . ." I gasped.

Heat swept through my body, radiating ecstasy outward until every inch of me was tingling with bliss. As I shuddered, it was just enough to break the contact from Troy's mouth and he straightened, looking down at me as my climax rolled through.

He didn't say anything as I slowly recovered, but he didn't have to. His expression announced exactly how pleased he was with himself, and 'smug' was a good look on him. Having this gorgeous guy with a sculpted chest loom over me was amazing, but as he wiped a hand over his mouth and delivered a satisfied smile, it was nearly too much. Aftershocks of pleasure rocketed through my system.

Blood pumped loudly in my ears, but when it began to slow, I closed my eyes and threaded a hand through my long bangs, brushing them back. What was he thinking about as I lay there motionless before him, my trembling legs loosely wrapped around his hips? He'd confessed he'd wanted this for a long time. Had I even come close to meeting his expectations? He'd exceeded mine so spectacularly.

The first orgasm I hadn't achieved by myself in *years*.

He stood there and smiled like I'd given him pleasure and it wasn't the other way around.

I pushed up onto an elbow, hooked a hand behind his neck, and jerked him down to my lips. He had to slap a palm down on the counter beside me to keep from falling into me. My action hadn't been graceful. I'd put too much force into it, but it got the job done, and our fumbling kiss strengthened as I plunged my tongue into his mouth.

While my body was cooling post-orgasm, his was heating up.

The heavy sigh of satisfaction Troy gave . . . it echoed in my center. I'd trailed a hand down his chest and cupped him through his shorts, stroking the bulge pressing at the center seam.

Shit, he was so huge.

And *hard*.

I slowly traced the outline of him, which maybe was teasing, but I was enjoyed it way too much to go any faster. As I explored, he hooked the fingers of his free hand into the neckline of my bodysuit and jerked it down. My breast was only bare from the lace for a second before his mouth latched on.

The orgasm he'd delivered had only temporarily taken the edge off of my desire, and a new ache swelled in me. It had me forcing a hand inside his board shorts and curling my fingers around the thick girth of him. His skin was hot and velvety soft.

Air went sharply in through his clenched teeth, like a reversed hiss. His shoulders shuddered with pleasure when I awkwardly pumped my hand on him, making him throb. It was a tight fit inside his shorts, and I wanted them gone. I needed to touch every inch of him and revel at what we'd both been denied for so long.

"Get these off," I demanded.

"Yes, ma'am." His grin made him look impossibly young and even more attractive.

I'd never seen a guy get naked so quickly, and the second he was, I couldn't control myself. I clasped both hands around his dick.

"*Shit*," he groaned while my fists slid back and forth in steady strokes.

I squeezed even harder. "Is this for me?"

In response, he nudged his hips forward, essentially fucking my hands, and brought his mouth right beside my ear. "Every . . . last . . . inch."

His words were like a drummer slapping his drumsticks together to set the tempo for the opening song. There was no going back now, and we let the rush of performing carry us away.

I scrambled to unhook the clasp at the back of the bodysuit and pull down the straps. I wanted to be as naked as he was, but it was awkward trying to get the lingerie off while I hopped down.

"What are you—" he started, but I grabbed his shoulders and spun him around, pushing him back against the counter. He threw out his hands to brace himself, and it sent the silver dish full of decorative lemons flying. The fake food bounced and rolled, while the dish clattered loudly to the floor.

But Troy didn't pay any attention to it.

His focus was fixated on me as I dropped my knees to the expensive tile floor I'd let his mother talk me into.

Oh, God. His mother.

I forced her from my mind and focused on what I was desperate for. I was out of my mind and selfish with lust.

"I want you in my mouth," I said.

He'd given me so much pleasure, I was eager to return the favor. I curled my fingers around his hard cock, parted my lips, and took him inside my mouth. I'd only slid down a few inches on him before he began to thrust, and he wasn't gentle either.

He was . . . *urgent.*

Like he'd waited his whole damn life and wasn't going to waste another second.

The deep stroke of him between my lips was sexy and it caused fireworks to spark between my thighs. The steady thump of his hips crashing against the cabinets as he fucked my mouth, punctuated the quiet of the kitchen, rising over his gasps for air.

We would look insane if anyone were to walk in on us like this. For a single breath, I considered Clark showing up unannounced and witnessing Troy pinned against the kitchen counter, me on my knees and his dick in my mouth. It was scandalous. Shockingly out of character for me, and—*shit*—it was freeing.

But the thought vanished as quickly as it had arrived, evaporating as Troy moaned.

Was it really wrong, the two of us together? We were consenting adults who clearly enjoyed what they were doing. And I'd spent my whole life always doing the right thing, and what had it gotten me? A broken, sexless marriage, followed by an expensive and messy divorce.

No more.

I was reinventing myself, and what I was doing now with Troy helped to build the new version of Erika Graham. She was a woman who'd blow a guy half her age in her kitchen in the middle of the day. She was wild and unleashed. And she had no qualms about asking for what she wanted sexually.

This blowjob was murder on my knees, but so fucking worth it.

"Fuck," he said through tight teeth, "that feels so good."

I stared up at him as I bobbed my head, letting my tongue roll and cartwheel over his sensitive tip. His eyes were heavy, and his chest rose and fell rapidly with his hurried breath. God, he was so hot, it wasn't even fair.

His thrusts stopped, but I kept up the tempo. He buried a hand in my hair at the back of my neck, probably wanting to ease me back and slow me down. But he'd unlocked a secret part of me and set it free, and the feral creature I became was desperate to give him satisfaction.

I rocked on my knees, sliding my fist along the length of him in time with my mouth.

There was panic in his voice. "Erika, I'm close."

I set my free hand on his hip, telling him I wanted this. I tightened my grip on his cock, twisting on each stroke, and gave a hum of approval.

He'd been fighting the urge, trying to hold off, but I made it impossible, and he gave in seconds later. His thrusts resumed, and he pushed deep into my mouth.

"I'm gonna . . ." he gasped. "Fuck. *Fuck.*"

I froze in place as his movements became shallow and

erratic, and the grip in my hair tightened to the point it was uncomfortable, but that only turned me on more.

"*Fuck*," he moaned again.

Every rhythmic flex of him filled my mouth as the orgasm surged through, one pulse after another. I swallowed immediately, and that action made him shudder. When he finally stopped throbbing, I retreated.

He was leaning back on his arms, slumped against the counter as he continued to catch his breath, and he gaped at me like he wasn't sure if I was real. Or if what we'd done had really happened.

Emotion suddenly reared inside me, filling me with alarm. It was so overwhelming, I couldn't tell if I was about to laugh or cry. So, I did neither. I knelt at his feet and stared at him with wonder.

Dear lord, he stole my breath. His face was glossy with sweat, and his heartbeat seemed to be pulsing in the side of his neck. He gazed at me with satisfaction, but also with a touch of embarrassment, like a student about to admit he hadn't done his assignment.

I was buzzing, and my warm voice reflected my dreamy state. "What is it?"

His gaze shifted away. "That was over a lot sooner than I wanted it to be."

If anyone should have been embarrassed, it was me. I'd ruined our chances for anything else. "I know," I said. "I'm sorry. I was enjoying myself and got carried away."

He laughed like what I'd said was amazing. He bent and grasped my arms, helped me to my feet, and then pulled me close. "I need fifteen minutes," he said softly, "and I'll be ready again."

"What?"

The corner of his mouth lifted into a sultry smile, and his confidence returned faster than the snap of his fingers. "If you want to go down on me again," he drawled, "I bet I could be ready in ten."

TEN

Erika

I stared at the red bodysuit in a heap on the floor as the air conditioner kicked on. I was right under a vent, and when I shivered, Troy walked to my robe, picked it up, and held it out for me to put on.

And when that was done, he gently grasped my face and kissed me, dropping a quick series of playful pecks before growing more serious. His tenderness was disorienting. He was young and supposed to be inexperienced, yet he knew exactly what I needed.

His hand slid down my neck and inside the robe, cupping a breast, and heat began to pool inside my center. He thought he'd need ten minutes, but my body was ready whenever he was. I was dressed in my robe, but he made no effort to put on his clothes.

"You're still naked," I whispered.

He grinned lazily. "You noticed that, huh?"

It should have felt uncomfortable and awkward . . . but it didn't. It had to be him. He had no problem being alone with me in my house—which he'd never stepped foot inside before—and being here sans clothes, he acted like it was perfectly natural.

Like he'd been here all along and I hadn't noticed him

until now.

"Maybe," he sandwiched between kisses, "we can go somewhere more comfortable? Not that the counter wasn't fun."

I smiled. "Hey, that was all your idea."

"Yeah, I know." He shrugged. "I couldn't wait any longer."

His words caused flutters in my belly, and I tucked a lock of my hair behind an ear. "Well, I have a bedroom. It has a bed and everything."

He exaggerated his fascination. "You don't say? This I gotta see."

Troy released me, scooped up his shorts and t-shirt, and followed me through the doorway out into the living room. I passed the couch, the fireplace, and was nearly to my bedroom door, before I realized he'd stopped.

He stood with his gaze fixed on the wall, and my pulse quickened when he examined the pictures hanging there. It was a series of photos taken of me throughout my stalled career as a performer.

There was one photo from twenty years ago, where I was sitting on a stool with an acoustic guitar in my lap and a microphone in front of me. The background was blurry and indiscernible to anyone else, but I recognized it as the coffee shop I'd often performed at when I'd been a music major at Vanderbilt.

I'd been in a band for a hot minute right after graduating, and there were pictures of us on stage during the Tennessee State Fair. Beside that, my debut at the Opry House.

Last, and most important to me, was the framed artwork

consisting of two sheets of paper lined with bars and musical notes.

Troy gestured to it. "What's this?"

I fiddled with the belt to my robe, not wanting to give away how proud I was and risk sounding pompous. "It's 'Reckless.' The first song I ever sold."

You mean the only *song you ever sold.*

Troy's brow furrowed as he read the lyrics, and his gaze traced over the notes. He'd said he was learning the piano, so it was likely he knew how to read music.

"Have you heard it?" I asked.

Without prompting, I sang the first line of the chorus, which was the most recognizable part. The song had been a modest hit for Alan Foles six years ago, but since then, we'd both faded into obscurity.

Troy's mouth dropped open in surprise, but I wasn't sure if it was my abrupt singing—or if he recognized the song. He stared at me with unflinching eyes as I softly sang about secret love and being scared to tell the other person how I felt.

The atmosphere in the room grew enormously intense in a single heartbeat. The lyrics and their meaning were so powerful, it forced me to trail off.

Oh, Jesus.

Was this how he felt about me all these years?

"You make me want to be reckless," he sang back, completing the line in his smoky voice and with perfect pitch, and my hands tensed into fists beneath the long sleeves of my robe. I had to clamp down and squeeze my throat shut to stop the gasp from escaping. Hearing him sing my lyrics

was an emotional assault I was entirely unprepared for, and I blinked back the tears that stung my eyes.

It was so beautiful and perfect, I worried I'd fall apart.

And despite my effort to look unaffected, Troy could tell.

His expression warmed and his voice softened to a hush. "I like that song," he said. "I had no idea you wrote it. That's awesome."

"Yeah, well," I raised my eyes toward the ceiling to drain back the tears, forced a casual smile onto my lips, and shrugged. "Alan did a great job with it."

The sudden emotional turn in the conversation had put Troy off-balance because he dropped his clothes and pulled the throw blanket off the back of the couch, wrapping it around his waist and using a hand at his hip to hold it closed. I had the weird feeling that he hadn't covered himself because he felt vulnerable. He'd done it to make me more comfortable.

"What else have you written?" he asked.

I swallowed painfully. "Nothing."

He tilted his head in question, and I dropped my gaze to his hand clenching the gray blanket. The fabric draped loosely around his waist, dipping down on the side opposite where he held it closed, revealing paler skin that hadn't seen the light of the sun.

"Maybe it was my job, or the way things got with Clark, but the music dried up," I admitted. "I haven't been able to write at all the last two years."

He hesitated. There was a question he wanted to ask but wasn't sure if he should. Or maybe he didn't know how to phrase it. But he pressed forward. "It's none of my busi-ness, but can I ask what happened?" He frowned at himself. "You don't have to tell me. You probably don't want to talk about it."

I went with the easiest answer. "He fell in love with someone else. And he forgot he was still married to me."

"He cheated on you?"

I inhaled a deep breath. "Yeah."

I didn't tell him with who, because despite everything that had happened between us and how terrible Clark had treated me, I wasn't going to 'out' him. I hadn't even told Jenna the truth. Just that I'd caught my husband having sex with someone else, and I didn't correct her when she made the assumption it'd been a woman.

Anger flashed across Troy's face. "He's a fucking idiot."

I lifted a shoulder in response. What else was there to say? "You're not wrong."

"I got cheated on once." As soon as his statement was out, he frowned and waved a hand like he was trying to brush his comment away. "Okay, I get it's not the same. Doesn't com-pare to yours, but I just meant it sucks and people are stupid. If you want to be with someone else, go be with them. It ain't that hard."

I drew in a deep breath. "Again, you're not wrong."

We lapsed into silence, and it grew cold and awkward.

He scrubbed his palm over his chin as he contemplated what he'd said, making his scruff bristle against his fingertips. "I made it weird." He gave an apologetic smile. "Sorry about the boner-killing conversation."

A short, unexpected laugh burst from me. "Boner-killing?"

"Yeah."

As he strolled toward me, the mood in the room shifted yet again, but it lightened. How the hell did he do that? The promise of sex lurked in his eyes, and I couldn't help but see dollar signs in his future. I'd given up any attempt to be professional with him, but when he strutted to stand in front of me, I had a vision of him in a music video, crooning a love ballad and making every woman in America swoon over his bedroom eyes.

They'd go as weak kneed as I was now.

He let go of the blanket and it dropped to our feet. "I promised you another round, didn't I?"

Excitement edged my voice, but I tamped it down and bit my bottom lip. "Troy—"

Too late. He threaded his hands into my hair and lowered his mouth to mine. He kissed me as if it were do-or-die, like an audition where he'd have to give it his all, leaving everything on the table.

Instantly, I was drowning in him. I succumbed to his lips and the desire coiling inside me, not fighting him as he tugged at the knot on my belt to undo it. I followed him blindly as he led me to the couch, slipped a hand inside my open robe, and eased me down to sit on the cushions.

Did he know his kiss was just as powerful as his singing voice was to me?

He knelt beside the couch and nibbled on my lips, his hands roaming over my bare skin.

"How is it," I murmured between his slow kisses, "you're

so good at this? More YouTube tutorials?"

His grin was lopsided. "Those kinds of tutorials aren't YouTube."

Troy's hands scooped under my legs and he jerked me to the edge of the couch, making me flop back on the cushions at an angle. My legs straddled his waist, and I was still technically wearing my robe because my arms were in the sleeves, but the sides were wide open. It gave him a perfectly naked ribbon of my body to drink in.

A moan seeped from me as his hands took full advantage of the access he had. His palms smoothed over my breasts. They caressed my stomach, my hips, my legs. His musician hands played me like an instrument he'd studied, and I made all the sounds he'd hoped for because lust flared across his face.

The way he looked at me was amazing. And sort of terrifying because he gazed at me with reverence. He'd put me up on an unwarranted pedestal and it was much too high.

His blue eyes were focused as his hand glided over my waist, inched downward, and brushed between my legs. His featherlight touch sizzled.

"Oh, my God," I whimpered as he pushed his middle two fingers inside me, all the way until his knuckles pressed against my sensitized skin. I arched up, bowing off the couch cushions at the sudden pleasure. I reached out, grabbing onto the thickest parts of his arms, and my gaze was drawn to his fingers as they slowly eased out and disappeared inside me again.

The sensation made my toes curl into points and I dug

my fingernails into his skin, unable to control myself. Shit, it felt good. So different and new and better than anything I'd had before.

Troy was kneeling next to the couch, but he sat back on his heels and dipped down, running his tongue up the length of my slit. It tore a cry of satisfaction from my lungs.

"Yeah?" His question was teasing, seductive, and one hundred percent rhetorical.

He swiped the tip of his tongue over me again and chuckled wickedly when my legs trembled as he passed over my clit. Blood rushed through me, hotter than lava, and I struggled to catch my breath.

While he licked and teased, his fingers continued to pump, and goosebumps burst down my calves. I'd had to give up my hold on him when he'd started going down on me, so now I clutched at the couch, fisting whatever part of the upholstery I could latch on to.

"I could eat this pussy all day," he said.

The room tumbled as his tongue swirled, and it spun faster still when he pulled his mouth away and used his fingers to rub. He'd had his arm under my thigh and a hand on my stomach, but he trailed it down so his first two fingers could manipulate the swollen nub of flesh that gave me the most pleasure.

My moans filled the room, overpowering the sounds of enjoyment he made. He liked watching what he was doing to me. His lips were parted, and his eyes were magnetic.

Back and forth his fingers rolled, filling me with a powerful, urgent need. He was absolutely going to make me come again. The only question now was when, and my body wanted the answer to be, "right fucking *now*."

He adjusted the angle of his thrusts, sliding deeper.

"Oh," I breathed, "right there."

He moved faster, sliding his fingers so quickly we could both hear the sound they made against my wet skin. If I wasn't so frantic, I might have blushed, but there wasn't room to think about this sound as anything other than sexy.

I pinched my eyes closed and savored his possession. He was young and gorgeous—he could probably get any girl he wanted. What on earth was he doing with me?

It was unavoidable, the way my body began to writhe, as I approached my orgasm, but luckily his hands moved in sync with me. Troy's thick fingers plunged and retreated while he rubbed me viciously with the ones from his other hand, causing sparks to fire behind my eyelids.

"Oh, my God," I cried in warning, but it only made him ratchet up the intensity. Tremors skirted up my legs as the storm of ecstasy took me over.

"Fuck yeah," he groaned. "Come all over my fingers."

His dirty talk was shockingly sexy, and it poured gasoline on the fire of my orgasm. Bliss exploded, forcing me to buck, but once again he moved with me, keeping his fingers lodged inside. It prolonged my climax, making wave after wave crash into me and causing my nails to drive into my palms.

I floated in a daze, unable to do anything but breathe while the pleasure began to recede. As I recovered, Troy straightened and set his warm hands on the tops of my thighs, gently squeezing as if wanting to remind me of his presence.

To be connected to me throughout the experience.

My heart was still hammering in my chest as I propped myself up on my elbows and peered at him. I couldn't imagine what I looked like, although my face had to be flushed. The robe around my shoulders was a cloak of fire, making me sweat even more than I'd been before. Surely my hair was a mess. I could feel it plastered to the back of my neck.

Yet, he blinked seductively as his gaze drifted up over my naked skin, and he stared back at me like I was flawless. The hunger was back in his eyes and his body. His erection was nearly as hard as it'd been when I was on the counter.

His tone was flirtatious. "Do you have a condom I could use?"

If I wasn't already out of breath, that would have done it. "Yeah," I said. "In the drawer of my nightstand." I collapsed back on the couch. "Give me a minute and I'll be able to walk again. My legs are still shaking."

Troy chuckled proudly, leaned over, and dropped a kiss on my lips. "I'll be right back."

There wasn't time to stop him, even if I'd wanted to. He was up on his feet instantly and disappeared into my bedroom, leaving me to recover while I was strewn across the couch cushions. He'd gone with such urgency; he'd practically bounded from the room.

There was a pang in my heart. He was *eager* to have sex with me. Lord, I'd spent so much of my life with someone who didn't initiate and certainly never was excited for intimacy. All those years with one man, while another was right there, secretly wanting and willing to give me exactly what I craved.

The sound of the drawer sliding open came through the doorway, followed by rustling and the tearing of perforated foil. But then it went silent and still.

My heart thudded, slowing down with each quiet second that ticked by. There was no noise of him shutting the drawer, and no footsteps thudded closer to announce his return. What was he doing in there, alone in my bedroom?

"Troy?"

There came a thump as the drawer closed, and he emerged from my bedroom with a smile tilting on his lips.

"Did you get lost?" I teased to mask my relief.

He lifted a shoulder in a half shrug. "A little. That's some collection you've got there, Erika."

When I realized what he meant, my mouth went dry. I sat up on the couch and swiped a hand over my hair to smooth it back into place while my face burned. "Oh, shit."

In my disoriented state, I'd forgotten about the rest of the contents of my bedside drawer. When he'd paused in my room, it was because he'd been staring at the various vibrators, dildos, and toys I used to get myself off at night.

The muscles in his chest and arm flexed and rolled while he stroked a hand over his dick to maintain his erection. It was unavoidable the way my gaze caught the glint of the pale blue wrapper in his free hand as he sat down beside me.

His voice was low and pure seduction. "You should show me how some of those toys work."

My heart stumbled over itself. "Now?"

He grinned and shook his head. "No." He tore open the

condom wrapper and began to fit it over himself. "Some other time, because right now I just want it to be us. Me fucking you exactly how you want it."

He finished rolling on the condom and ringed his fingers around the base of his cock, holding it proudly out from his body. His words sent a jolt of pleasure down my spine that settled between my legs, and grew more acute when he asked his question.

"So, how do you want it?"

It felt like someone else was in command when I stared at his sheathed dick, awaiting me to climb on, and his direct question unleashed my thoughts. "I want your mouth on my tits as you fuck me."

Air left him in a sharp exhale and desire consumed his face. My words had surprised him, and he not only approved, he looked utterly thrilled. As I rose onto my knees and turned to straddle him, he pushed a hand inside my open robe to grasp my hip and help guide me.

The sheathed tip of him began to intrude, and I gasped with pleasure.

The stretch of my body around his cock filled me with delicious tension. The sensation went on endlessly as I slowly yielded to him, taking more and more and *more*.

We breathed together in a shuddering breath as I slid down. My warm skin was flattened against his. It was a lot to take, and I controlled my breathing, struggling to adjust. Holy shit, there was someone else inside my body.

Troy's head thudded against the back of the couch for a second as pleasure ripped through his expression, and it was as if he needed a moment to regroup. To mentally prepare for what we were about to do.

He straightened with focus in his eyes.

I was the one on top, yet he was the one in command. Beneath me, the muscles in his thighs went taut and he flexed up into me. His hands were firm on my waist, urging me to rock back and forth and ride him. It flipped a switch in me, and unstoppable moans swelled up from my throat.

Was it supposed to feel this amazing? Or had it simply just been so long I'd forgotten?

We must have had the thought at the same moment because our hands tangled as we tried to get the robe off my shoulders. It hung on my elbows as Troy abandoned that task and cupped my breasts in his hands. He squeezed and massaged, his thumbs brushing over my hardened nipples, but it was the caress of his gaze I enjoyed the most.

He licked his lips before nuzzling into me, his hot mouth latching on and sucking until I whimpered with satisfaction. The way he feasted on me was pornographic. Better than any fantasy my mind could have cooked up.

Time lost all meaning as we ground our bodies together, taking pleasure from each other. I shed the robe completely and shivered in enjoyment as the dull edges of his fingernails raked down my bare back. His short beard grazed over my nipples and was followed by the gentle bite of his teeth. It poured heat into me, swirling like an inferno.

Sweat beaded on his forehead, but he didn't slow his thrusts, some of them so powerful they nearly lifted me off the couch. Tingles washed over my legs. The friction of our bodies rubbing together was stimulating my clit, just enough to make me think another orgasm could be in my future.

But it'd need help.

I leaned back, bracing a hand behind me on his knee, and walked the fingers of my other hand down to where we were connected. Troy's eyes widened with excitement as he realized what I was doing.

His voice rasped like it'd been dragged over gravel. "You're so fucking sexy."

I rubbed myself as his compliment caused sparks to fire inside my body. He was doing more of the work than I was, but it still required a ton of exertion from me, and I was grateful I was in the best shape of my life. Sex with him would leave me blissfully sore all over.

"Tell me you're close," he demanded.

I was, but I slowed the roll of my body and peeled my lips back in a victorious smile. "Maybe I want to enjoy you like this for a little while longer. You can keep up, can't you, Troy?"

Dark heat flashed in his eyes. "Yeah, I fucking can."

"It's okay if you can't," I whispered, stunned by my mocking tone. "I have a drawer of toys that I can always—"

His fingers bit into my waist, commanding me to move. "Maybe you don't need them anymore. You want to get off? I'm right here."

He licked the pad of his thumb, shoved it between my legs, and pushed my hand out of the way. The way he touched me was indecent. Shocks ran along the insides of my thighs.

His tone reflected his ruthless determination. "You like

the sound of that? Me being your personal sex toy?"

"Fuck," I cried. My mind went white-hot at the idea.

"Yeah, I thought so." He rubbed circles on my swollen clit while he continued to pound at me from beneath. "You can use me however you want to."

My heart sprinted frantically, flying toward explosion. Even though I wasn't scared, something like panic filled my voice. "You're going to make me come."

"You're goddamn right," he growled.

Pleasure gripped my body and mind so all I could do was endure the sensations flooding through my limbs. The orgasm swept through me so abruptly, I gave a choked-off cry and collapsed on him, my legs quaking.

His arms locked around me to hold me still as he found his end. I was still falling apart with ecstasy as he joined me, slowing to a stop, and throbbing deep inside. Our gasps for breath were loud in each other's ears, and beneath my palm on his chest, I could feel his heart racing.

Our bodies cooled as he held me shuddering in his arms.

It felt so good tears pricked at my eyes, but I hid it by pressing my lips against the spot in his neck where his quick pulse was beginning to ease.

My voice was so quiet, it was barely audible. "You're kind of amazing."

His chest lifted with a deep breath. "I was hoping you thought so."

ELEVEN

Erika

When Troy returned from the bathroom, he dropped down beside me and cast a thick arm over the back of the couch. It was meant to look casual, but there was a subtle possessiveness to it that I adored. It made it easy to fit myself against him.

How long would this last, where every little thing he did revealed how much I'd been missing?

I tentatively used a fingertip to trace a pattern on his thigh. "We never made it to the bedroom."

The corner of his mouth lifted. "Got sidetracked. Next time."

His statement hung in the silence of the room. Not because there wouldn't be a next time, but because I had guilt knowing that there *would* be one. It seemed inevitable. I'd given in to all my desires, and I was sure I'd only crave him more now.

When Jenna found out, I was going to lose her. And I deserved to, didn't I?

I didn't want to think about it right now. The guilt would come soon enough, and it'd be crushing.

The electronic trill of my phone came from my bedroom, and for a moment I considered ignoring that too and staying cozied up under Troy's arm. But it was likely Ardy, wanting to know how my meeting had gone with the potential new client. He didn't like how mysterious I'd been, and curiosity was eating him up.

"I should get that," I said, reaching for my robe.

Only when I dashed into my room, picked up my cell phone, and saw the caller ID, I rolled my eyes. What the fuck was Clark's deal? I punched the screen to send the call to voicemail. He wouldn't leave a voicemail and was incapable of sending a text message. I suspected he didn't want to put anything in writing or a recording. Had he forgotten the divorce was official?

When I came back to the living room, Troy had pulled on his shorts and was knotting the strings at his waist. It gave me a view of his sculpted chest and the ridges of muscles surrounding his rib cage.

He was in such great shape, maybe I should suggest we work out together sometime.

What do you think you just did?

"Didn't recognize the number?" he asked, since he knew I hadn't taken the call.

I skewed my mouth to one side. "No, I recognized it."

His shoulders lifted with a deep breath. "Ah. You weren't kidding. He does call a lot." He set his hands on his waist. "What does he want?"

"The fuck if I know," I admitted. "I don't answer, and he never leaves messages."

A dark cast fell over Troy's face. "So . . . he's, like, harassing you?"

"No, no." I frowned. Clark's calls were annoying, but calling them harassment felt extreme. "It's no big deal. He'll give up eventually."

Troy was skeptical. "You know you can block his number, right?"

I despised how feeble my voice sounded. "Yeah, of course."

Yet I hadn't been able to bring myself to do it. It didn't make sense why I couldn't cut him off. I didn't love Clark anymore, but I'd spent so much of my life with him, it was impossible not to care, at least a little. I kept telling myself that if it was important enough to get ahold of me, he'd leave a message or text me.

What it boiled down to was I wasn't ready to shut him out forever.

It looked like Troy wasn't all that satisfied with my answer but he wasn't going to push either. He motioned toward the phone in my hand. "I left my cell in my car. What time is it?"

"Quarter to five."

His posture went stiff. "Fuck. Really?" He didn't wait for confirmation. Instead, he scooped up his t-shirt and jerked it on. "I was supposed to help Bill with cabinets at four. He's going to be so pissed." He raked a hand through his wavy brown hair and focused on me. "I should probably go."

I nodded in understanding, but he didn't move. He stood beside the couch, hesitating. I was about to ask him what was wrong when he strode to me, grabbed the knot of my robe, and hauled me into his hurried kiss.

"I meant it," he said. "You call me next time you're thinking about reaching into that drawer."

Thankfully, he couldn't see beneath my robe, otherwise he might have noticed the shiver he caused. I smiled provocatively. "I will."

He grinned as he backed away, not taking his eyes off me until the final second—and then disappeared through the door.

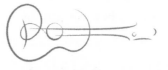

It was late when I climbed into bed. I'd put it off all evening, unsure of how to broach the subject with Troy after what we'd done today.

> Me: Are you still awake? Everything work out with Bill and the cabinets?

> Troy: I'm up and yeah.

> Me: That's good. We didn't get a chance to talk business this afternoon.

> Troy: We can now. Wanna call me?

I swallowed a breath, tapped his name, and waited nervously like a schoolgirl for him to answer.

"Hey," he said over the sound of gunfire and explosions.

"Hi." The background noise became more bombastic. "Are you watching a movie?"

He sounded distracted. "No, it's *Call of Duty*. Just a

second." The sound cut off, and I pictured him pausing the video game. "What's up?"

I sat up straighter in my bed and forced myself into professional mode. "I was thinking we could operate with a verbal agreement until your audition. Assuming you're on board with me acting on your behalf until you officially sign."

He said it like I'd caught him off guard and now he was playing catch-up. "Yeah, sure. That sounds good."

"Do you have a demo you can send me?"

There was a pause. "Uh—"

"Or a recording? I'd like to have a sample on hand for Ardy. He's Stella's manager."

"I can record something on my phone," he said.

I smiled at his eager tone. He was trying to be helpful, but it wasn't needed. "No, let's have you come by the office. There's a small studio setup we can use. What's your schedule tomorrow?"

"I'll be at the gym until noon, then I'm supposed to help Bill with demo at one o'clock. That'll take the rest of the day."

He was going to spend all morning at the gym? No wonder he looked so good. "Can you shave an hour off your gym time, so we can lock down a track?"

"Not really, unless I can come by early? My class is at ten, and I have two clients after."

Class? Clients? "You're taking a class?"

He chuckled. "No, I'm leading it. I do the Bootcamp Burn on Wednesdays." When I didn't say anything, it prompted him to continue. "I'm one of the trainers at Motivation Gym."

Fuck me, he was a pool boy *and* a personal trainer. I was

like the ultimate cougar, snatching up the hottest boy toy. "I didn't know you did that."

"Yeah. My degree is in Athletic Training. Being a personal trainer ain't exactly what I had in mind, but it's a start."

My laugh was tight with embarrassment. "I almost asked you today if you wanted to work out together sometime."

"Totally. I'm always looking for new clients." He said it laced with innuendo. "I could even give you a discount."

Was I blushing right now? At least he wouldn't be able to tell. His effect on me was powerful, and I sucked in a preparing breath. "Hey, listen. Since we're going to be working together, we need to talk boundaries."

The single word from him made it impossible to tell how he felt about my statement. "Yeah?"

"Is it stupid to think we can keep business separate from what we did today?"

His answer came quick. "No, it's not stupid." He paused, likely composing what to say next. "Boundaries. What did you have in mind?"

I pressed my lips together. I hadn't dated anyone in forever—not that what we were doing was dating anyway—but I was horribly out of practice. He had far more experience than I did in this department. That imbalance left me unsure, but there was a bigger issue at work too. "No one can know. If word got out I was sleeping with a client, it could be bad for my career."

"Erika," he said, his voice deadly serious, "I'm not going to say anything. You can trust me."

It felt as if my heart were made of rubber bands, and his

words stretched the outer band until it was taut. If he let go, it'd snap back with a sharp, stinging pain. All the trust I'd poured into my marriage had been rewarded with heartache.

"Okay," I said quickly, trying to gloss over my anxiety. "But just to be safe, can we keep it professional anytime we're not alone? Or talking business?"

He paused for so long, I wasn't sure if we'd been disconnected, but then his tone was rich, telling me he was smiling on the other end. "Are you telling me not to flirt with you?"

I tried to be practical. "I need to deal with Troy 'the artist' right now, not Troy 'the guy I'm banging.'"

His laugh was loud. "Banging," he repeated. "Okay, okay." He settled, and his sigh was colored with amusement. "I get it. When you want it strictly business, you let me know and I'll give you that."

"Good," I said, feeling a sliver of relief. "I need it business tonight because we're behind where we should be. The audition is in a week."

"Oh." He'd said it the same way I expected he said 'oh, shit.'

"Yeah. I'd like to schedule you for as many performances as we can before then. Get you as comfortable as possible with your material in front of a crowd." There was nothing like the pressure of an audition, but I'd do my best to prepare him. "We can talk specifics about that tomorrow. Can you come in at eight?"

To the rest of the artists I dealt with, eight in the morning was an unheard of time. Ungodly early for the people who were up late every night. But Troy didn't hesitate. "Yeah, sure."

We talked a bit more about how the audition would be handled and the web series Stella was planning to run, and true to his word, he never slipped out of professional mode. We didn't talk about the crazy hot sex we'd had, or when it was going to happen again, or whether he was currently having crazy hot sex with anyone else.

Just the idea of that soured my stomach. After we said goodbye and I'd hung up, that was the thing that needled at me. What if I asked him if he was seeing anyone else, and he said yes?

Would I be able to believe him if he said no? He hadn't done anything to make me distrust him, but I was plenty aware at how good he was at keeping secrets.

I focused elsewhere. Tomorrow he'd come into the studio, record a sample, and Ardy would help evaluate. Then I'd know for certain the talent I'd seen in Troy was real, and not clouded by my personal feelings.

As predicted, my pool boy and personal sex toy had left me blissfully sore. I gingerly slid under the sheets, tired but sexually satisfied for once, turned out the light, and laid my head down on the pillow.

I'd only just shut my eyes when the melody echoed in my mind. It was only a few notes, barely two measures, but I blinked in surprise. And as I stared into the darkness of the room, the melodic line fleshed itself out and took further shape. I heard it as plain as day, the up-tempo music with a sexy, playful vibe.

Like Troy in the form of music.

I bolted upright in the bed, reaching blindly for the lamp

switch, and blinked rapidly against the overly bright light as I clicked it back on. I was breathing hard, but sat utterly motionless, worried if I moved, the music would flit away like a scared bird.

But it stayed.

My heart lurched forward with excitement as I launched myself from the bed and hurried toward my home office where my acoustic guitar waited for me on its stand.

A new song.

TWELVE

Troy

Warbler Talent was easier to find than a place to park once I got there. I considered driving my Jeep right over the Toyota Yaris someone had parked like an asshole, taking up a space and a half of valuable street parking. Which was impressive because the car was stupid tiny.

It was too early for that shit, but I tried not to get pissed off because this meeting was important. I grabbed the strap on my guitar case and crossed the quiet street, heading for the agency's entrance.

I was in jeans and a button-down shirt and already sweating, but it wasn't the heat causing it. It was normal for my nerves to act up right before a performance, but usually it was more excitement than anxiety.

Today was . . . different.

One bad show wouldn't hurt me. It definitely wouldn't make or break whatever 'career' I thought was possible for me. But this? If I sucked or didn't impress Erika's boss, she'd pump the brakes on the whole thing. I understood this was an audition I had to nail before I could get the *real* audition.

The floorboards of the entryway creaked as I came in and I liked the sound of it. Maybe because it sighed with age and history, rather than the gleaming floors I'd spent most of last week helping Bill install. And by helping, I really meant doing. He was using me as a crutch more and more.

In the main room, there was a girl sitting behind the desk facing the front door, and the groan of the floor drew her gaze up from her phone. She was pretty, with light brown hair down past her shoulders, and a face full of perfect make-up. She seemed to be about the same age as I was. If I weren't so focused on the woman I'd come here to see, I might have labeled this girl hot. But today I was completely uninterested.

It was clearly not the same for her. The girl's gaze swept over me and her face lit up. She wasn't subtle, and her bright, teasing voice wasn't either.

"Well, hi there. Who are you?"

I pasted on a polite smile. "Troy Osbourne. I've got an appointment with Erika." Was it cool I was so informal? "Ms. Graham," I amended.

The girl's smile hung. She'd expected her friendly tone to warm me up and was confused it hadn't.

Movement to the side caught my attention. Erika appeared from one of the doorways, and my body heated just at the sight of her. I'd been inside her less than twenty-four hours ago and I was still so fucking horny for her.

Be professional, Troy.

She had her hair pulled back, and although I loved her hair down, she looked great like this too. She had on a black sleeveless shirt that showed off her toned arms and was cut low to hint at her amazing rack, and white pants that clung to her thighs. Fuck, I wanted to be between them again.

Any hope of keeping it professional went out the window.

If I had my way, I'd push her inside her office, shut the door, and make her moan my name. But this was business and as usual, Erika was oblivious to the torch I carried for her. She crossed her arms and leaned casually against the door frame.

"Hey, Troy," she said. "Did you find the place okay?"

I shifted the guitar bag from one hand to the other. "Yeah," I said. "Other than someone parked a Toyota Yaris out front like a jerk."

She pressed her fingers to her mouth, and I didn't understand she'd done it to hide her smile until the girl abruptly stood and grabbed her purse off her desk.

"Oh, I didn't realize." The girl sounded mortified. "I'll go move it right now."

She disappeared out the door, and when it banged shut behind her—

"Well, shit," I said. "Now I feel bad."

"Don't." Erika's eyebrow arched up. "Charlotte parks like that almost every day. She's gotten three tickets, but I guess it hasn't fazed her because she keeps doing it." Her focus dropped down to my hand holding the case, and then she nodded toward the stairs at the back of the room. "C'mon. The studio is upstairs."

There was a nervous flutter in my stomach. *Seriously? Butterflies?* I swallowed thickly and followed her up the steps.

We turned the corner at the top, and once I stared down the long hallway, it was obvious which room I'd be recording in. There was a red light over the door and everything. But Erika bypassed it, turning into a room beside the studio, and flipped on the lights.

The mix room had a cool vibe to it. The walls were red, the furniture black, and mounted over the desk full of mixing equipment was a huge TV monitor displaying Warbler's logo. Even though the room was carpeted, there was a red patterned rug in front of the leather couch. It looked comfortable but was currently occupied by a guitar case.

This room was a place of business, but it felt cozy and inviting. The small fireplace on the back wall had probably been functional when this old house was built, but now it was purely decorative. A framed black and white photograph of Stella hung over the mantle. She had on headphones and a microphone in front of her, and she looked much younger than she was now. This must have been taken when she was first starting out.

The wall opposite the fireplace had a door and a window, allowing me to see into the recording studio. It was also painted red, and black sound dampening panels bowed away from the walls. The floor was hardwood, but a microphone stood on top of a square rug in the center of the space. Otherwise, the room was empty and . . . waiting.

My cold sweat got worse. This was, like, *legit*.

I motioned toward the desk and the mixing console with all its knobs and sliders. "You know how to use that?"

She gave a half smile. "I know enough to be dangerous. But don't worry, we'll trust this session to a professional. Once you're ready to go, I'll call Ardy in and he'll handle it." She walked to the couch and reached for the handle of the hard-sided guitar case that was worn and scuffed. "Sorry, I'll get this out of your way. You can put your stuff here."

There'd been a black book on top the guitar, and when she moved the case to make room for me, the book tumbled to the floor, landing open and bending its pages. Trying to be a gentleman, I picked it up and smoothed my hand over the paper to flatten the bent pages—

"What's this?" My name was scrawled in handwriting at the top, followed by lines in stanzas.

Poetry?

No. *Lyrics.*

The thin red ribbon to mark the page hadn't lost its place because it was still tucked against the spine.

Erika let out a nervous laugh and reached for the journal. "It's nothing. Something I was playing around with last night." She added it like an afterthought in a quiet voice. "And maybe a little this morning while I was waiting for you."

My pulse skidded to a stop. "A new song?"

Her gaze darted away. "It might be, yeah."

Holy shit. My heart clanged awkwardly in my chest. "And it's about me?"

Erika clasped her hands around the journal and hugged it to her chest like she wanted to seal the book closed forever. "No, not about you. But . . ."

It was hard to breathe. "But what?"

She lifted her gaze to connect with mine, and the rest of the world faded. I'd watched her enough to understand how emotions played through her, but this one was new. It looked like she was both terrified, and yet excited. "This song might be *for* you."

I'd been disappointed when she'd said it wasn't about

me. This was way better. It was almost too good to be true, and my enthusiasm made it come out like a demand. "Sing it for me."

Her laugh was embarrassed. "Oh, Lord, no. It's not ready. I just started working on it last night."

"You're writing again." I grinned. "After two years."

She drew in a deep breath. "I had music in my head last night."

Fucking hell. Even though I'd saved and scraped every dollar I'd had in college to afford my guitar, I tossed it carelessly down on the couch now, freeing my hands so I could grab her waist.

I made my voice sound as sexy as possible. "I wonder what's changed?" The question was rhetorical, but I didn't give her a chance to answer anyway. "It's okay if you want to say my dick is magic."

"Oh, my God!" She spun out of my hold and her expression was shock, but I wasn't fooled. She was trying hard not to laugh at the truth I'd just laid down. But then her eyebrows pulled together in thought, and her lips turned down in a scowl. "This is business, Troy. You can't talk like that here."

My amusement faded as I realized I'd blown right by the boundary she'd asked for last night. And the boundary was there for a good reason too. This was her job, and I shouldn't be fucking around with it.

"You're right, I'm sorry." I jammed my hands in the back pockets of my jeans to keep them to myself. "I got excited and wasn't thinking." The space she'd put between us helped cool me off and refocus. "I'm glad you're hearing music again, and I can't wait to hear what you've written—when it's ready."

The tension in her shoulders eased and she nodded subtly. The intimate spell was broken, and she shifted her attention toward the couch and my guitar. "How long do you need to warm up?"

Her message was loud and clear. I needed to get on with it. I leaned over and unzipped the case. "I sang on the drive over, so I'm ready whenever y'all are."

"Good. I'll let Ardy know."

Her boss was a guy with a broad chest and a thick beard patched with gray, and I expected him to make my anxiety worse, but he had a calming effect the second he stepped into the recording studio. I had the strap to my guitar on a shoulder, so I tucked my pick into the strings on the fret board and shook his hand. His handshake was firm and sort of fatherly.

"He's got a good look about him," he lobbed over his shoulder to Erika, who lingered in the door between the studio and the mix room. Finishing his visual evaluation, his eyes sharpened on mine. "Okay, kid. Let's hear what you got."

Ardy was stone cold as I played, giving off zero reaction while I belted out the first verse. He crossed his thick arms over his chest, and the only movement he made after that was to blink slowly.

Oh, fuck, this audition wasn't going well.

When I hit the chorus, sweat trickled down my spine, my fingers were clumsy on the strings, and my tongue suddenly felt too big for my mouth. I didn't glance over at Erika because I didn't want to see the disappointment in her—

Shit.

Ardy lifted a hand, signaling for me to stop, and I tightened my left hand around the fretboard to stop the strings from vibrating. My heart pounded in my throat. This was where he thanked me for my time and sent me on my way, I was sure of it. Forty-five seconds was all he needed to hear to know I wasn't good enough.

He didn't speak, though. Instead, he nodded to himself and stroked his short beard with his thumb and forefinger, considering. "Yeah, all right," he announced, turning his head toward Erika. "He needs some polish, but I'm with you. Think you can have him ready in time?"

If I weren't reeling with surprise, I probably would have thought the certainty in her voice was sexy. "Absolutely."

"Where'd you find him?" he asked.

"He's, uh . . . my pool boy."

A smile widened on the man's face and he looked at me for confirmation. "No shit, really?"

"Yeah," I said.

She could have said she'd discovered me at Blanche's, but this made sense too. It was hard pretending I wasn't interested in her, but it would have been impossible to act like we were strangers. And if she had said I was her best friend's son, her boss might have wondered about her friendship impacting her judgement.

Ardy's amusement continued. "Did you know she's one of my best agents? Or was it blind luck you happened to work for her?"

Was he asking if I'd sought her out for opportunity? Because I'd absolutely positioned myself to get close to her—just not for the reason he thought. I tilted my head and pulled the corner of my mouth up into a lopsided smile. "I knew she was an agent."

"Well," he said, "you're not afraid to hustle to get your foot in the door and I can respect that." He strolled toward the door. "You need some hustle if you're going to make it in this business. Let's get your track recorded and then we can talk about the next step."

Everything I was feeling—the thrill making my heart ricochet wildly inside my chest—intensified when my gaze locked onto Erika. She didn't speak, but the proud thought was loud on her face.

You did it.

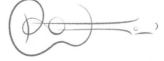

I rode high the rest of the day. It didn't bother me when Bill asked for my help in tearing out the brick fireplace at the new jobsite, or when he stood back to supervise and left all the work to me. I wasn't irritated for once when my best friend Preston bailed on drinks to go hang out with his new girlfriend.

Nothing could ruin this perfect day—although my mom sure tried.

Since I was staying in the guest house, I came and went through the back gate, bypassing the main house completely. Maybe my mom was genuinely hanging out beside the pool, but it seemed unlikely because it was miserably humid out-side, and the gnats buzzing around were always the most an-noying in the evenings. When she spotted me, she stood from her patio chair.

It was clear I'd just walked into an ambush.

"Hey," she said, putting her hand to her forehead to shield her eyes, even though she was in the shade of the um-brella. "How was work? Did you see Bill's text message?"

"I was driving." I pulled out my phone and glanced at it.

> Bill: Just checked the schedule. We're putting
> in a header on Tuesday. Can you take off
> Thursday instead?

Irritation tightened the muscles in my back, and I sighed loudly. My mother was just as involved in the business as my stepfather, if not more. She was the one who helped order things and schedule deliveries.

"No," I said, assuming she knew what the text was about. "I can't come in on Tuesday." I thumbed out the same re-sponse to him.

"Why not?" she asked.

Because I have an audition to open for Stella Mills.

Technically for her team, who'd package the auditions and present them to her and her fans—but the artist had fi-nal say. Not that I could tell my mom any of that. Always the realist, she'd lose her freaking mind and be a buzzkill of epic proportions.

"I've got a business thing all day at the gym," I lied.

"Can you do it some other time? We can't risk Bill helping

install it. You know how bad his back is right now."

She pulled her usual routine of looking distraught. It worked on her husband, but not as well on me. My stepfather's company made good money. Either one of them could hire more workers, but I was cheap and reliable labor. Plus, they had me over a fucking barrel. I lived rent free, and I was sure that would change the instant I stopped "helping" out at the family business.

It was a steady paycheck, but hard work I hated, and I didn't want to end up with a fucked-up back like Bill had. I'd gone to college to train athletes and prevent injuries. Instead, I had to grit my teeth every day and hope I didn't end up with one myself.

I enjoyed the few clients I worked with at the gym, but they were hard to find and it wasn't anywhere near enough income for me to afford my own place. And a few performances a month wasn't netting me much cash either.

But I wouldn't allow myself to dream of anything bigger when it came to music. Erika was incredibly talented, far more than I was . . . but she never 'made' it. What hope did I have?

So, I never expected performing to be more than just a hobby. And I tried not to think about how the audition could change all that.

My tone was firm. "I can't push it. It's scheduled for Tuesday."

"Troy, this is important. The Tanner project is huge, and we're already behind schedule. We really need you. I'm sure if you talk to the gym, they'll understand."

It came out more forceful than I'd meant it to. *"No."*

My mom's shoulders pulled back. "We don't ask much of you, you know. You've got a pretty sweet deal here. We paid for your college and the Jeep. We let you live here, where you've got your own space, with free utilities and rent. You can come and go whenever you please." She frowned and put her hands on her hips. "We even gave you a job while you search for something you want, so I think we have been more than understanding. It feels like you're being ungrateful."

Maybe I was, but— "Don't act like you're doing me a huge favor by giving me that job. We both know that isn't the case." They needed me just as much as I needed them, if not more.

"What are you talking about?" She frowned. "You make good money when you work for Bill—a lot more than you do at the gym, I might add. At least with Bill it could lead somewhere." Her posture straightened and she lifted her chin. It was what she did right before saying something important. "He built his company from scratch, but you know he doesn't want to do it forever. He'd much rather hand it down to you than sell it off."

I pressed my palms to my forehead. I'd suspected this for the last year, but it'd never been said out loud before, and my stomach flipped over. I filled my lungs with air and picked through words in my mind, trying to find the right thing to say. It put me in a tough spot.

But in the end, I went with the plain truth.

My tone was quiet and sad. "I don't want it."

Bill had been more of a father to me than my biological

dad, who had walked out on my mom and me back when I was a toddler. My stepfather was kind and loving and funny. I couldn't have asked for a better man to become part of our family. We didn't share blood or a last name, but I was happy to be his son.

The problem was I was his only child.

His company meant the world to him, second only to our family, so I had to tread carefully. Bill was sensitive. If I turned it down, it was likely he'd see this as my rejection of him as a father, rather than what it simply was—a business I had zero fucking interest in running.

It was Bill's dream. Not mine.

And if I wasn't careful, I'd get sucked into that dream to make my parents happy and wind up miserable for the rest of my life.

"How can you not want it?" My mother wasn't just shocked—she was *hurt.* "I'm sorry, but you need to get your head out of the clouds. You think something better than this is going to come along?"

"Probably not," I said.

But *maybe.*

That was the only answer I gave, and my mom didn't like my attitude . . . or lack thereof. She pressed her lips into a thin line. "Fine. We can talk about the future some other time, but you didn't give us much warning to fill your spot for Tuesday. All the other guys give us more of a heads-up."

That was bullshit. Guys asked for vacations the next day or called off sick all the time. Last week when we'd been working on an addition and the HVAC wasn't installed yet, it'd climbed above a hundred degrees inside the house. It wasn't surprising that two of the guys on the crew "came down with something" and were miraculously better once the air conditioner was turned on.

"It's last minute, but I can't reschedule." I gave her a pointed look. "It's an opportunity, and when I said I'd work for Bill, we all agreed that wouldn't get in the way if something better for me came along."

"Better," she repeated, annoyed. "What is it?"

Since she'd literally just told me to get my head out of the clouds, I wasn't about to say. I played up a shrug. "It could be good, or it could be nothing. I promise I'll tell you about it afterward, though."

I walked past her, wanting the conversation over. I didn't like lying to my mom, and a better use of my time right now would be practicing.

My pads of my fingers were sore, and my wrists ached. I'd spent the last three hours playing the guitar and filming myself with my phone to watch my performance. It made me cringe the first few times with how stupid I looked. Without a crowd, the whole thing felt forced, but Erika had said to keep doing it until I was comfortable. An audience of one was still an audience.

It was after nine when my phone buzzed with a

text message.

> Erika: Got a second to talk?

> Me: Yup.

I tried to play it cool, but I was dying to hear from her. After I'd finished recording with Ardy, we'd gone right into talking about the audition and then I'd had to book it to make my class on time at the gym. I hadn't gotten a chance alone with her.

My phone rang and I didn't bother saying hi. I needed to know right off the bat. "Is this call business," I asked, "or pleasure?"

There was a pause like my question had thrown her.

"It's pleasure." Her voice was surprisingly sure. "Come over, and make sure to bring that magical dick with you."

I grinned bigger than I ever had in my life. "Yes, ma'am."

THIRTEEN

Erika

Waiting to text Troy nearly killed me. I must have picked up my phone a dozen times throughout the day with the intent to tell him how badly I wanted him, only to pocket my phone instead.

I told myself there was work to do first, and once that was taken care of, then we could play. But I couldn't get a handle on the desire sizzling through my bloodstream. When he'd sung at Blanche's, it'd been dark and late, and there had been my shock at seeing him perform for the first time.

Today in the studio, there'd been no shadows to hide away my desire. I had to linger in the doorway behind Ardy so he wouldn't see my face or the way I'd clenched a hand on the doorframe to keep control of myself. Troy's voice, his beautiful hands on the guitar, and his powerful body were sin in the flesh.

I was coming unglued.

So, I gave up on the idea of work, then play. I needed fucking relief, to get the lust out of my system, so we could get back to focusing on other things.

I'd been anxious after we'd ended the call and I waited for him to show up on my doorstep, but the second he did and flashed his bright smile, my nerves evaporated.

"Hi," I said, pulling the door open wider to let him in.

He stepped inside, bringing us nearly chest to chest. There was electricity in his eyes, and sex in his voice. "Hey."

Good lord, my knees went weak with a single word. No wonder I'd gone boneless when he'd sang this morning. He pushed the door closed behind him and as he peered down at me, I caught a faint woodsy smell.

Cologne?

He smelled amazing and looked even better.

"I set up some things for you this week." I sounded breathless because that was what he did to me. "We need to talk about it after."

He blinked in confusion. "After?"

I felt like a woman possessed as my hand fisted the front of his shirt and jerked him forward, making him crash into me. I lifted onto my toes and pressed my mouth to his, desperate to have his lips against mine.

"Oh, I got it." He chuckled. "Business after the pleasure."

"I tried waiting," I said in between kisses, "but I can't." I slid a hand up to cup the back of his neck. "I don't think you understand how badly I want you."

I hadn't meant it as a challenge, but he must have taken it as one, because he had me stumbling backward until I was against the side of the staircase. The edge of a stair tread nudged gently into my back as Troy eased a hand down the front of my pants. He hadn't bothered to undo them, and his forearm was big, but somehow he made it fit and worked his fingers down inside my panties.

I slumped against the staircase and my vision hazed as

the pads of his fingers slid over me, exploring.

His smile was victorious. "You're so wet already."

"Yes," I sighed. I hurried to release the button and unzip my pants, giving him more room. "I've been like this all day."

He grunted his approval and claimed my mouth, his tongue slashing at mine. Trembles moved up my legs in waves. His wicked mouth had my hands balling his shirt into my fists and dragging them up.

But to take off his shirt as I was demanding meant he had to stop touching me, and the conflicting desires waged war in my head.

"All day?" His seductive tone and the brush of his fingers made the ache inside me worse. "Try waiting five years, Erika."

My knees threatened to buckle, but it was like he knew. His free hand latched onto my waist and pinned me to the wall, keeping me upright. His fingers teased like he wanted to be cruel, but he kissed me with adoration.

It popped out before I could stop it. "Why me?"

His fingers slowed as his lips pulled away from me, leaving my skin damp with his kiss.

"I bet you can get any girl you want," I whispered.

"But I want one woman in particular."

He thought I was being playful when I was entirely genuine. "Why?"

Troy's gaze slid down me in an evaluating look and he matched my serious demeanor. "Because you're confident, sexy as hell, and know exactly what you want."

It was shocking he saw me like that, especially when I struggled to believe any of that was true. "I'm faking a lot of it."

His hand withdrew from my pants and he grasped my hip so both of his hands were on my waist, steadying me. His expression said he wasn't buying it. "I watched you get up on a stage and sing like it was the easiest thing in the world. And after that, I heard you tell your husband *exactly* how you wanted him to fuck you. I'd never heard a girl talk like that, and—fuck—I never wanted to be someone else so badly in my life than I wanted to be him." He tore his gaze away, like he didn't want to look at me while he admitted it. "And you don't even want to know how many times I fantasized about it."

Fear fluttered in my heart. "Being my husband?"

"No." A half of a laugh slipped out of him. "You telling me what to do, exactly how you wanted it." He softened back into me and his lips brushed over the shell of my ear. "Every dirty, nasty thing you like."

The idea of it sucked all the air from my body and heat flooded in its place.

I wanted this now too. His fantasy became mine in an instant. Excitement twisted inside my center like a screw being tightened, and my voice dipped low. "What dirty, nasty things do I like?"

He didn't miss a beat. "Oh, all sorts of stuff." He grinned wickedly. "You've got a filthy fucking mind."

I swallowed thickly. "I do."

"So," his teeth grazed against the side of my neck, "tell me how you want it."

This question was exhilarating and a little scary, because it was him handing all of the power between us to me. Given the keys to the kingdom, my mind raced with ideas. All I had to do was vocalize my desires, but which one to lead with?

"Well," I sucked in a breath and tried to sound strong, "I don't want it here, up against the stairs in my entryway."

Amusement glinted in his eyes. "Where, then?"

I pushed off the wall, wordlessly asking him to follow me. Thankfully, my undone pants stayed up around my hips, making it possible to walk through the living room and into my bedroom. I flipped on the bedside lamp and when my gaze fell to the end table, I zeroed in on the brass drawer pull. Until recently, that drawer had contained all my devices of pleasure, but my new, best one was currently standing near the foot of the bed waiting for direction.

"Have a seat on the bed," I requested.

He did, but his focus was pinned on me. He watched intently as I sauntered to him and placed my hands on his broad shoulders.

"You said you'd be my personal sex toy." It was shocking how seductive my own voice sounded to me. "That I could use you however I want." I coasted my hands down his chest as I lowered onto a knee between his legs. "So, I plan to."

He took in an enormous breath, his eyes hazed, and he parted his thighs wider to give me more room. My intent was clear, and he was absolutely on board with it. Troy put his hands on the bed behind him and leaned back, staring at me as I skimmed my palms painstakingly slow over the front of his jeans.

Although he was positioned to make it easy on me, I still struggled to undo the button at the top, and then he had a hand there to help.

"No," I said softly. "I want to do it."

Because there was satisfaction in doing it. Not just the physical pleasure of my hand's teasing brush, either. It was the same satisfaction of unwrapping a present when you already knew what it was, but you wanted it so badly, you were just as excited anyway.

A smile tilted his lips, and he settled back on his arms. "Okay."

He let out a heavy breath when I inched his zipper down and explored the rapidly hardening length of him beneath his underwear. I cupped my hand and massaged, enjoying the quiet groan from him. It was louder the second time when I settled on my knees, curled my fingers under the waistband and lifted, freeing his erection.

"Can I ask you something?" I whispered it as I wrapped my fingers around him.

His chin tipped up to the ceiling, like he was regrouping, and then his gaze locked onto me. "Anything."

It was a simple word, but it carried so much meaning. As if whatever I asked, he'd not only do, but he also wouldn't judge.

He shuddered as I tightened my grip, slid it up to close around the tip, then pushed my fist all the way down to the base of him. White-hot desire seared through me. Would I ever get used to my touch bringing someone else pleasure? I wanted to keep him here forever and watch every sigh he made. Find out if his moans had a melody to them.

"I'm on birth control," I said, "and I got tested when I

found out Clark had been unfaithful. I'm clean."

Troy's lips parted to say something, but nothing came out. He blinked, unsure.

"Are you?" I asked.

"Clean?" He nodded. "Yeah. I'm careful."

I was inclined to believe him. He took such good care of himself physically, it seemed unlikely he'd risk his health and his body like that. I stroked my fist over him and watched the hurried rise and fall of his chest.

"Good," I said. "And what we're doing . . . you're not doing it with anyone else, right?"

"No." He peered at me like it was a question I didn't need to ask. "Trust me. I'm not going to fuck around on you, Erika."

This was harder to believe, but I wanted to. His expression was full of conviction. "What about you?" He strove for a teasing tone, but I heard the truth beneath. "Are you doing this with anyone else besides me?"

Now it was my turn to give him the look that said his question wasn't needed. "You know I'm not."

"Cool." He licked his lips, savoring how I was touching him. "Glad we figured that out." His voice was tight with need. "Curious about why you said you're on birth control."

I wanted to laugh. I'd told him that for a reason, and he was eager to confirm his suspicions.

"Because I was going to ask, if I said I was okay to go without condoms—"

"You want me to fuck you raw?"

All the moisture in my body flooded directly between my legs at his vulgar language. For all his 'yes, ma'am's, he didn't talk like a gentleman in the bedroom, and my mind responded enthusiastically to it, as did my body. I didn't want proper, respectable sex with a gentleman.

I hungered for something . . . darker.

Primal, basic fucking.

Through the connection of our gazes, I didn't need to use words to tell him my answer was yes. I parted my lips, lowered into his lap, and closed my mouth around the head of his dick.

Air left his body in a hiss through his clenched teeth. The sound was pleasure so acute, it was nearly killing him.

His skin was so soft against my tongue, yet firm as steel. I traced circles, swirling my tongue over the tip before pushing farther down on him. Every trick I could think of to maximize his enjoyment, I threw at him. I used my fingers to ring his cock and pumped them in time with my lips. I sucked so hard, it hollowed out my cheeks. He gasped and moaned as we both found pleasure in what I was doing. It was uncomfortable for my jaw because he was so fucking hard, but I didn't slow down.

I was so lost in my desire, once again I didn't heed his warning signs. I didn't pay attention to the way the cadence of his breathing changed, or how his moans went short and sharp. Not even his dick pulsing and throbbing inside my mouth was enough to get me to stop.

It was his hand gently grasping the side of my face that got me to ease back. I looked up at him, stunned to see how he struggled for control. It looked like he was finishing a marathon. Determined and focused, but also laboring to find air.

"You're, like, really good at that." His smile was tight. "I don't want to ruin your fun, but . . . I'm not going to last long if you keep at it."

I went back to using my hand, gliding my fingers teasingly over his dick that was wet with my saliva. "You think it'll be easier when you're all bare inside me?"

He pressed his lips together. "Yeah, it's a concern."

I laughed gently, but my amusement couldn't last under the tension filling the room. This new sexual creature I was transforming into ventured further outside of her cocoon.

I put my hands on his knees, pushed onto my feet, and began to peel off my clothes. The pants went first since they were undone already and sagging low across my hips. Then, my top was pulled up and cast aside. I stood before him in a pink, barely-there bra and panty set, shifted my weight to one side, and put my hand on my hip.

I forced my voice to sound powerful and confident. "Get naked."

Troy reached behind himself and grabbed the back of his shirt, showing off the flex of his thick bicep, and jerked the t-shirt over his head. He tossed it away as he stood, hooked his thumbs into the waistband of his pants and underwear, and down his legs they went.

God, his body.

It was a thing of beauty that made it impossible to hold thoughts in my head.

I motioned toward the bed. "Lie down."

A sexy smirk flashed on his lips just before he climbed on top of it, spread out, and settled down with his back on the sheets. As I undid the clasp on my bra, my hands shook, but it was with anticipation and not anxiety. I had to control my movements to prevent myself from leaping on top of him. It was because I wasn't prepared for how amazing all of this was.

There was a man ready and waiting for me in my bed.

And he was dying for me to tell him what to do. To fulfill my fantasies.

I shimmied out of the scrap of fabric that was my thong and put a knee on the mattress, then the other. I crawled along his body, just as naked as he was, moving until I was over him and tendrils of my hair fell in his face. He used a hand to push them out of our way, lifting his head until our lips met.

The kiss was slow and lingering, more smoldering heat instead of the raging fire he was capable of.

I slid a leg over his waist and straddled him. His notched abs and the warmth of his skin felt incredible against the insides of my thighs, and I metered my breath to stay in control.

It was harder when his palms swept over my nipples and he filled his hands with my breasts. His dick rested on his stomach, which meant when it jerked, the damp tip of him brushed against my ass. He'd gotten close during the blow job, and I wanted this to last a lot longer than that had.

My heartbeat quickened. "I'm going to tell you how I want it."

His focus was split as he continued to knead my breasts and pinch at my nipples, but his eyes sharpened on me. "Yeah?"

"Put your hands behind your head."

He liked me telling him what to do, but there was disappointment now that I was taking away his ability to touch. His fingers trailed over my bare skin as they reluctantly went, and he slid his hands under the pillow beneath his head. It accentuated his casual, almost frat-boy look. Like he planned to sit back and let me do all the work.

It was exactly what I intended.

FOURTEEN

Erika

Troy had said he was my personal sex toy and I was going to enjoy him that way tonight.

"Don't move," I said, lifting onto my knees and shifting back so we were better aligned. I reached into the space between us and palmed his cock, drawing a deep groan from him. He was thick in my hand as I lifted him and teased his bare tip against my clit.

His gaze was focused between our legs, and when I moaned in enjoyment, he canted his hips, trying to gain entry, but I adjusted and moved out of his reach. It made me plant a hand in the center of his chest and give him a strict look.

"Stay still." It was both an order and a plea. I rubbed him against me again and shuddered at how pleasurable this felt. It was torturous anticipation for both of us. The muscles in his arms flexed and corded. He had to be fisting the pillow beneath his head to keep from grabbing me and slamming me down on his cock.

I sounded evil. "You want to fuck me?"

"*Yes.*" His lust-soaked word made me shiver.

"That's too bad," I said with a mocking tone. "Because *I'm* going to fuck you."

I lined him up and slid down, taking him inch by inch

until he was seated deep inside my body. His mouth rounded into an 'oh' and mine probably did too—since it felt unbelievable. With nothing between us, I could feel everything.

"Your pussy's so warm," he gasped. "You're like fire."

The muscles inside me clenched, squeezing at him and giving both of us more enjoyment. He rocked his hips, pressing up into me and I flattened my palm harder against his chest.

"No moving," I warned, "or I'll stop. Understand?"

He both liked and didn't like my rule, but he'd do his best to obey. He gritted it out. "Yes, ma'am."

Whether it was the conditioned response of a southern gentleman or his upbringing to respect authority, it didn't matter. Whenever the polite reply came from him, it strengthened the powerful, sexually confident woman I hoped to become. I wanted to be the fantasy of me he'd created.

The one who liked fucking with the lights on and being in charge. The one who believed her pleasure was just as important as her partner's.

The muscles of Troy's jaw tightened when I began to ride him. A look of concentration swept over his handsome face as I established my tempo. His gaze flitted between mine and the sway of my breasts as I swiveled my hips, rocking back and forth.

The slick push and pull of him made my heart go out of rhythm. It felt like everything inside me was morphing into something new as heat and bliss built at a feverish pace.

He turned his head to the side and groaned it into the pillow. "Fuck."

I'd thought having him stay still and not allowing him to touch would help him last, but maybe it made it harder for him. He sounded as out of breath as I was. Low grunts of satisfaction poured from his lips. Was he already struggling?

I had both my hands on his chest, using them as leverage, but I slowed my hips to a stop and stroked my fingers over the ridges of his muscles.

"Don't come yet," I said.

"Well, don't be so fucking hot," he shot back.

The smile that spread across my face was unstoppable. I'd never thought of myself as a cruel person, but he brought out a side of me that liked to tease. I dragged my palms down his stomach, up my own, and clasped my hands around my full breast. I flaunted what I could touch, but he couldn't.

His eyes filled with music, inked in a hand hurried with longing and white-hot desire. And he moaned like I was tormenting him in the best way possible.

There was one way to make sure I got my orgasm before his, and the memory of him watching me in the pool house while I touched myself seared through my mind. I could get myself off even faster with something other than my hand . . .

I leaned over and reached for the drawer.

He sounded more curious than alarmed. "What are you doing?"

I didn't answer right away, too focused on my task. The rose gold toy I liked best was right on top, and I grabbed it by the handle, then pushed the drawer closed and straightened to sit upright.

"You wanted to see how some of my toys worked." I held

it up for him to see. "I'll show you."

His intrigued gaze was glued to the weirdly shaped toy that had an O-shaped mouth protruding at one end, and was sheathed in silicone. I set my fingers of my free hand over my pussy and spread myself wide so my clit was exposed.

"This," I pressed the button on the handle, making the toy quietly buzz, "uses suction on my clit." I placed the toy over my damp skin, and as soon as it was sealed, I shuddered. "It feels so nice."

Inside me, his dick jerked.

The pleasure of the toy was so intense and distracting, it took a long moment to become aware that the man beneath me was moving again. It was so subtle. Just a fraction of an inch to entice me to allow more.

To bend the rule. To seduce me.

But it felt like the power I'd gained was starting to shift away, and I was enjoying it too much to give up yet. I'd barely started.

"Hold still," I begged. "And don't come before I do."

He exhaled loudly, and the muscles of his abs strained when I resumed moving on his cock. "That's . . . not . . . easy." He lay perfectly still, other than the way he panted. "You feel so fucking good."

Everything was buzzing from the toy and the fullness of him inside me, and it wouldn't be long before an orgasm roared through my body. Trembles shook my legs as I moved faster, and the slap of my body against his grew louder. My hair swayed while I rocked, the ends tickling the bare skin of my back.

"Slow," he groaned, staring at the rise and fall of my body on his. "Careful."

But I didn't want to go slow or be cautious. I was locked inside a pressure cooker filling with steam. My need made me a slave, and I fucked him how my body demanded me to.

His warning was serious and accompanied by a firm hand on my hip. "You're going to make me come."

His attempt to get me to stop moving didn't work. I wrapped my fingers around his wrist and flung his hand off me.

"Shit, Erika. I'm close."

The edge of desperation in his voice not only excited the darkest part of me—it unlocked it. I slowed my hips, grinding to a halt and gazed down at this gorgeous man who'd told me he thought I had a filthy mind. I was determined to prove him right.

"Maybe you need some motivation," I whispered.

Tension crept into his body like he sensed whatever I was about to say would be worse than making him lie still.

"If you come before I say you can . . ." I swallowed so hard it was audible. "As punishment, you have to clean it up."

He stopped breathing. Stopped blinking. "What?"

"If you come inside this pussy without my permission, you'll use your mouth to take care of your mess."

An enormous shudder shook his body, as if he'd tried to hold it back and couldn't.

Because my shocking, filthy decree had turned him on when he hadn't expected it to. He'd barely finished processing it before I resumed moving. His teeth were clenched and the muscles in his neck corded, but he held still and endured the pleasurable way I heaved my body over his.

But it took its toll. No matter how he tried to concentrate, it was getting to him. Not just the slide of my pussy, but the sights and sounds. I couldn't stay quiet as the toy pulsed against my sensitive clit, and I writhed on top of him, arching my back and making my hardened nipples point toward the ceiling.

"Goddamnit," he growled. Although it was so desperate, maybe it was a whine.

I watched porn and knew some of the terms, and I doubted there was anything I could say that would shock a twenty-four-year-old guy. He had internet and was probably into more things than I was.

"Maybe you're a dirty boy who wants to eat his own creampie," I murmured.

He exhaled loudly and flinched beneath me. His dick throbbed, announcing that he'd gotten very, *very* close. The idea of it was too much and pushed me over the edge.

"Oh, my God," I gasped. "Oh, God, *ohmigod . . .*"

As the frenzy built inside me, it was mirrored on Troy's face. Excitement lit his eyes. "Yeah? Come all over me."

My orgasm took me in its grip, and everything contracted—then burst open. I flinched with shocks of pleasure and pulled the mouth of the toy away, the suction now far too intense.

"Fuck, yeah," he groaned. "*Fuck.*"

I was still shuddering when I fumbled to turn the toy off and then dropped it to the mattress beside us.

His warm, rough hands were around my waist, but it

seemed like he'd done it to hold me steady, not to try to control. I'd been wild in the throes of my climax, and he hadn't wanted me to accidentally pull off him. He'd enjoyed me coming almost as much as I had.

"Holy shit," I breathed.

He grinned. "That good, huh?"

It was like the ecstasy had disrupted my brain and I could only produce single words. "Yes," I said. "Good."

As I recovered, he grew bolder. His fingertips skated up my back and urged me forward. He wanted to kiss me, and I wasn't going to deny him that. I needed it more than anything else right now, and our greedy lips collided, lighting a new fire inside me.

The song playing in my head was different than the one last night. It was deeper and more emotional, and my heart panicked at it. I'd told myself the only feelings I was allowed to develop for this man were the ones in my pants. I was coming out of a marriage and besides that, getting emotionally involved with him would further complicate things with both Jenna and our careers.

Yet . . .

I couldn't stop kissing him, and I couldn't stop the wave of longing that swept through me.

When I began moving again, slower this time, Troy stayed a statue. Only his face twisted with satisfaction as I eased up and down. Stroke after long stroke, I found my tempo. When I lifted up and braced my hands against the headboard, I could move faster.

His question came from the back of his throat.

"Can I come?"

It felt so fucking good, I was sure I could wring another orgasm quickly from my body. "Not yet," I cried.

It was not the answer he wanted, and in my greed, I hadn't realized I'd pushed him to the brink. He sat up and wrapped his arms around me, then suddenly turned us over so I was flat on my back, the sheets beneath me.

I gasped as he guided himself inside my body and drove deep, his hands cuffing my wrists and pressing them to the mattress. Denied too long, Troy took control. I gaped up at him in awe, utterly thrilled by the ruthless way he took me. He rutted like a beast.

Determination etched his face and burned in his eyes as he fucked me. The slam of his body against mine was violent and it shook the bed. This wasn't a man wanting to please . . . he'd done that already.

This was a man wanting to find his end.

I marveled at his raw display, how he acted as if his need for me was consuming him. The sexual creature inside me wanted to burst. It was beyond sexy and whispered the power I thought I'd relinquished was still there—it'd only shifted.

His grip on my wrists tightened as he approached his climax, and the furious tempo of his thrusts became uneven. A deep moan climbed out of his chest on his final thrust, and as he came, Troy collapsed forward onto me, flattening his sweat-damp skin to mine.

The rhythmic pulses of his orgasm felt so incredibly good, I moaned in sync with him. He lay on top of me for a long moment, shuddering and spent, before collecting himself and rising onto his arms.

I didn't understand the expression he was wearing. Was he ashamed of how rough he'd been?

Oh.

My breath caught as he sank down my body, making the sheets beneath us rustle as he shifted over them. Was he going to—

Yes.

He was.

I arched my back, bowing off the bed in surprise when he nuzzled his face between my thighs. Holy shit, it was fucking *dirty.*

And I loved it. My hands speared into his hair, holding onto him as he worked to complete his task. Every flick of his tongue was a jolt of bliss.

My voice was heavy, weighed down with debauchery. "Oh, God, yes. Make me come again."

He issued a sound of approval, and hearing him enjoying what he was doing was all it took to send me flying.

The orgasm ripped through me as fire and I was left blissfully tingling in its aftermath. As soon as I stopped shuddering, he dropped a line of kisses across my belly, working his way back to me.

He'd gone from reluctant submissive to dominant and back again, and I couldn't tell which version of him I enjoyed more. I liked playing either role myself. We were so perfectly matched in the bedroom and in music, and if I could be honest with myself for once, I would admit how I wanted to know where else we aligned.

If I could have ordered the universe to send me the perfect man, custom made just for me . . . how close did Troy
come to that?

FIFTEEN

My disoriented eyes blinked open. Where the fuck was I? The bedroom was unfamiliar, and then my gaze went to the empty spot beside me in the bed. Erika's bed. I'd passed out after the mind-blowing sex and now I had no idea what time it was or where she had run off to.

The clock on her side of the bed said it was nearly two a.m.

I was parched, and I needed to find her, so I kicked off the covers, pulled on my underwear, and headed for the kitchen. Hopefully she'd gone there to get a drink and that was all. She wasn't hiding from me in some other room of the house, freaked out by what we'd done and that I hadn't left yet.

It was possible, because I was a guy, and I didn't always understand what a girl was thinking, or if I'd made a mistake.

The kitchen was empty, though.

I figured out where the glasses were, filled one with water from the dispenser in the fridge door, and then drank it in large gulps while I stood in the dark room. Fucking her had been a workout and I needed to hydrate.

When I went back for a refill, the dispenser lighting up my glass, I heard music coming from somewhere else in the house. It was only a few chords before it stopped, and I tilted my head, trying to determine where it had come from.

Like a weird game of Marco Polo, I got snippets from a guitar to help guide me in the right direction. I carried my glass down the hall and toward a set of French doors. Only one side was cracked open, but it didn't matter. They were made of glass, so I could see inside the music room.

Erika sat on the edge of a leather couch with an acoustic guitar in her lap. She wasn't wearing anything but her long reddish-brown hair, and the guitar teasingly hid her nakedness. The sight of her like that squeezed my lungs.

She looked down at the strings as she searched for the right chord, ignoring the open journal beside her on the couch, and she was lit by the moonlight pouring in through the arched window.

She was fucking gorgeous.

Shit, she was going to ruin other women for me.

Maybe that was a stupid thought. I was kind of convinced she already had.

Like an idiot, I stood in the shadows of the hall and watched as she plucked her way through another measure and looked satisfied with the results. She picked up her pen, scribbled something in the journal, and then dropped it with a hurried thud like she was eager to get back to the strings.

Whatever she'd been struggling with, apparently it'd been solved, because she didn't start and stop this time. Erika straightened her shoulders, adjusted her grip on the neck of the guitar, and began to play. Even if I didn't know a thing about song structure, I would have recognized she was starting at the beginning.

The melody was . . . beautiful.

It took its time and reminded me of someone breathing in deep breaths.

When she began to softly sing, the hairs on the back of my neck stood. Goosebumps lifted on my arms. While the volume of her voice was low, the intensity behind it was so powerful I tightened my hold on my glass of water.

It made me a willing slave, unable to do anything but listen to her music and try not to disrupt her. The moment was magic, even more than the last time I'd heard her sing, and I didn't want to break the spell.

Her song was about desire. How she was a prisoner beneath it and whoever she was singing about had such power over her. She sang it was scary, but . . . she didn't want them to release her. She only wanted more.

My pulse sped so fast, I wondered if my heart was going to explode. She couldn't write for two years, and now it seemed like she couldn't stop.

Was this the song she was creating . . . for me?

Because I wanted it to be, but—*fuck*—I really wanted it to be how she felt about me.

Erika strummed her guitar, singing to herself as she stared off into the empty room, concentrating on the lyrics and the notes. When she ran out of song, I was lost. It was fucking heartbreaking there wasn't more.

"Is that my song?" I asked.

"Jesus Christ!" she cried, jerking backward.

"Sorry. I didn't mean to scare you." I pushed the door open and stepped into the room while she glared up at me. Her heart was pumping hard with shock, judging by how rapidly her chest was moving, but it would probably match mine. I was still recovering from hearing part of her song.

"Is this like your thing?" she asked. "Sneaking up on me when I'm naked?"

I laughed. "Do you want it to be? It worked out pretty great last time."

She pointed to the glass of water I was holding, and I handed it to her. She took a long sip, and warmth spread through me at this simple act of sharing. We'd shared way bigger things than this, but I liked it anyway.

I sat down on the couch beside her, resisting the urge to sit too close. I didn't want her to feel like I was crowding her.

She pretended it wasn't important to her, when it clearly was. "How much did you hear?"

"All of it, I'm guessing." I was dying inside but did my best not to show it. "I mean, of what you have so far, I think."

She clutched the guitar so tightly, her fingers squealed against the veneer. "And?"

"And . . . it's amazing." Hopefully, she understood how serious I was.

It seemed like it because air seeped out of her in a re-laxed sigh.

"Is it the song for me?" I asked.

Her eyebrows pulled together, creating a crease between them. "I . . . This wasn't what I was working on this morning."

Interesting.

"Another song?" I grinned. "You weren't hearing music for two years, and all of a sudden, it's nonstop."

She cocked an eyebrow, unamused. "Are you going to

tell me your dick is magic again?"

"Do I need to? I think the evidence speaks for itself."

She smiled and shook her head, humoring me. It made the long curtain of her hair shimmer, and I slid closer, looping a strand around my finger. The atmosphere in the room shifted, becoming intense and serious.

My voice dipped to a hush. "Still haven't answered my question, Erika."

Her eyes were wild and her expression anxious, like she worried her answer was signing the song rights over to me alone and for all time. I opened my mouth to tell her that wasn't true. She hadn't even finished—

"Yes," she whispered. "It's for you."

I kissed her, because how could I not? I'd only heard part of the song, but I'd wanted it so badly, it felt like an enormous gift. No, not felt—it *was* a gift.

Our kiss wasn't like the ones we'd had before.

Until this moment, kissing her had been foreplay. Part of something larger, working toward a goal of getting us naked and sweaty. But this slow, deep kiss wasn't about that at all. It echoed what she'd sung about, how she was scared but didn't want to be released. Our mouths moved together, silently singing how we both wanted more.

The intense kiss faded until she ended it. If I had any doubt it hadn't gotten to her, it disappeared when she touched her fingertips to her lips, like my kiss lingered there.

My voice was full of gravel. "What's my song called?"

"I was thinking of calling it 'Power.'"

I nodded, liking that. "Will you play it again?"

She did, and when she finished, she then began to teach it to me.

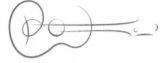

I wasn't sure where the best place would be to throw up in the green room of the Grand Ole Opry House. It was called a green room, but the dressing room had cream-colored walls and furniture decorated in purple velvet. It was fancy as fuck, and basically wallpapered with framed photos and show posters of all the legends who had performed here. Willie Nelson stared down at me.

No pressure.

There was a bathroom attached that I could use, but it was shared with another dressing room, and I wasn't quiet when I hurled. Whoever was waiting in the other room was my competition, and I didn't want them to hear me being a pussy.

Hopefully, it didn't come to me using the trashcan in the corner. My stomach was bubbling and acidic, but it usually went away when I stepped on stage. This waiting was fucking killing me though, and why the hell hadn't I taken more time to distract myself while tuning my guitar?

I checked my phone again to see if I had any new text messages from Erika, but there was only the one from thirty minutes ago.

Erika: We're behind schedule, so sit tight.

Probably another 20 minutes.

I'd warmed up my voice, so now I paced the room to stay loose. It was weird to be alone right now, but there was nothing I could do about it. Preston had work, so I didn't bother asking him to come, and if I had, he might have flaked anyway. Erika was the only one who knew I was here, and she couldn't be back in the green room with me. She was sitting in the audience with Ardy and the rest of Stella's crew, judging.

Plus, I wasn't her only client auditioning today.

I didn't have a clue how many acts were auditioning in total, but she'd told me to block off the entire day. It was a bare minimum of fifteen performers, but probably more. My call time had been eleven a.m., and while I'd been escorted to my room to prepare, I'd heard music coming from the main stage. The auditions were already happening.

Pacing was making my cold sweat worse, and I glanced in the lighted mirror to make sure I still looked okay. I wore the same thing I usually wore when I performed. Jeans, a blue plaid shirt with the sleeves rolled back to the elbows, and my leather cuff. My hair looked decent and my face wasn't shiny yet, so that was good.

A knock at the dressing room door made me flinch. "Osbourne?"

"Yeah," I answered.

"It's time," the production assistant announced.

Fuck. I should have thrown up and gotten it out of the way. Now that window had closed. I grabbed my guitar, pulled open the door, and followed the guy wearing a headset down the hall.

I'd been backstage in the famed theatre before, but that had been years ago during a middle school class tour. It was really hitting me what was about to happen. If this was it—as far as I ever made it as a singer—I couldn't complain, could I? I was getting to perform on the same stage as Johnny Cash, Elvis Presley, and Dolly Parton. Last week, Dierks Bentley had sold this place out.

We wound through the hall, passing other production people and what I assumed was the band that had gone on before me, because they were carrying instruments. My brain could barely register it over the noise that played as nervous static in my head.

The guy I'd been following wasn't much older than I was, but he looked serious and was dressed head-to-toe in black, so he reminded me of an executioner. Maybe he was. It kind of felt like I was walking toward my doom.

What if I bombed?

What if I let Erika down?

Pressure mounted at the base of my spine and crawled up my back. Over the last week, I'd spent every available moment either practicing or thinking about the audition. Erika had gotten me a gig at a bar on the far side of town this past Thursday. It was dark and cramped, a total dive. The crowd had been more interested in their drinks than me when I'd started my set, but I'd been able to convince most of them to come around by the end.

I was as prepared as I could be, she'd told me last night, and she believed in me. She'd invited me over to her house to talk business, but after hearing that, it'd been impossible to keep my hands off her. It led to a quick fuck, both of us needing to let off some steam, before she sent me packing. I needed my rest, she told me.

"Hold here. Don't go out until I tell you to," the assistant said when we reached the curtains at the side of the stage. "When I say so, you'll walk to the mic, someone will get you plugged in, and there will be a quick sound check."

There was a lump the size of a baseball in my throat as I peered ahead. The stage was brightly lit and empty, other than a microphone stand in the center. It was placed on top of a six-foot circle of yellow hardwood, while the rest of the stage was made of darker planks of wood, lightly scratched and scuffed from years of performances. The ring in the center was made from the original stage at the Ryman Auditorium, where the Grand Ole Opry Show was born nearly a hundred years ago. It even miraculously survived the catastrophic Nashville flood in 2010, while the rest of the stage couldn't be salvaged.

The assistant nodded to whatever was said to him through the headset and put his focus on me. "Okay, we're all set. Good luck."

My heart thudded in my chest and my guitar weighed a million pounds, but luckily my feet still seemed to work. I rolled my shoulders back, took a deep breath, and stepped onto the stage.

The lights were so powerful I had to blink against them, but I forced an easy smile onto my face. I'd fake it until I made it in the confidence department, because who'd want to watch some nervous kid as the opening act for a superstar?

The stage was huge as I crossed it. Overhead, red curtains were draped as scallops, and the lights from beneath the balcony tier winked back at me. When I approached the legendary circle of oak, my anxiety vanished. Yeah, this wasn't the same as performing a show at the Grand Ole Opry, and the red seats of the large theatre were mostly empty, but—

This was a moment I'd remember the rest of my life.

And it was all thanks to Erika Graham, who I was finally able to find through the blinding lights and see the big, encouraging smile on her face.

I wasn't going to blow this audition.

I knew because I'd be performing for her.

Once my feet were planted in the ring, I lifted the guitar strap over my head and settled into playing position. A tech guy appeared from out of nowhere, clipped a microphone onto the edge of my guitar's sound hole, and asked me to play a chord.

He got a thumbs up from the guy working the board in the booth, which made him scurry off stage.

"Hey, Troy," Ardy said in his booming voice. He was sitting near Erika, both of them on the main floor center seats. "We're going to start by having you introduce yourself."

I glanced at the camera up on a tripod a few rows behind the team from Warbler. There was a second camera up on a guy's shoulder, who stood in the floor aisle down below the end of the stage. I didn't want to ignore the camera entirely, since the videos were what Stella would judge as she kept her tour going, but I needed to show how I performed live.

I lifted my chin and spoke clearly into the microphone.

"Hi, I'm Troy Osbourne, from right here in Nashville. Today, I'm going to be performing U2's 'Still Haven't Found What I'm Looking For.'"

I'd been kind of a mess when I'd played for Ardy last week, and this was so much bigger than that. So it was shocking when a calm moved over me and took hold. I flashed a relaxed smile at the crowd, positioned my fingers for the opening chord, and readied my pick.

Three, two, one . . . go.

My hands moved easily, and I strummed with energy, letting the music keep me loose. Although I wouldn't move from my spot during the song, I didn't want the performance to be static. I filled my lungs with air to support my vocals and belted out the opening lyric. As my voice and instrument flooded the music hall, I gathered strength.

There wasn't anything like the sound of it.

Everything I felt, I channeled into the emotion of the song. I knew all about being restless. About striving for something and not getting it. But for the first time, I found meaning in the song that was uplifting. I hadn't found what I was looking for yet, but there was a promise that I could.

It was hard not to keep my gaze fixated on Erika as I sang. I was looking for even more from her than we had, and a spark ignited inside me. I could find whatever I needed to and convince her to truly give us a chance.

Her expression as she watched me was . . . intense. Captivated. She stared at me like how I was sure I'd gazed at her the night she'd sang 'Power.' The rest of the small crowd watched with different levels of interest. One of the other agents, a dude in the back, nodded along in time with the music, but stared at his phone.

The only person who seemed as mesmerized as Erika was by my performance was the girl who worked the front desk at Warbler. Charlotte, Erika had said her name was.

The girl gaped at me like I was naked. It wasn't an entirely new experience for me. I'd had some girls legit toss their panties at me at bars, usually a bachelorette party where the women wanted to be wild and show off for their friends. Charlotte's gobsmacked look didn't hurt my ego either, but it also couldn't compare with how Erika seemed to hang on each line I sang.

I could feel her with me on every note.

The three and a half minutes it took to play went so fast. I brought the song to a close, winding down the volume, the tempo, and power to demonstrate my control. Hopefully, I had the rest of the audience on the edge of their seats like Charlotte was. I sang the final refrain, struck the last note, and held still to let it wash over the crowd.

Their applause broke me from my daze and unleashed a smile from my lips.

"Thank you," I said.

"How long have you been playing?" someone in the crowd asked.

I'd been told there was an interview at the end, and this was what I sensed Erika dreaded. My inexperience was a clear disadvantage. I relaxed my grip on the guitar neck and stood tall. "About five years."

The next question came from a woman in the row in

front of Erika. "Are you doing music full-time?"

"No, ma'am." It was clear she wanted me to elaborate, and I struggled to maintain my smile. "I just finished school, so I'm taking as many gigs as I can get."

"What do you do for work?"

"Sports training and some construction. Like, home remodels."

"I thought you were a pool boy," Ardy quipped.

I laughed to downplay my embarrassment. "Oh yeah. I do pools too."

The interview turned serious. It continued with questions about what kind of show I'd like to put on if I landed the opening act. Who my musical influences were. If I were to perform a song from Stella's library, which one would it be and why?

I was crushing my answers . . . all until the last question.

"What's the largest audience you've performed to?"

The smile on my face froze and my voice wasn't as solid as I wanted it to be. "I did a friend's wedding that was, uh, probably four hundred people."

This was Nashville, the music city, with venues on Broadway that could accommodate twenty-five hundred covers. Even more if it were outside, or in one of the auditoriums.

And it was likely my competitors had played them. I was up against people who'd moved to this town from all across the country with dreams of making it. Performers who had years of experience and far more skill than I did.

Hell, I'd met a guy one night at Blanche's before my set who was a bouncer at Blake Shelton's bar. He'd come from

Vermont and taken the job only so he could fill in and do acoustics whenever they had a light entertainment week. Maybe he deserved to be up here more than I did. I hadn't been hungry like that until recently.

But . . . wait. Fuck that. I hadn't been hungry because I hadn't believed it was even possible. Now that it was? I craved it with every inch of my soul. Standing on the stage felt *right*. I knew that I belonged here.

Although a lot of the people in the audience were looking at me like I didn't. There was distrust in their eyes. This kid Troy from Nashville was unproven, and probably not a risk Stella should take with her brand.

"Can I say something?" I asked.

Ardy motioned for me to go ahead.

"I just wanted to thank y'all for letting me come out and perform today." I glanced around the theatre, taking it all in. "It's an honor to stand on this stage, especially for an unknown like me, and to get this opportunity. I don't know if Stella sees this part of the process, but either way . . . I appreciate what y'all have done."

I genuinely meant what I said, but I also hoped the words would reach Stella personally. She wanted to pay it forward and help someone launch their career, and she couldn't find anyone more unknown than me.

"No, thank you." Did Ardy sound this friendly and warm as he said goodbye to everyone else who'd auditioned? "We appreciate your time. Erika will let you know if we need anything else."

The sound tech reappeared and unclipped the small

microphone from my guitar.

Audition over, I exited the stage the way I'd come and walked in a trance-like state back to the green room where my stuff was. All the prep and anxiety over it, and the whole thing had taken less than twenty minutes. I wouldn't find out how I'd done for weeks. The auditions would be edited together and posted to Stella's website.

I moved methodically as I put the guitar back in its case, wondering how I'd survive the waiting, but then . . . I didn't have to. My phone buzzed with a text message.

Erika: You fucking nailed it.

SIXTEEN

Erika

As soon as Ardy ended our team meeting, Charlotte practically climbed over the Opry House seats to get to me. It'd been a long day of listening to auditions, and the consensus among Warbler was to recommend Lauren as the agency's pick to Stella. Like Troy, she'd also knocked her audition out of the park, but she had a terrific résumé, including touring experience, to back her performance up.

Ardy wanted to play it safe.

I was thrilled for my client, but the personal disappointment inside me was crushing. I wanted this so badly for Troy. All hope wasn't lost though, I reminded myself. Stella's fans would have a say when the series aired on her site, and the artist herself would make the final decision.

Charlotte's smile was bright and energetic. "Hey, can I ask you a question?"

I stood from my seat and stretched, tired from sitting all afternoon. "Sure. What's up?"

She glanced around mischievously and lowered her voice, like she didn't want anyone else to hear. "The pool boy. He's yours, right?"

My body was suddenly made out of concrete. "What?"

"Your client? Troy."

"Oh." It was embarrassing where my mind had automatically gone. Of course she'd meant professionally. "Yeah, I brought him in."

This was the answer she was hoping for because her smile widened. "So, I know I'm probably not supposed to ask this, but like . . . what's his deal? Do you know if he has a girlfriend?"

The concrete was back, solidifying my bones. I could give her a line about not getting into the personal lives of my clients, but it'd be utter bullshit. Instead, I gave her the most honest answer I could. "No, I don't know if he has a girlfriend."

Because while Troy and I were exclusive, we'd never put those labels on each other. It wasn't like we dated. We had wild sex and I used him both as my personal sex toy and my muse to write music. That didn't mean I was his girlfriend.

Charlotte looked pleased. "Then he probably doesn't. I think she would have been here if he did, or he would have mentioned her to you." She quirked her head to the side. "I mean, it's none of my business. It's not like I can date him even if I wanted to. My dad would freak out."

The idea of Charlotte and Troy dating was a punch to my stomach. It wasn't just how we were secretly together. It was the fact that Troy and Charlotte were the same age. They were both attractive, and no one would think twice about them if they went out. On the surface, she made a lot more sense for him than I did.

I fucking hated it.

And what happened when Troy eventually realized I was

too old for him? He'd leave me for a girl half my age . . . probably one who looked just like Charlotte.

"You look worried," she said, "but you shouldn't be." She waved to her father across the theatre, signaling she'd be right along. "Everyone from Warbler can vote for Lauren, but there's no way Troy doesn't win the popular vote."

"Why do you say that?"

She laughed like I was being ridiculous. "Hello, do your eyes work? Lauren's great and all, but he's gorgeous and all of Stella's fans are like me—girls." She kept her gaze glued on me as she backed out of the row, her eyes sparkling. "I'd vote for him every day, and twice on Sundays."

I couldn't help but share her smile.

My plan was to call Troy after I'd finished the final verse of 'Power,' and he'd come over as my reward. We'd celebrate his audition, I'd play the full song for him to see what notes he had, and once I'd taught him the whole thing, he'd smile . . . and I'd be done for. I'd tear off his clothes and demand he make me come, and he'd happily oblige.

I'd stopped by the gym, squeezed in a quick workout, and hopped in the shower as soon as I came home. I was still drying my hair when my phone rang, and excitement flashed through me. Was Troy unable to wait, and calling me? I raced to grab my phone like a teenager with a crush.

The number wasn't his though.

"Hey, there," I said.

Jenna didn't give me a greeting. "Are you at home?"

"Yeah. Why?"

"Because I'm in your driveway." She sounded upset. "Troy told me everything, Erika. We need to talk."

She said the word *talk* like a threat, and my heart leapt into my throat.

"Oh," was all I could get out before the call disconnected.

When I unlocked my front door and pulled it open, she came through in a huff, her gaze not meeting mine as she barreled straight for my kitchen. I followed her heavy footsteps and stood by the sink, watching her as she dropped her purse on the counter, reached into my fridge, and popped the top of a . . . Diet Coke?

Unbearable tension gripped me as she drank. I expected her to be furious, but she looked more irritated than anything else, which was strange.

"I'm not happy with either of you," she announced. "He not only kept it a secret, he straight-up lied to me. You did too." Hurt filled her expression. "How could you not tell me? I thought I was your best friend."

"You are," I said quickly.

She didn't look like she believed me. "This is a huge deal, and you kept me in the dark."

The guilt I'd shoved away into a closet, suddenly burst open and swept me away. "I'm so sorry. It just happened, and we—"

"It just happened," she repeated dubiously. "Yeah, this

huge audition for Stella just fell out of the sky, and there was no way either of you could do anything about it, including mentioning it."

She took another swig of the Diet Coke, and if I wasn't so flustered, I might have found the angry way she drank comical. He'd told her everything, and *this* was what she was upset about? How we'd kept the audition secret, and not that we were sleeping together?

A voice in my head warned me I was being stupid. She'd said he'd told her everything, and in her mind, maybe he had.

But there was no way it was true. If it were, she would have come in like an inferno and likely reached for something a hell of a lot stronger than a soft drink.

"But Troy had enough time to ask off for it," she said. "And lie to me about what he was doing."

My emotions scattered everywhere. There was relief at not having the immediate confrontation, and then my guilt was back, where I promptly began hiding it away again, and finally, irritation. Wasn't she proud that he'd gotten to perform and was being considered for such a huge opportunity?

"I'm sorry we lied, but," I swallowed a breath, "aren't you happy for him?"

Jenna gave me a flat look. "Of course, but it's hard to be happy when I know what's coming." Her eyes filled with sadness. "He's going to be crushed when he doesn't get it."

My heart hurt for Troy because she didn't believe in him, but also at how she could be right. "He might, Jenna. He's really good."

She said it hesitantly. "You were really good."

It wasn't meant to be mean, but her point stung anyway. I pushed the professional, agent side of my personality to the front as a shield. "That's not a fair comparison. The market is different between men and women."

She sighed. "I just don't want him to get hurt and see him go through it all again."

Everything in my kitchen went still. "Again?"

"Like what happened with baseball. He wanted to play in the Major League all through high school. It was because he had this coach—bless his heart—filling his head with big ideas. I told him not to listen to it. Troy was a great third baseman, but what he didn't understand was great kids aren't actually all that rare. He wasn't prepared to get cut from the team his freshman year at Randhurst."

Oh, my God.

I remembered how busy she'd been when he was finishing up his senior year because she'd gone to every one of his games, including regionals and state. He'd been on a traveling team too all summer. She'd mentioned he was disappointed about not making the team in college, but that had been years ago, and honestly, I hadn't paid that much attention.

"He nearly quit school," Jenna said. "So, y'all have to forgive me if I don't want to watch his dreams die a second time."

I couldn't catch my breath. The ache in my chest was too constricting.

Failing at your dream once was awful, but to have it happen twice? I didn't want that to happen to anyone, much less to Troy, and my desire for him to land the opening spot increased exponentially.

I stared at my friend, hoping she could see my conviction. "I can't guarantee he'll get it, but what I can promise is I'll do everything I can to help him with his career."

"Career?" She said it with disdain, before softening to a pleading tone. "Please, Erika. No one understands more than you how hard it is to make it in this town. The odds of it are so fucking slim. All I want is to protect him from getting hurt."

I understood her concern stemmed from a good place, but . . . "I get it, but he's an adult."

Irritation flitted through her. "Yeah. One who still lives at home."

Once again, she wasn't exactly being fair. He was her only child, and she was rather attached. I smiled to soften the point I was about to make. "You're telling me you'd prefer he didn't? You seemed pretty happy when he came home from college."

"Of course I was happy. Randhurst is ten hours away." She set her drink down with a thud, but kept her hand wrapped around the can as she contemplated what to say next. "Look, I want him to be practical. Don't get his hopes up, because if it doesn't work out, it won't just be devastating to him. It'll be the same for me too."

It was true you couldn't fail if you never tried for anything, but what was the cost? "You want him to give up on his dreams just because he might not get them?"

"Are they his?" she accused. "Or are you pushing yours onto him?"

Her question cut right to the bone, possibly because

there was truth to it. Troy and I teased last night how I was using him for sex, but was I also using him for this? To fulfill the dream I'd held for myself?

"Again," I said tightly, "he's an adult. He gets to decide what he wants."

I stuck a nerve because her shoulders snapped back. She put her hand on her waist and her voice took on a hard edge.

"Bill needs back surgery. He's been putting it off because he knows he'll be out of commission for months, and I can't run the company by myself. He wanted more than anything for Troy to step up, because . . ." Her eyes abruptly went wet with tears, but she blinked rapidly to hold them back. "Troy's just as much his son as he is mine. It would mean a lot for him to take over, for Bill to know he was leaving all his hard work in good hands. Family hands."

The kitchen was fraught with tension, and I sensed where she was going before she said it.

"Bill offered it to him tonight. The company he spent the last twenty years building." Her stare was inescapable. "Troy turned him down. Want to guess why?"

I pressed my fingertips to the base of my neck. "Oh, Jenna."

"This was an incredible opportunity he just passed up, all for a chance at something that I think, frankly, is a fantasy."

With the way she was looking at me, there was no need to say it out loud. She blamed me for putting this fantasy in Troy's head.

I opened my mouth to defend him, but she cut me off.

"Troy turned down what Bill and I hoped for, so he could

follow this dream. So, I don't want you to promise us anything, except you won't let him get hurt. Can you do that?"

How the fuck was I supposed to answer that, as either his manager or the woman he was secretly involved with? Nothing was guaranteed in music or life. Certainly not in love.

Love?

I must have made a face because Jenna's soured. "Yeah, I thought so."

She left the half-empty drink on my counter, snatched up her purse, and headed for the front door.

"Wait, wait," I said, catching her arm in the entryway, finally coming to my senses. She was upset, and she could argue she had a decent reason to be, but I'd let her control the conversation far too long. "I need to say something."

Jenna lifted a wary eyebrow.

"Just you wait," I told her, "until you see the video of his performance. When he sings, Jenna? Everything *stops*." I drew in a deep breath. "I didn't fill his head with bullshit. You can be mad at me, but I'm not wrong. He's incredibly talented. In fact, he might have the best vocals I've ever heard, as an agent and a musician."

She paused. My friend wanted to believe, but her practical side was reluctant. "Really?"

The word was a whisper from her, but mine was loud and confident. "Really."

I wanted her to see his potential like I did. I'd had parents who didn't believe in me, and their doubt set me up for failure. It made it so much easier for me to give up. I didn't want that for Troy.

"You're going to be so proud," I said.

If she didn't believe in him after that, then I'd have to believe for her too.

I was in the hot tub with a glass of wine when I heard the back gate creak open, and longing fired through me as Troy appeared in the lamplight from the patio. He had on a simple white t-shirt and his red board shorts. The sun had set recently, and fireflies sparkled in the night air as he set his guitar case down on a deck chair.

He was so attractive it was disorienting.

Or perhaps the dizzy feeling he caused was something else. It wasn't just his body I desired or his music. I wanted all of him now.

Which was crazy.

But when he set his gaze on me and flashed a sexy smile, I couldn't help myself. I wondered if this feeling could last. It was scary how much I wanted it to.

"Hey. There's beer in the fridge," I said, "if you want some."

If he noticed I was affected by the sight of him, he hid it well. Troy nodded, disappeared into the house, and emerged with an open can clasped in his hand a minute later. As he sauntered up to the edge of the hot tub, his eyes studied my bikini top like he was determining the fastest way to get it off, and my heart went into overdrive.

He plunked his beer down in the cupholder on the ledge, grasped the sides of his t-shirt, and lifted. His smooth, tanned skin came into view, and I sucked in a breath. He could be on the cover of a fitness magazines.

Once he got big, maybe that was something I should look into.

Crap. It was getting harder to keep the business side separate from our personal relationship when we were alone, and I wondered if I should quit trying to do it.

Troy stepped out of his flipflops, and I moved to make way for him to climb into the hot tub beside me. The water sloshed around as he dropped into the seat opposite me and spread his arms out across the back edge. It was an invitation to climb into his lap, but I couldn't take him up on it yet.

"You told your mom about your audition." I said it soft and conversational, just loud enough to be heard over the jets.

The ease in his body vanished. "She called you, huh?"

"Actually, she came over."

He scrubbed a hand over his face, then lifted it as if in surrender. "Sorry I didn't give you a heads-up. I was going to, but she was mad enough with me, I didn't think she'd want to talk to you right away." He peered at me cautiously. "How'd it go?"

"Okay-ish?" I said. "She was upset in the beginning, but we got to talking, and I think that helped." I'd been able to convince her to stay longer, and by the time she'd left, we seemed to be back on solid ground. "I think she just needs a little more time to process it. It sounded like there were high hopes for you to take over the business."

His expression turned grim. "Yeah."

"How was your conversation with them? Are you okay?"

His gaze drifted away from mine as he contemplated how to answer me. "It wasn't great. I know how much he wanted me to have it, and when I turned it down that hurt his feelings, but . . . I had to. I don't want it."

His attention shifted back to me and his hand dipped down into the water, finding mine resting on my thigh. He pulled my hand up until it broke the surface, and then his fingers played with mine, enticing me to lace ours together.

The color of his eyes was deeper in the low light. "I'm glad it's finally done. It feels good to have it out there, not hanging over my head anymore."

His subtext came through loud and clear, but I frowned as I stared at our joined hands. "I want to tell her about this too, but we can't right now. One thing at a time." I felt flushed and it had nothing to do with the temperature of the water. "I'm not sure what we'd say. I don't even know what 'this' is yet."

Our hands sank together under the water, but the connection wasn't enough for him anymore. Troy leaned forward and scooped me up into his arms, pulling me into his lap.

His lips brushed against the edge of my ear. "What do you want it to be?"

It was strange how I had no problem telling him how I wanted sex . . . but talking about emotions or our relationship? It made me skittish. I squirmed in his hold, both against the discomfort of his question and the rush of desire his embrace caused.

So, I lobbed the ball right back into his court. "Well, what do you want it to be?"

His laugh was throaty. "No way. I asked first."

Instead of answering, I stalled. "Charlotte was curious about you after the auditions. She asked if you have a girlfriend."

He ran the tip of his nose along the curve of my neck and enjoyed the pleasurable shiver that ran through my body. "What'd you tell her?"

"I said I didn't know." I was short of breath from his seduction. "Is that how you think of me?"

He hesitated, but not out of fear. It was cautious optimism. "Do you think of me as your boyfriend?"

"No way, I asked first," I teased, although I was entirely serious.

He sighed dramatically and slid his arms tighter around me. "I thought you weren't the kind of girl," he mumbled against my shoulder, "to get all twisted and suddenly be too scared to do something. But it's okay, Erika. I'm not scared." He planted a kiss on my skin right beside my bikini strap. "You've made me reckless like that."

I inhaled sharply at his reference to the song I'd written years ago. It seemed to carry far more meaning now. Did 'Reckless'—a love song—describe the way he felt about me?

"Yeah, you're my girlfriend." He stated it as a fact. "My amazing girlfriend, who wrote me a song and got me an audition and said she believes in me." His warm mouth roved up my neck. "She's also hot as fuck." His fingers skimmed up my spine, finding the hook at the back of my top and undid it with lightning speed. "And she loves being topless too."

I laughed softly as the tension went out of the fabric and the peach swimsuit top began to float in the churning water, tethered to me by the tie still done behind my neck. I made quick work of it and slung the sopping swimsuit over the side of the tub.

I wasn't worried about the neighbors seeing. The jets were running, and my breasts were below the bubbling water line, making it hard for Troy to even see me. He used his hands instead to discover my curves and I wrapped my arms around his damp shoulders.

I whispered it in his ear, my voice rasping with need. "Are you going to fuck me out here?"

His smile was sly. "Maybe. Why? You think someone might see?"

"More like hear. Dr. Lowe's girlfriend isn't quiet when they use their hot tub."

He went stiff and awkward.

"What is it?"

He made a face. "You know I'm friends with Cassidy, right? I mean, I was in high school when she was with Preston. That whole situation is fucked up."

I wasn't sure what he was talking about, but I tried to piece it together. "Dr. Lowe's girlfriend . . . used to date his son?"

"Yup."

"Well, I guess that explains how Dr. Lowe met her," I said quietly. "She's half his age."

"Like I said, fucked up."

I gave Troy a plain look. "Yes, we should definitely cast stones from our glass house."

He laughed like I was being ridiculous. "I didn't mean because of the age thing. You know I don't care about that." He softened, returning to his playful self. "What I do care about is getting the rest of this bikini off, and then getting you on my dick."

I feigned a dreamy, dramatic look. "God, you say the most romantic things."

He chuckled knowingly. "You love it."

I really did.

SEVENTEEN

It was three days before the videos were posted on Stella's site, and by Monday my life became chaos. When I walked in to teach my bootcamp class, one of the other trainers joked loudly, "Hey, the pool boy's here!"

Two of the women at the gym asked for my autograph, which was just fucking weird. What else was surprising was how I was leading in the fan poll. But Erika said she wasn't surprised at all.

She'd been the one to tell me my audition video was up, right after it was posted last Friday afternoon. I'd been at a jobsite, helping the guys hang drywall when my phone buzzed.

> Erika: Auditions just went live on the site.
> Here's the link.

I'd stepped outside, gone down the lawn until I was away from everyone else, and watched the clip with my hand covering the sides of the screen to cut the sun's glare. It was shitty conditions for the first viewing, because my screen was small and I wanted to hear the audio through headphones, but it didn't make the thing any less surreal.

When I got home that night, I streamed the entire series to the TV so my folks could watch with me. There were five auditions and six videos in total, because the first was Stella's intro. She'd shot it backstage before one of her shows, explaining the contest and that fans could vote once a day for the next week.

My mom cried.

Which of course, got Bill worked up too, and then someone somewhere was cutting onions because my eyes began to sting. I held it together though. Plus, any pride I felt was quickly overridden by unease when I watched the other auditions. They were so freaking good.

"There were only five videos," my mom commented. "I thought you said the auditions went all day."

"They did. These were the ones they liked best."

Or, as Erika had said, the five that Stella and her team had approved. The artist felt comfortable with any one of these acts opening her show. Erika didn't say it, and maybe I was being pessimistic, but it kind of felt like I'd barely squeaked in.

My mom beamed. "Lord, Troy. We're so proud of you."

My chest expanded as I took in a deep breath. Of course it was great to hear, but it felt different than I'd expected it to. I'd thought it'd be vindicating, but instead it just felt . . . nice. Good.

It didn't last though.

"I just want you to keep in mind," she continued, "some of the other auditions were really good too, so if you don't go any further, you should still feel proud of yourself for making it to this far. Top five! Honey, that's so great."

It was painful to smile. Could she not be practical for

once in her fucking life?

"Oh, you have to call your Mimi," she said abruptly, nearly bouncing off the couch. "She's going to love this."

Inside, I sighed. I loved my grandmother but sending her a link wasn't a thing you could just do, and walking her through using her ancient desktop computer was the *worst*.

Over the weekend, my social media exploded. I gained a shit-ton of Instagram followers overnight. I got recognized at the Taco Bell drive-thru window. The cashier girl sputtered and dropped my change on the ground, but thankfully not my cheesy gordita crunches. While I was pumping gas, some woman catcalled me out of her car window as she drove by.

"Looking good, pool boy!"

Damn Ardy's question during the interview. Beneath my name on the title card of the video, it had listed "Pool Boy" as one of the details about me. I didn't mind the attention—honestly, it was a trip. But I didn't want to be thought of as a joke.

Saturday night I did a set at Blanche's and it was the largest crowd I'd ever played. Erika sat at the bar, videoing and evaluating the performance. She'd delivered her critique afterward, and once we got back to her place, she gave me plenty more direction.

There'd been champagne in her fridge to celebrate my considerable lead in the fan poll. I wasn't big on champagne, but I appreciated the gesture, and by the time we'd finished the bottle, Erika had me on the couch with my jeans down around my ankles.

"How do you want it tonight?" I asked, pushing her hair out of the way so I could watch better as she wrapped her mouth around my dick.

She was buzzed and her eyes were shining with mischief. "I want it dirty."

I was going to ask her to expand on that, but it was taking all my focus not to thrust into her mouth, and if she described what she meant, I'd probably lose control anyway.

I had an idea though, and when she was riding me reverse cowgirl, I licked the pad of my thumb and tested if she was squeamish about anal play. All it did was make her moan encouragingly.

"Yeah?" I grinned.

She didn't give her answer with words, but her body screamed, *hell yes*. I was slow and deliberate as I worked my thumb inside her ass, and by the time I made it all the way to my second knuckle, she came so hard I was a goner.

My girl was a wild freak like me, and I couldn't get enough. It didn't seem like she could either.

We clicked when it came to sex and music, but the few times I'd brought up our relationship outside of that, Erika would shut down. She wasn't ready to talk to my mom about us, and she *still* hadn't blocked her ex's number. The guy kept bothering her with calls and he was getting on my damn nerves.

I tried not to push, because I was a lot younger than she was and I hadn't been married. The longest I'd ever been with someone was fourteen months, but she'd been with Mr. Graham for twenty years. I figured she was scared and just needed more time. I wasn't going to give up, and while I waited, I'd keep being awesome.

She'd get there eventually.

The next morning, after sex and breakfast, I'd gotten dressed in the same clothes from last night, kissed Erika goodbye, and headed out to my Jeep parked in her driveway.

"You cleaning her pool on Sunday mornings now?" a familiar voice asked.

Preston was in his driveway, just on the other side of Erika's lawn, his hand on a push lawnmower. His tone said he knew his question was bullshit.

I grinned at my friend as I walked across the grass toward him. "What can I say? She needed an emergency service."

He nodded, wanting to play along. "Took all night too, because your Jeep's been there all morning."

"Well, I had to make sure I did it right."

Preston snorted. "And how long has this emergency been going on, bro?"

We were only a few feet apart now, so I lowered my voice. "A few weeks."

"No shit." He glanced up at her house, then back to me. "Is it serious?"

"I don't know. Maybe."

My friend could be self-involved, but he'd gotten better over the last year. Dealing with his dad and Cassidy hooking up had changed him, and he wasn't always the center of the universe anymore. He cocked his head as he evaluated me, like he actually wanted to know how I felt.

"Dude," he whispered. "You're into her."

I tried not to be defensive, but it happened anyway. "Yeah. So what if I am?"

He lifted his hands as if to say, *no offense.* "I'm not try-ing to be an asshole. I'm just surprised, is all." His lips lifted in a half-smile. "Maybe a little jealous. You bagged a cougar, man. How's the sex? Is it insane?"

Talking with my boys about fucking wasn't a big deal. We liked to brag about numbers and how often we go laid, but now? Talking about Erika this way felt invasive and wrong.

"Yeah," I answered, giving him nothing else to go on.

His eyes widened and his smile was incredulous. "Oh, you're *really* into her."

Irritation heated in my chest. "Okay, I gotta get going."

I didn't want to be a dick, but Preston wasn't trying that hard not to be one, and if I didn't get home soon, my parents would notice I'd spent the night out. I was an adult, but they struggled to give me space and not ask questions. Plus, my track record on honesty had taken a hit with them since I'd hidden my music side-hustle.

"She got any hot friends?" he teased. "I mean, besides your mom?"

I didn't mean it, but it was a required response. "Fuck you, man." But then realization hit me, and I dropped my voice. "Hey, seriously, though. Don't tell anyone about this. Erika's my manager, and it might be bad for her if word got around."

"Oh." His amusement faded into seriousness. "Yeah. I gotcha, Troy."

A year ago, I might not have trusted him with anything important, but now? It seemed like I could.

By Wednesday, my lead over Lauren had widened, but my mom was quick to remind me not to get cocky. Stella had stated in her intro video that she'd be taking the voting results into consideration when making her pick. Winning the poll did not equal winning the spot.

I barely slept Thursday night. Erika had work with one of her other clients, so I stayed home and was up late playing *Call of Duty* with Preston and Colin. I was jittery most of the night, aware that in a few hours, I'd either be fucking ecstatic or depressed beyond belief.

I tried to mentally prepare for the worst.

Really, all I had to do was think about freshman year and the moment the coach had pulled me aside at training. He'd done it while the team was moving to the weight room so the other guys wouldn't notice. I remembered that long-ass walk back to the dorm with my equipment bag in hand, knowing the team was still back at the gym working out. Training went another two hours for them.

But not me.

I needed it to be different this time.

I wasn't the only one who hoped I got the spot. Erika was right there with me, and it felt like this wasn't just my dream anymore—

It was *ours*.

Morning sunlight crept through the window but I stayed

in bed, staring vacantly at the ceiling while I tried to get a handle on my expectations. My schedule was light today. I didn't need to be at the gym until my lunchtime burn class, but for once I wished I had something earlier. What the fuck was I going to do with myself for the next few hours?

If I needed any evidence of how nervous I was, I discovered I was too distracted to jerk off.

I considered texting Erika, but she'd be in work mode now when I wanted to talk to my girlfriend.

The universe must have known my frustration because my phone rattled on the nightstand. I vaulted up out of bed, yanking the charging cord out of the port and sliding my finger across the screen when 'Warbler Talent' flashed on it.

Only I hadn't realized until I'd already accepted it that the call was coming through via FaceTime.

Ardy popped up on my screen, wearing a confused expression as he stared back at me. "Hey, kid, I know it's early. Sorry to wake you."

It wasn't early, he was being polite. "No, it's fine. I was up."

He lifted an eyebrow. I was in my bedroom and shirtless, and my hair was a mess, so he clearly didn't believe me. "Right. Anyway, we've got a bit of a situation on our hands. You got a minute?" When I nodded, he said, "Great. Let's have you put on a shirt first."

"Yes, sir." I set the phone down on the dresser and scrambled for the first half-decent thing I could find. Fuck, my room was a mess. I snatched up a gray t-shirt off the floor and tugged it on, raked a hand through my hair to make it presentable, and picked my phone back up, turning so the only background was the tan wall behind me. "What's the situation?"

Ardy was satisfied with my transition. "I'm going to let her explain." He winked at me. "I just needed to make sure you were camera ready." His image blurred as he lowered his phone, and the screen abruptly rolled over to a new caller.

"Troy?" the girl asked. "You there?"

For a second, thoughts vanished from my brain. It made it really fucking hard to remember how to speak. "Yeah." I fumbled. "Hi, I'm here."

Stella Mills was only a few years older than I was. She had sandy blonde hair and eyebrows that were like notches. When she'd started out, she'd been the down-to-earth girl next door, but she'd shed that image with her latest album. Now she was more like a lioness. Elegant and classy, and not afraid to flash her claws.

This girl on the other end of the call was the OG Stella. Her hair was piled on top of her head in a messy bun, and she was wrapped in an oversized sweatshirt from Vanderbilt. Her makeup was minimal, and the lighting on her tour bus was harsh as it sped along, making her look very real and normal.

But she was still Stella Mills, on my phone, talking to me.

"Hi!" She brightened. "It's nice to meet you."

Don't be weird, don't be weird . . . "Yeah, you too!"

It came out too loud and excited, making me cringe.

She didn't seem to notice. "So, listen. I've been talking with Ardy, and the concern over at Warbler is about your level of experience."

My heart thudded to a stop. This was where she told me

they'd decided to go in a different direction. My shoulders sagged. "Okay."

"I don't have those concerns," she added.

I blinked, unsure of what to say. That sounded good, but I didn't trust it.

"My concern," she continued, "is with who you are as an artist. Like, I love your tone, but I'm not looking for a good cover band. I want to discover someone who has a *voice*. Do you know what I mean?"

"Sure." I didn't really, but I was kind of starstruck, and my brain wasn't functioning at full capacity.

She lifted her gaze away from the camera so she could glance out the window and appeared deep in thought. Then, her attention abruptly snapped back to me. "I really liked what you said. I felt it in my soul when you talked about how much it meant to you to be on that stage. It's been a while since I thought about it, but I remember being there at that point in my career, just starting out."

When she smiled, it was so genuine and contagious, I smiled too.

She squeezed her earlobe with her fingers, thinking. "I guess what it comes down to is, what kind of show are my fans going to get from Troy Osbourne? I know what I get with Lauren, because she's put out an album, but I don't have anything else to go on with you."

My heart banged a furious tempo. It felt like my and Erika's dream all hinged on the next thing I said or did. I swallowed an enormous breath. "Can I play you something?"

Her smile was polite and bright. Hopefully, she wasn't

just humoring me. "Sure."

"Let me grab my guitar."

And some pants since I'm not wearing any.

I'd never gotten ready so fast. I tugged on jeans and cleared my throat as I stumbled into the living area. I wasn't warmed up at all, and I fumbled to get the phone angled right on the TV so she could see me, but it didn't seem to matter. I got out my guitar and sat on the edge of the couch with the guitar positioned across my leg.

"What are you playing for me?" Stella asked.

"This is 'Power.'" I was relieved at how confident I sounded. "An original written by Erika Graham."

The U2 cover I'd done was up-tempo and energetic, but Erika's song was deep and deliberate. Even if I wasn't in a relationship with the songwriter, it was likely I'd have felt a connection to the lyrics. Who couldn't relate to feeling like they were under someone's spell?

Like my performance at the Opry House, I was calm and in command. Erika wasn't here physically, but I felt her all around. She seeped through the music and sang the lyrics with me as a duet in my head. I barely checked in with the screen to see how I was doing.

I got lost in the song. Every time I'd sung it before, Erika had been beside me, and I'd leashed my intensity. I didn't have to worry about scaring her off now, so there was nothing to lose. I played and sang my fucking heart out, feeling every lyric in the marrow of my bones.

Was it a cliché to say I put it all out there? When I closed the song, I was spent and drained. It'd taken everything I had emotionally to get through it, and my voice broke on the final word. When I lifted my hand from the strings, my gaze went to the phone propped up on the cabinet across the way.

Stella had her hand tucked under her chin, and a slow smile worked across her lips. "Yes," she breathed. "*Now* I know who you are. Thank you, Troy."

My chest was still tight with unexpected emotion, so I pressed a hand to it, trying to work the knot loose. "Of course. Thanks for letting me play it for you."

"I need to talk to Ardy again and discuss some things, but as soon as I've made my decision, you'll know. Okay?"

I nodded, even though my head felt like it was filled with bees. "Sounds good."

"All right, thanks." She gave a wave. "Have a great day."

"Yeah, you too—" I started, but she was already gone.

EIGHTEEN

Erika

The gym where Troy worked was decorated in burnt orange and black, and had a warehouse feel. It was so different from the one I went to. It was serious, and I suspected the big bros on the floor would be there all day, hogging the machines.

I stood in the lobby and watched Troy through the glass, because not only was I a visitor, I was wearing my favorite hot pink heels. They'd brought me luck in the past, so I figured it couldn't hurt Troy's chances of getting picked.

He didn't notice me. He wore a black tank top with the gym's orange logo stretched across his chest, and as he called out the exercises to the class of people on the mat, I wondered how much money it'd cost if I switched gyms. He had the same confidence leading the group as he had on stage.

A cute guy approached me and flashed a smile. He was wearing the same black shirt Troy had on and a name badge that read 'Colin.' He looked vaguely familiar, but then again, he had the college frat boy look to him, so that was probably all it was.

"You interested in our lunchtime burn class?" he asked.

"Oh, no thank you. I'm actually not a member." I motioned through the glass. "I'm just waiting for Troy."

He looked at me critically, like he was worried I was

some stalker fan. I was about to tell him I was Troy's manager, when Colin's expression shifted. He snapped his fingers and then pointed at me with honest-to-God finger guns.
"Ms. Graham?"

I went rigid. How the hell did this kid know me?

Oh my God.

Had Troy told him about us? I was uncomfortable at the
idea of this stranger knowing, but sort of excited because that
meant Troy was talking about me, and wasn't embarrassed
for people to know he was dating an older woman.

Whatever face I'd made, it was enough confirmation for
Colin. His friendly demeanor snapped back into place. "You
live next door to Preston Lowe."

"Yes." Relief washed through me in a wave. Colin looked
familiar because I had seen him before. Every summer,
he spent tons of time hanging out in Dr. Lowe's pool with
Preston and Troy.

I returned his easy smile. "I'm also Troy's manager."

"Yup."

Was I imagining the knowing look in Colin's eyes? He
gazed back like he was in on some private joke with me. It
made my mouth go dry.

He knew.

"Right." I tried not to sound flustered. "How much longer
is the class?"

He glanced down at his smartwatch. "Just another minute or two. Is it important? You want me to go get him?"

"No, no, it's fine."

My focus drifted back to the man on the other side of the

glass. He rested his hands on his hips, flaunting his powerfully toned arms, and I was struck by how much had changed for me in such a short time. It wasn't a lifetime ago when I'd hidden behind the curtains in my living room, watching him through the window as he cleaned my pool—but it felt like it.

And now as I stared at him, I was filled with so much more than basic lust.

I *longed* for him.

Longed for his voice, his laugh, his kiss. For his fingers to pluck the strings of his guitar and touch me in the places that lit up my body. For years, I hadn't thought about Troy, and now time made up for it.

He was all I could think about.

He must have sensed my gaze on him, because as he took off the microphone headset, he glanced in my direction and did a double-take. I hadn't texted him I was coming, so he wasn't expecting to see me here, standing in the lobby beside his friend and coworker. But he looked thrilled with the surprise and had no shame as he grinned back flirtatiously. It flooded me with so much heat I had to look away.

Unfortunately, that meant my attention landed on Colin, who'd witnessed the whole thing, and wore a smug smile. "I guess I don't need to get him for you."

Because Troy was moving swiftly across the mat toward the glass door to the lobby. I swallowed thickly as he pulled it open and came over, close enough that he could touch me, only just stopping himself from doing so.

"Hey." He was so pleased to see me. "What are you doing here?"

"Stella made her pick." Anxiety twisted my stomach. "I asked Ardy if I could tell you before it's announced."

Troy turned to stone, and his bright smile died until it hung awkwardly on his face. "Oh."

I'd been numb on the drive over to his gym, unable to process. My voice dropped to a whisper. "It's you, Troy."

He blinked. Like me when I'd been told, he went numb from shock. "What?"

"She picked you."

His eyes widened and he opened his mouth to say something, but it was like he'd forgotten how to speak. Finally, the question tumbled out. "Are you shitting me?"

It was hard to catch my breath, like I was running too fast down a steep hill. It was exhilarating and scary. "Nope." I gulped down air. "Congratulations."

The excitement spread like wildfire inside us both, and maybe it was why I hadn't been able to process the news until this moment. I'd wanted so badly for this to happen for him, the joy was shared. It became ours.

I'd needed to be with him as soon as I'd learned he'd gotten it.

Our smiles grew into stunned laughs, and abruptly I was crushed by his warm arms, pulled into a hug that made me want to melt. That was why I allowed it to go on so long, even as a warning alarm blared in my head about how unprofessional it looked.

"Okay," I breathed, putting my hands on his chest to ease him back, although I was dying to stay right as we'd been.

"Sorry." He dropped the embrace and straightened, but

he didn't sound sorry. His eyes were wild and dazzling. "What are you doing right now? Let's go somewhere to celebrate."

I knew exactly what he was insinuating. He wanted to go where we could talk and act freely, and I was desperate for it—but we couldn't. My heart was racing, but I smoothed my hands down the sides of my slacks to try to even myself out. I needed to return to the manager I was supposed to be.

"I wish I could, but I've got a lunch meeting across town." Could he see how much I longed to connect? I was a bomb of emotions, primed to explode, but I forced it down. "The announcement's going out at five p.m. Eastern, so any time after four o'clock today, you can start talking about it, either online or in person. I'll email you a copy of the press release when I have it."

He nodded, but his focus wasn't on my face. Instead, his gaze was pinned over my shoulder, looking at whatever was behind me.

"There are also a few old Facebook posts of yours," I continued, "that Warbler's marketing team flagged for removal, so I . . ."

Was he listening?

Abruptly, his gaze flew back to me and his voice was urgent. "Come with me, just for a second."

"What?"

He put his hand on the small of my back and guided me toward the hallway branching off the lobby. The first open door he found was what he'd been looking for, and as soon as he had us inside the small room, he shut the door and locked it.

It wasn't much bigger than a bathroom stall. There was a full-length mirror on the back wall, along with hooks, and a bench seat on one side. My gym had similar rooms for clients who came straight from the office and wanted to change into their workout clothes.

But I didn't get much of a chance to look at anything because Troy spun me around and flattened my back against the cold mirror. His hands captured my face and tilted it up so he could deliver a deep, blistering kiss. Tingles burst across my skin as his mouth moved over mine. It was passionate and uninhibited. So powerful, I sagged against the glass, sinking under the weight of his kiss.

This wasn't the kiss of a man who desired me physically. It said he wanted . . . more.

So much more.

Whenever I heard new music in my head, it was usually just fragments. Like a few fingers absentmindedly touching the keys of a piano. The melody in my mind now? It was strong and confident and nearly complete. It played in a beautiful, endless loop as Troy's lips made wordless pleas and promises about our future.

Oh, God, I was drowning in this man.

How had I let this happen?

When the kiss ended, he tipped his forehead to mine and closed his eyes. "Okay, that's better. I needed that."

"Me too," I whispered.

It was like I'd told him he was opening for Stella all over again, he looked that happy. His eyes burst open and searched mine to make sure he'd heard me right. I adjusted on my heels, which continued to prove they were lucky, straightening against the mirror.

"Let's go out tomorrow night," he said.

My heart skipped. "Like a date?"

He laughed softly. "Yeah, a date. You are my girlfriend, Erika."

Part of me wanted this fiercely, but . . . "Are you sure that's a good idea?"

"Nashville's a huge town." His expression said he thought I was being overly cautious. "We'll be fine. No one's going to know."

"You mean, besides Colin?"

Confusion made him pull his shoulders back. "What?"

"You told him we're dating."

Troy's expression filled with alarm. "I didn't."

Annoyance moved through me and I put a hand on my hip. "Okay, then you told him we're fucking, because he obviously knows."

He looked like he was about to defend himself until the realization slammed into him. He wiped a hand over his mouth and grumbled it under his breath. "Fucking Preston."

Seriously? I sighed. "You told Preston too?"

"No," he said quickly. Then, he thought better of his answer. "Well, kind of? It wasn't hard for him to figure out. My Jeep was in your driveway all night."

My irritation dissipated. "Oh."

"I asked him not to tell anyone, but I guess he couldn't keep his fucking mouth shut." He glared off, perhaps planning the next conversation he was going to have with his friend, but then Troy's focus swung back to me. "Don't worry about it. I'll talk to them both, and Colin will be cool. He knows how to keep shit on the down-low." He looked remorseful. "Sorry about that."

It wasn't his fault, and really . . . was it that bad if his friends knew? Other than it made me envious? As long as they stayed quiet a little longer, it'd be all right. Troy and I needed to deal with the balance of work and our relationship, plus telling Jenna and Bill, but I had an idea for that.

"It's okay." I gave him a sweet smile. "And I'm sorry I can't stay to celebrate, but I have to get going."

He nodded in understanding, unlocked the door, and held it open for me. "Thanks for coming."

"I didn't want you to be on pins and needles all day," I said. "Plus, when I found out, I couldn't wait to tell you."

His grin was devious. "Still on pins and needles though. You didn't say yes about tomorrow night."

I laughed, strangely shy and tucked my hair behind my ear as I walked out of the changing room. Thankfully, the hall was empty. I turned and looked at him, marveling that this gorgeous man wanted to take me out.

"Yes," I said.

His chest lifted as he took in a breath. "Cool. See you then."

My pumps clicked against the tile as I strode toward the exit, but I only made it a few steps before Troy's voice rang out.

"Hey . . . I forgot to tell you. I really like your shoes."

I glanced back at him over my shoulder. "Thanks." I grinned. "They're my lucky heels."

He smiled back at me.

The sun was glaring outside, and I dug inside my purse for my sunglasses as I walked across the parking lot toward my car. By the time I was seated inside it, my phone buzzed with a text message.

Troy: You wore them for good luck for me?

Me: For us.

I'd tried on three different tops before reaching for the black silk one with lace trim along the neckline. It had been cute and flirty before my breast augmentation, but with its deep V, I had cleavage for days and transformed into a bombshell. I'd avoided trying it on for my date, even though I knew I'd wear it. I'd needed to see the other tops first to justify it was the right choice. Or to work up the courage.

I had the silk shirt halfway on, my head through the neck hole, when my phone rang. It was Jenna, wanting to know if I was interested in joining her and Bill for dinner. Which I appreciated, but also found odd. They wanted me to be their third wheel?

"Oh, thanks," I said, "but I have plans."

Plans that include your son.

"It's just dinner," she said lightly. "Come on. You can do whatever work thing you have after."

I couldn't fault her for assuming my plans were work since it was all I'd done until the divorce was finalized. "I appreciate the offer, but—"

"Bill's cousin is joining us, and I thought it'd be fun if we all got together. He's a nice guy."

I paused. "Like a double-date?"

"Yeah." My friend's voice was bright and excited. "I think you'll like him, and if not—no big deal. He'll be good practice as you get back out there. Plus, he's really funny."

Her desire to set me up came from a good place. She just wanted to see me happy, but a voice in the back of my mind whined that she was doing the same thing to me that she did to Troy. She made decisions without consulting anyone else.

"Sorry, but I can't," I said.

There was a sigh of frustration on the other end of the line, and I clenched a hand into a fist. She thought she knew what was best for me. Or at least, better than I did.

"I can't," I snapped, "because I already have a date tonight."

There was stunned silence for a long moment before Jenna spoke, and when she did, I pictured my friend bouncing with excitement on her feet. "You do? With who? How'd you two meet?" Her mouth couldn't keep up with her brain. "Oh, my God, spill."

I closed my eyes. "Uh, I'd prefer not to say." That wasn't going to do anything to satisfy her curiosity, so I gave her a bent version of the truth. "It's our first date, and . . . well, we work together, so we're not telling anyone about it just yet."

"Oh." She said it like I was being scandalous, which . . . she was not wrong. "Okay, at least give me something to chew on. Is he good looking?"

Oh no. "Um . . . extremely."

"Been married before? Does he have kids?"

She had no idea, but her questions stung. She was imagining a man much older than Troy. One who was more 'age-appropriate.'

I did my best to keep my tone even. "No, and no kids."

"All right, one more question and then I'll stop." Her voice went serious. "Please tell me you're going to wear that black top tonight. You know the one. Your boobs look amazing in it."

My mouth went dry. "That's not a question."

"You're right." She laughed. "Are you going to wear it?"

There was no power in my voice. "Yeah."

"Good, show the girls off. You paid for them." I could hear the smile in her words. "He'll think he died and went to heaven when he sees you."

Too bad I was going to hell.

NINETEEN

Erika

Jenna had been correct. When Troy came to pick me up, his tongue nearly fell out of his mouth. His gaze had started at my leopard print sandals, worked up my skinny jeans, and came to a screeching halt at the center of my chest. It took him time to restart his brain, and finally his gaze lifted to meet mine.

"Maybe we could stay here," he suggested.

I laughed and shook my head. "No way. This was your idea and I want to celebrate."

When he scrambled to open the door to his Jeep for me, I had nervous flutters in my stomach, but they were the good kind. Yes, I hadn't been on a date in two decades, but it'd be like riding a bicycle, right? Plus, it was silly to be anxious. We'd slept together a bunch of times.

"You okay?" he asked as he climbed into the driver's seat and buckled his seatbelt.

"Yeah, why?"

He smiled, curious. "You look nervous." His eyes widened a degree, like he'd made a mistake. "I mean, you look amazing."

"Thanks. You too." Fuck, I was nervous, but he didn't have to know that. I shot him an exaggerated, hard look. "I'm nervous you might not put out," I deadpanned. "You're a sure thing tonight, right?"

A surprised laugh burst from him. "Oh, yes, ma'am."

My gaze trailed over the interior of his Jeep, which was spotless, as he started the engine. Of course his car was perfect. It didn't matter how messy a guy could be at home—in my experience, they always took care of their car.

Troy drove to a restaurant in Brentwood, a suburb on the far side of the city where the chances of running into anyone we knew were nonexistent. Not that it mattered if we did. I could always say it was a work dinner. Plus, we *were* celebrating his big break.

Conversation flowed so easily during dinner. We laughed as the server carded us when ordering drinks, although I had no idea if she'd done it because Troy looked young and she carded me because she was being polite.

We talked about the first concerts we'd ever been to. The best and worst experiences we'd had when performing. Favorite song to sing.

"Easy." Troy set down his nearly empty pint of beer. "'Power.'"

It was a Saturday night and the restaurant was bustling, but the sound faded away. I gave him a dubious look. "All the songs in the world, and you're picking that one?"

"You wrote it," he said simply. "And you wrote it for me."

"I did." I licked my lips to stop myself from mentioning I wrote it about the way I felt about him.

"Can we talk business for a second?" He leaned forward, and his eyes turned serious. "I want 'Power' to be my closing song when I perform. Is that okay with you?"

Breath caught in my lungs. He was only allowed three songs in his set, because Stella already had an opening act she was touring with.

"We'd need to get Ardy and Stella to—"

"Yeah, I know. What I'm asking," he said, "is if everyone else signs off on it, will you?"

Didn't he know this question was silly? That he didn't even need to ask? "Yes." I smiled. "If you want to sing it—I'd be honored."

Our phones were face down on the table, and when it vibrated, we both flipped ours over. He glanced at my screen and saw the name Clark at the top. To his credit, Troy attempted not to react, but I could see how irritated he was.

I sucked in a breath. "Okay, so you're a young'un . . . How do I block a number?"

Relief swept through him and was quickly replaced by a victorious smile.

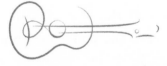

I spent Sunday recovering from the marathon sex I'd had with Troy and dodging Jenna's questions about how my date had gone.

"Great," was all I said.

By Monday I was back to being consumed by my job. There were fall festivals I was trying to get two of my clients booked into, a debut album launch for a singer-songwriting duo I'd signed in January, and an international tour of a bluegrass band on my list to help set up.

On top of all that, on Tuesday there was a contract sitting on my desk which had come over from Warbler's legal attorney. I spent my lunch break reviewing it, and the packaging Warbler was putting together for Troy's set. He'd sat for headshots this morning and texted me that it went well.

I left the office a little before five, grabbed the mail from my mailbox when I got home, and sorted it as I walked toward the house. My footsteps slowed as I tore open the envelope with my homeowner's association logo in the corner, dreading its contents before even reading the letter. Ever since Judy Maligner, my neighbor two doors down, had been elected president, the HOA had become a headache to deal with.

"What now?" I groaned.

When I read the contents of the letter, I got so angry, I turned and headed for her house, cutting across the Lowes' lawn and marching up her front porch steps. I stabbed my finger on the doorbell and crossed my arms over my chest, waiting for her to answer.

Like me, Judy was a relatively young divorcee who lived alone, but that was where our similarities stopped. She'd been married to a wealthy attorney, and the rumor was she simply lived off her cushy alimony. She didn't have a job, other than making ridiculous rules for her neighbors.

Either Judy wasn't home, or she was purposefully not coming to the door when she saw it was me, clutching her letter in my angry fist. I sighed, both impatient and frustrated.

"This is bullshit," I said, not caring if she heard.

I stomped off her porch and was halfway back to my house when I heard water splashing, music playing, and conversations coming from the Lowes' backyard. Was Dr. Lowe having a pool party?

I went to the gate on the side and stuck my head over the top. Sure enough, there were several people on floats in the pool or lounging on the deck with drinks in hand. Most of them looked to be Preston's age. Dr. Lowe was close by, manning the grill while wearing only his swim trunks.

Since he was a trauma surgeon at the hospital, it was rare he was home. I needed to take the opportunity to talk to him while I could.

"Hey, Greg," I called. "You got a second?"

Greg's gaze lifted from the hamburgers and he spotted me through the haze of the grill. "Sure, come on in."

I opened the gate and followed the landscaped stone steps toward him.

He flipped one of the burgers confidently with a spatula. This was a man who was an expert with a tool in his hand, although typically it was a scalpel.

He took a sip from his can of beer and then put his focus on me. "What's up?"

"Honestly? I just need to vent," I said. "I got a fifty dollar fine today from the HOA for putting my trash out too early." I lifted the letter and read the section out loud. "Per our rules, trash receptacles must not be placed at the curb before dark, however yours were witnessed this past Sunday at the end of your drive at 8:03 p.m. Twilight does not conclude until after 8:20." I gave him a pointed look. "Are you freaking kidding me?"

He shook his head and looked pissed on my behalf. "She's out of control."

"Who are we talking about?" Greg's girlfriend asked, padding over to the grill. Troy had said her name was Cassidy.

She was young and beautiful, looking effortless in her black string bikini. She stood close to Greg and, as if their bodies were attuned to each other, he leaned back toward her. He was in his forties and she in her twenties, but they made a handsome couple despite the age difference. Maybe it was because they looked very much in love.

"Judy Maligner," Greg said. "Erika got fined for putting out her garbage too early."

Cassidy's smile died and she shot a glare over her shoulder toward Judy's house. "I kind of hate her."

As he focused on me, his expression was filled with regret. "So, I kind of think this is my fault."

I tilted my head. "What?"

He let out a tight breath. "Judy thinks my relationship with Cassidy is . . . inappropriate."

His girlfriend snorted. "Yeah, because she's a sore loser and doesn't know how to mind her business."

Sore loser? Had Judy wanted to date Greg?

That made sense. He was attractive, young, and a doctor.

Whatever face I was making must have asked for an explanation, because he set down his spatula and turned serious.

"Last year, Judy and I exchanged words, and not too

many of them were nice. Things escalated, and since then, she looks for every opportunity to make our lives difficult. All these bullshit rules the HOA is implementing? They're hers, designed to get at us."

"She's got the whole board wrapped around her finger," Cassidy added. "They do whatever she says." Her expression shifted and she looked smug. "I'm the devil girl who seduced Greg to the dark side. What they don't know is I draw my power from their dirty looks."

All my anger about the stupid fine Judy had slapped on me channeled toward this new information. Who the hell did this judgmental woman think she was? Cassidy was right. Who Greg dated was none of Judy Maligner's business.

"Judy has always had a giant stick up her ass," I said, "and a holier-than-thou attitude. I thought that was why she was doing this. I didn't realize she was targeting y'all."

He either took it in stride or put on a brave face for his girlfriend's benefit. "It's all right. Nothing we can't handle." He nodded toward the people in the pool. "What's the verdict?"

Cassidy brightened. "Everyone wants a burger except Lilith."

He nodded and began counting the patties on the grill but paused as he thought about something. "You want one, Erika?"

"Oh, that's nice and it smells great, but no. Thank you."

"You sure? We've got plenty of food."

I smiled. "I'm sure. Are you celebrating something?"

His tone was warm as he exchanged a look with his girl-friend. "It's Cassidy's birthday."

"Oh. Happy birthday," I told her.

She grinned. "Thanks." And then she leaned in, setting a hand on Greg's shoulder. "You need anything? Another beer?"

He picked up his can to evaluate how much he had left. "That'd be great."

As Cassidy left us, it was good timing for me to make my exit. I was out of place in slacks and a blouse, while everyone else at the party was in swimsuits. Plus, Greg and I were the only ones who didn't appear to be in their twenties. But I didn't move. I was rooted to the ground beside the grill, partially obscured from the partygoers' view by a crepe myrtle bush.

My voice was low, but loud enough for Greg to hear over the music and sizzling grill. "Can I ask you a personal question?"

If that made him nervous, he didn't show it. "Sure."

"Dating someone a lot younger than you are. Is it hard?" I frowned. "I mean, do you worry about what other people think, or—"

"No," he answered quickly. "In the beginning, yeah, it was tough. Especially for her because people assumed the worst. I was just the guy with the trophy girlfriend. And Judy's been a real piece of work." His gaze drifted toward the pool and all the people there, oblivious to our conversation. "The hardest part for us was our situation with Preston. Once we got a handle on that, we didn't really care what other people thought."

I nodded, not sure what to say. His priorities were absolutely in the right place.

"It gets easier too," he added. "In a few more years, she'll be in her late twenties and no one will care we're together."

He saw his relationship with Cassidy going the distance, even with how complicated the dynamic was with his son. My relationship with Troy had less obstacles. Just my friendship with Jenna, and how Troy was my client. Easy by comparison to Greg and Cassidy.

"So . . ." Greg's expression turned devious, "you and Troy, huh?"

"What?" I blurted out. His direct question rattled me, and I groaned my irritation. "Did Preston tell you?"

He laughed. "No, I made an educated guess. I was on-call last week, and when I came home, I noticed Troy's Jeep in your driveway—at four a.m."

I threw my hands up in the air, because why fight it? It felt sort of good that people knew, and there was no judgment in his eyes. I tucked my mail under my arm and twined my fingers together. "Okay, yeah. Troy and I . . . I don't know how it happened. But it has."

"Hey," he sounded amused, "if anyone's going to understand, it's going to be me." His expression turned thoughtful. "My unsolicited and clichéd advice? Do what makes you happy. That's coming from someone who spends a lot of time dealing with the unexpected, like motorcycle accidents, strokes, and aneurysms." It carried far more weight than a simple platitude. "Life is short."

There was a loud splash from the pool, followed by the playful screams of those who'd gotten drenched.

"You're an asshole, Preston," a girl scolded.

It broke the tension between Greg and I, and he turned, pulling down a branch of the crepe myrtle to check on his son. What I didn't realize until the flowering branch was out of my way, was I recognized one of the guys sitting at the edge of the pool, his feet dangling in the water. He laughed as a girl wrapped her arms around Preston's shoulders and tried to dunk him.

Greg heard my sharp intake of breath. "Oh, yeah. Preston invited him."

It was surreal to see Troy like this, and an uncomfortable pain banded across my midsection. Wasn't this how he was supposed to be? Hanging out with friends who were the same age as him? Dating a girl who didn't know what the other side of twenty years of marriage looked like?

But then his posture stiffened as he went on alert, and it only took a single heartbeat for me to know what had set him off. His eyes, hidden from me behind his sunglasses, had discovered me lurking behind the bush with the other adult. He put his hand down on the concrete so he could pull his feet from the water, and when he stood, he no longer belonged with the rest of these twenty-something-year-olds.

He was meant to be with me.

"You can grab your suit and join us," Greg said.

I had no idea if he was being genuine or simply polite, but I flashed him a hurried smile. Troy was stalking across the pool deck toward me, and I was coming apart at the seams, both dying to talk to him and desperately not ready. Our date had been fantastic, but it was a baby step to being a true couple and hanging out with Troy's friends was a gigantic leap I hadn't prepared for.

"Ms. Graham." Troy's hair was wet from the pool, and he wiped a hand over it to push it back out of his eyes. His gaze bounced from me to Greg and back again. "Hey, I haven't checked on your pool yet. Should I do it now?"

I bit down on my bottom lip, feeling Greg's knowing gaze burrow into me. "Uh, sure."

"Cool." Troy's coy smile was dazzling. "Let me grab my stuff and I'll be right over."

He bounded back the way he'd come, reaching for his bag with his towel, phone, and presumably a shirt.

Greg cleared his throat. "Let him park in your garage. It won't be long before Judy notices his Jeep, and then I expect she'll find a way to complain about it."

"Fucking Judy," I muttered.

"Yup," Greg agreed.

TWENTY

Troy

As I got my shit together and stepped into my flipflops, Preston slapped the surface of the pool and flung water at me.

"Where the fuck are you going?" he asked.

His grin said he already knew the answer. He'd seen Erika talking to his dad, and then the way I'd hurried over to her. Could he blame me? She looked so fucking hot today, standing on the stone paver in her skinny pants and off-white shirt, her reddish-brown hair falling past her shoulders.

I wanted to grab a fistful of that hair, jerk her head back, and kiss her until she begged me to fuck her. It was what I'd been planning since Preston invited me over this afternoon. Yeah, I'd wanted to be there for him as he dealt with helping his dad celebrate Cassidy's birthday, but I'd also been biding my time until Erika got home.

But when I left the Lowe house, let myself in through her gate, and walked up the hill toward her pool, she was nowhere to be found.

"Erika?"

I dropped my bag on one of the loungers and peered toward the windows of the house. We'd come a long way in our relationship but barging in uninvited to her house wasn't something I felt comfortable doing yet, plus I was still wet from the pool. Maybe she was in her pool house.

Heat rose inside me at that idea. We could role play and reenact when we'd watched each other jerk off, only this time we'd get to do all the things we'd wanted to do then. That could be hot.

But she wasn't in the pool house either.

I stared at the work bench where she kept her chemicals. Fuck it. I was here and I was supposed to do it anyway. I grabbed the water test kit, went outside, and plunged the plastic collection block elbow deep into the pool, turning it right side up to let it fill with a sample.

I put the drops in and swirled the block, checking all the levels—which were fine. The skimmers were mostly clean, but I emptied them anyway. I dumped the sample water in her rock bed, repeated the process for the spa, put the kit back in the pool house, and measured out the chemicals I needed. She didn't use her pool much, but it'd been a few weeks since I'd shocked it.

When I came out of the pool house carrying the measuring cup, Erika was standing in the shade of her covered patio. I tossed the cup of powder into the deep end, then set the plastic measuring cup on the table beside the lounger, making my way up the two steps to meet her.

Holy shit.

Around her shoulders was a white, gauzy cover-up, but I was more focused on what was beneath. I gazed at her blue-green bikini with a small ruffle accentuating her magnificent cleavage. "Is that new?" I grinned. "I like it."

"Thanks." She seemed distracted as she pulled out a

chair at the table to sit. "Can we talk business for a minute?"

"Yup." I sat in the chair opposite her. "Before I forget, you're almost out of shock for the pool. Want me to order more for you?"

"What?" She blinked. "Uh, sure, but I need to find someone else to handle that going forward."

I couldn't help my teasing, hurt tone, and pressed my hand to my bare chest. "Are you saying I can't be your pool boy anymore?"

Her smile was humoring me. "I highly doubt you're going to have the time." She drew in a deep breath. "And also . . . I can't be your manager anymore."

It was warm outside, but the way her voice broke as she said it left me cold. "Sorry, what?"

I hadn't noticed the papers on the table until she pushed them toward me. "This transfers the copyright of 'Power' over to you. I retain the credit, but it's your song, Troy."

I picked up the paper and stared at the dense, legal text, but couldn't process any of it. She was just giving me the song she'd written? "Wait, go back to the part where you said you can't be my manager anymore."

Her eyes were wide and full of fear, and it turned my stomach. "Ardy has offered to pay me a finder's fee and take you on as a client."

Anger flared inside me. "And you're just going to let him?"

"No," she said. "I asked him to."

"*What?*" I stood fast, making the chair chatter over the wooden planks of her deck. "Why the hell would you do that?"

She swallowed so hard I saw the bob of her throat.

"Because," she whispered, "if we're going to have a chance at a future, I can't be your manager."

My body froze as her meaning hit me. *Future.* This was fucking huge. The power of it was enough to drive me to my knees beside her chair and slide a hand into her hair, cupping her cheek.

"Okay, wait." My voice was as uneven as I felt inside. "Just wait a minute."

"I don't want to hide anymore. We do this, and no one's going to say I took advantage of you, or that you're just fucking me to get ahead."

I scowled. Would people think that? Ardy had said he respected my hustle when he'd found out I cleaned Erika's pool. If he knew we were dating, it was possible he'd think that was true.

Oh, shit. "You don't think that, do you?"

The corner of her mouth lifted like she was amused I'd even had to ask that question. She covered my hand on her cheek, moving it enough so she could plant a kiss in the center of my palm. Her stunning tenderness lit me on fire. She'd been bossy and needy with me, but never like this.

"We can tell your parents," she said.

I wanted that.

Fuck, I wanted all of it out in the open, where I could show her off and not worry about who'd see us together. But I was smart enough to understand there wasn't much risk for me. My mom was going to love me no matter what, but Erika had a boss who might fire her, and a friendship that could be destroyed.

"I want that," I said, "but not like this. I don't want to do it without you."

Her gorgeous face twisted with anxiety. "Troy."

My hand firmed beneath hers, and I shot her the most determined look I possessed. "Remember when I wasn't going to audition if you wouldn't give me a chance? We do this together."

"I'm doing this so we can *be* together." She lifted my hand away from her face, threaded her fingers through mine, and matched my determination. "Look, I don't want to hand you off to someone else either, but this is the best I can come up with. I'll still be a part of the things Warbler offers you."

"No," I said. "This is ours."

Resignation swept through her. She knew I was going to fight her on this, and now she was willing to play the card she didn't want to have to. "The rights to 'Power' are contingent on this deal."

I shot to my feet, breaking the connection of our hands. "You said it was mine."

"It is." Her eyebrows pulled together. "I want you to have it, and I want us together. Don't you want that too?"

"Yeah, I do, but I also—"

"Part of being an adult is compromise, not getting everything you want."

I should have been happy. She was giving me so much of what I wanted. The chance at a career with a top-tier manager. The rights to her song. The acknowledgement that what we had wasn't just casual sex, but more.

But her statement pissed me off.

I hauled her up to her feet, tightening my grasp on her arms. "I'm not some kid you can boss around."

It was the wrong thing to say because . . . wasn't that exactly who I'd asked to be to her?

Her eyes thickened with irritation, but lust was buried beneath. "You're not?"

I liked when she told me what to do, but I wasn't a pushover, and I had no problem being the one in charge. Half the time, I let Erika think she was the one taking the lead when it was really me.

Who was actually in control anyway when one person ordered the other to take the reins?

"Is that what I am to you?" I gripped her hair at the base of her scalp and tugged hard enough to get her attention. "Just some kid? Because you let me do some very *adult* things to you."

It excited me when she went weak at my words, her lips parting to drag in a shallow breath.

"You want that, don't you?" I demanded. "For me to fuck you all the ways your husband wouldn't?" I dropped the volume of my voice until it was a growl. "In all the *places* he wouldn't?"

"Oh, Christ," she gasped.

She'd confessed to me she'd never had anal sex. I hadn't either, really. The one girl from my past who'd been open to the idea changed her mind five seconds in.

I was excited to try it with Erika at some point, and she'd dropped plenty of hints she was eager too. But right now, I was more talk than promise. She'd gone over my head to make this decision about my career, and I needed to remind her I was capable of making decisions too.

I slammed my mouth over hers, silencing her moan of approval. I wasn't going to ask how she wanted it this time, and I didn't need to either. We'd been together long enough I could tell. Plus, we were both angry at the situation and looking for a way to blow off steam.

When I stroked a hand between her legs, right over the fabric of her bikini bottom, she jolted and broke the kiss. Her gaze flew down the slope of her lawn toward the party still going on around Preston's pool. The sound was quieter up here, but we could still hear the music and the people laughing over it. We were partially obscured in the shade, but not exactly hidden from their view.

I'd expected her to drag me into the air conditioning of her house, but instead she clamped a hand on my wrist and tugged me toward the pool house. Not to the workshop door, but to the side of it.

There was a slatted partition wrapping around the outside of the brick building and covered by the overhang of the roof. I'd never had a reason to go into her outdoor shower before. If I'd needed to rinse off my hands, I'd used the garden hose or the sink inside the pool house.

The open-air shower was spacious and bare, other than a hanging wire rack full of shampoo and lotions. I stood on the textured concrete floor as Erika cranked the handle attached to the chrome pipe that climbed up the brick wall and ended in a large rainfall showerhead. Right before the water began to pour and drip from it, she stepped back, shed her cover-up, and hung it on one of the hooks at the doorway.

Fucking her in the shower had been on my to-do list, but this? It was so much hotter. We were secluded back here, but it felt like we were out in the open. There was a party going on just across her lawn.

"If you get too loud," I set a hand on her hip and eased us both under the falling water, "someone might hear us."

The shower was barely warm, but that was good. It was hot enough outside and between us. In seconds, we were drenched, and her nipples poking through her bikini top begged for attention.

She sucked in a breath through clenched teeth as I pinched one of them, surprise making her blink her pretty blue eyes rapidly.

That's right, Erika. I'm in charge.

As soon as my message had been received, I put a hand on her shoulder and turned her around. Now we were both facing the partition, and I jerked her back into me, so her ass pressed against the top of my thigh. It put my hard-on right beside her hand that dangled at her hip.

To show her what I wanted, I tugged open my trunks and let them fall to the water pooling at our feet, and my dick swung free. Shit, it felt fucking amazing when she closed her fist around me. Her grip was tight, and stayed snug as I moved my hips, slowly sawing my dick back and forth through her hand.

My mouth was beside her ear, and I grunted with pleasure at her touch. I could touch too, though. I wrapped my arms around her, one hand to cup her tits and the other to play with her pussy. I started over the bikini. I toyed with her through the damp fabric as she worked me over.

The stroke of her hand made my heart go out of rhythm. I did a fair share of cardio along with my lifting schedule, but it blew my mind how quickly Erika could raise my heartrate. It was already difficult to catch my breath.

At least I had the same effect on her.

I shoved my hand inside her bikini bottom, rubbed her clit, and when she began to pant, I pushed my middle finger inside. A sinful chuckle broke from me as she arched her back and her hand stopped moving on me mid-pump. Like the sensation of it was almost too much to handle.

"That's just one finger," I whispered. "But this pussy's so wet, you want another?"

She shivered. "*Yes.*"

Her body was hot and slick, and she moaned when I eased my ring finger in to join the one already fucking her. I liked using my middle fingers in this position. It meant I could rub my palm against her clit and give her stimulation, inside and out.

Her hand that wasn't wrapped around my dick reached up behind her, until she could grab onto the back of my neck. The curve she created with her body made me wild. My hand jerked at her top, trying to get it up, or down, or sideways . . . whatever would get it out of my fucking way.

She let go of the back of my neck and undid the hook on hers. The band around her was still hooked closed, but I ignored it at first because her straps hung down and her tits were finally free, and I could see what I wanted.

Her smooth skin was damp from the swimsuit and the mist of the water falling nearby, and I ran my palm from the globe of one perfect breast to the other. The last five years of guitar had taught me to be good with my hands, and I used my skills to tease her to the point her sighs became whines of need.

Fuck it. Enough foreplay. I needed to get my dick inside her.

I stepped back, pulling my throbbing dick out of her hand, and I quickly undid the other hook that was keeping her top up. It fell onto the drain with a sopping noise, and I used a foot to push both it and my shorts off to the side.

Erika was as desperate as I was, because she hooked her thumbs into the sides of her bottoms and peeled them down her long legs. I clenched a hand on the cheek of her ass as it came into view. I was a classic guy. Tits and ass got the job done for me every time.

"This ass," I said appreciatively, "was made for trouble."

She liked hearing that, because she reached out, flattened her hands against the partition in front of her, and stepped out of the swimsuit wrapped around her ankles, spreading her feet on the shower floor. She was partially bent over, her ass presented to me.

Her question was rushed, like she wanted to ask it before she chickened out. "Is it an ass made for fucking?"

My dick jerked, and heat seared across my nerve endings. As excited as I was, it came from me in a dubious tone. "You want me to fuck your ass right now?"

"I want you to fuck my pussy." She wiggled her hips,

taunting me. Her voice was seductive, yet breathless. "There's a bottle of coconut oil in here, so you can use that for your fingers first, and then . . ." It was as if her directions were so hot, she could barely speak them. "Spread it all over your big cock, and when we're ready, you'll slide it inside my ass."

I nearly came.

Instead, I swallowed thickly. "Yes, ma'am."

She held perfectly still as I stepped up behind her and rubbed the head of my dick against her clit, both to tease her and orient myself. Her gasp dripped with satisfaction as I pushed inside her, and her hot pussy clamped down. I immediately set a fast tempo, because sometimes slow-fucking her felt *too* good. I needed to last.

I had one hand on her shoulder and the other anchored on her hip and drove into her. The slap of our wet bodies was loud and sharp, but I wasn't worried about anyone over at Preston's house hearing it. Erika's moans, though?

"Shh," I whispered, grinning.

She said it mindlessly, like it was a valid excuse. "It feels so good."

I agreed. It was why I reached behind me and searched for the bottle of oil among the shampoos and conditioners. As soon as I had it, I popped the top and poured some into my hand. It was like baby oil, but smelled much nicer, and I let the excess drip down onto her.

I'd slowed to a stop and was lodged deep inside her, and the noise of the shower water falling and gurgling down the drain was the only sound when I peeled her backside apart and dripped more coconut oil on her. I left the cap open and set it aside in the rack, then swirled the tip of my finger over her asshole.

She moaned encouragingly.

Her hands were splayed out on the partition slats, and as my finger pressed and began to intrude, her hands curled into loose fists. I went slowly and carefully, not wanting it to be uncomfortable, moving in and out until most of my finger was buried inside the tight ring of muscles.

"Good?" I whispered.

"Yeah." And to prove it, she gently rocked her hips, making her slide on both my finger and my dick.

My head swam with pleasure. Not only did it feel amazing, it looked amazing too. "You're so goddamn hot, Erika." I murmured. "Who said you could be so hot?"

She sighed with contentment, and her head hung down. I couldn't see her face, but I knew what pleasure looked like when it ran through her, and I was sure her eyes were closed and her lips were parted, rounding into silent 'oh's.

When she seemed relaxed enough with one finger, I tested her readiness with a second.

"Fuck," I groaned. "Your pussy just got ten times tighter."

Her moan in response was so loud, I froze. Okay, that one was definitely loud enough someone might question it. She whimpered, annoyed that I'd stopped, and I hesitantly resumed the glide of both my fingers and my dick inside her body.

Her legs were shaking, but it was obviously in pleasure. Our moans mingled together as I increased my speed. It was wild how I could feel my fingers on me from inside her pussy.

I was tingling and buzzing, and I clenched my jaw to hold back the desire to come.

"I want it now, Troy."

I withdrew my hips, sliding my dick out of her, and with the new space between our bodies, it gave me more room to maneuver. I thrust my first two fingers deep between her cheeks. "Yeah? You want me to fuck you right here?" The words tasted deliciously dirty. "In this virgin asshole?"

Once again, she shivered. She seemed to love my filthy mouth, and her plea was urgent. "*Please.*"

Hearing her beg was the sexiest fucking thing ever. I moved as a man with purpose, retreating from her completely so I could do what she'd asked. The bottle of coconut oil was snatched up and I dispensed a shit-ton of it into my hand, slathering it all over me.

I ignored how good the slick slide of my hand felt as I lubed up, and when that was done, the remaining oil on my hand was stroked between her ass cheeks.

The muscles in my chest were tense as I lined us up. Although she'd seemed to be enjoying it a few seconds ago, my dick was a lot bigger than two fingers. I wasn't going to be comfortable if she wasn't, and no way was I going to hurt her.

I asked it more for me than her. "Ready?"

She nodded.

With all the prep, her body was still kind of resistant, and it made me nervous with how much force I had to press into her with. Abruptly, the head of my dick pushed inside, and Erika's sharp gasp made me feel like I'd swallowed a brick. I froze, unsure.

The shower continued to run, but otherwise everything was still. I wasn't even breathing.

Her arms were tense, but her fingers unfurled from fists and pressed against the vinyl slats. And then she began to move minutely. Just a fraction of an inch at a time. I was only barely inside her, but I had to close my eyes. The visual of what we were doing was going to send me over the edge.

Her painstakingly slow movements began to increase, taking more of me with each pass as I held absolutely still. I couldn't help it, the words spilled from my mouth. "God, I love it when you fuck me."

She sighed dreamily. "Me too."

Warning lights flashed inside my body and bliss traveled up my spine in waves. *Don't come. Wait.*

Fingertips brushed against my sack and I glanced down. She was touching herself, and—fuck me—my dick was half-way inside her now. I palmed her ass cheeks and peeled her open so I had a better view.

"How does it feel?" I asked.

She didn't answer right away. Maybe she was struggling for the right word. I hoped for 'good' or some variation. Her tone was incredulous. "Crazy."

The brick in my stomach weighed me down some more. "Do you want to stop?"

There was no hesitation this time. "No." She kind of laughed. "You've got a big dick. Give a girl a second to get used to it."

I let out a tight breath.

When I relaxed, she did too, and suddenly it was easier

for her to take me deeper. I groaned from the sensation. It wasn't just how tight and different it felt, it was all the other shit that went along with it. How hot she looked with me inside her. That I was the first guy she'd wanted to try it with. How perfectly in sync we were.

I don't know how it happened, but at some point she handed control back to me. I was the one fucking her now, slow and deep, while she had one hand bracing herself against the wall and the other between her legs.

She said it like a warning. "I'm going to come so fast."

"That's going to make me come," I fired back.

I didn't want her so far away when it happened. I leaned over, setting my hand beside hers on the partition, and used my other hand to turn her head toward mine.

I drank in her moans as they swelled and crushed them under my kiss when she came. Her rhythmic pulses choked my dick, and I groaned as the orgasm roared toward me, feeling like my body had been cranked up to eleven.

We didn't talk about how she wanted it, so as I began to come, I pulled out. Hopefully, my timing hadn't been terrible or I'd ruined her orgasm, but it was impossible to hold back any longer. I pumped my fist on my dick, stroking a few furious thrusts, before shooting streaks of cum across her perfect ass.

"*Fuck*," I groaned, my whole body twitching with electricity and satisfaction.

Our hurried, labored breath was louder than the shower. I filled a hand with water and used it to gently wipe away the mess I'd created before she decided to get creative again.

Maybe it was my cooling body or the sudden breeze whipping through the slated partition that caused a chill to cling to my skin. An eerie awareness rolled through and my heart thudded oddly inside my rib cage.

There was a shadowy reflection in the water pooled at our feet that hadn't been there earlier. I glanced toward the shower's doorway—

Erika's ex-husband stood at the entrance, and judging by the horror running across his face, he'd been there a while.

TWENTY-ONE

Erika

When I felt Troy solidify into stone, I wiped the dampness from under my eyes, straightened, and followed his gaze.

No.

Clark stood at the entrance of the shower, backlit by the bright, sunny afternoon behind him, his gaze fixated on our naked bodies.

I said it both in my head and out loud. "What the *fuck*, Clark?"

There wasn't much point to shielding my nakedness from him. When we were married, we weren't shy about nudity. He had no right to look now, but still he had the audacity to do it anyway. In my surprise, my brain was slow to understand why he was looking at me like my body was unfamiliar.

It was because he hadn't seen my breasts since my surgery.

His stunned gaze flicked away from mine and landed on Troy, and his voice was hollow and powerless. It was as if he were shell-shocked. "This is a surprise."

And as suddenly as he'd appeared, Clark turned the corner and vanished from our sight. I scooped up my drenched bikini bottoms as Troy did the same, reaching for his shorts.

Hurried footsteps crunched over the pebbles in the rock

garden as Clark fled.

"Fuck," I spat out. "Wait."

My hands were flustered and clumsy. Putting on a swim-suit in a hurry was hard, but a wet one was *impossible*. Why the hell hadn't I brought a towel over? My cover-up was basically a useless accessory. Something cute I'd added to my cart when buying the swimsuit because it was on clearance.

Troy had it much easier than me and had finished doing up his fly when I reached for my top.

"Should I go after him?" He asked it in a hurried voice, but it couldn't hide how desperately he did not want to do that. Troy actively disliked my ex-husband, and surely saw this as another unwanted intrusion into my life. If anything, he'd want Clark gone as fast as possible.

What would Troy even say to him anyway?

I hesitated long enough that the gate crashed closed, making what I wanted irrelevant. Best case scenario, Clark would be backing out of the driveway by the time I made it to the fence.

"No, let him go." I struggled to put my top back in place as he shut off the shower.

"What was he doing here?"

I snatched the cover-up off the hook and jammed an arm into it. "Besides trespassing? No clue. I don't know why he would think it was okay for him to come back here without permission. This isn't his house, it's mine."

I marched out into the sun and to the end of the pool deck, peering down the slope of my lawn to spy the backend of Clark's BMW as he sped off. Frustration tightened inside me. He hadn't called or texted to ask if—

Shit.

I wouldn't know if he had because I'd blocked his number.

Troy stood beside me, the air between us tense. He watched me cautiously, not sure how to react or what to say, and it only grew more intense as time dragged on.

Finally, he broke the silence. "You okay?"

He had his hands on his hips, and water droplets clung to his bare chest. It dripped from his trunks and sluiced down his legs. The concern in his eyes nearly broke my heart and compelled me forward into his damp arms. Was he worried I was ashamed? I wasn't. We hadn't done anything wrong. That was all on Clark.

"I'm fine, just pissed at him." There were towels in the cabinet on the patio, so once I had some pulled out, I passed one to Troy. My heartrate was still up from the shock, and it disabled my filter. "Guess we're even," I said in a humorless joke. "We've both caught each other with a dick in our ass."

The moment I stopped speaking, all the air whooshed from my body.

Troy had been toweling off, but paused mid-wipe. "Wait. What?"

"Nothing." I couldn't get the words out fast enough. "Forget I said that."

A skeptical look crossed his face. "That's . . . doubtful." He straightened as he tried to figure it out, but he only looked more confused. "Okay, so Clark is—like—into pegging?"

Oh, God. I pressed my lips together.

I'd kept his sexuality private as Clark had asked me to. I

hadn't told a soul, outside of Derrick's wife, even as his affair had shaken me to my core and left me questioning everything.

Yet my ex had no problem violating my space or privacy. Why was I protecting him again?

Troy had proven he knew how to keep a secret, and I was desperate to share it with him. "I haven't told anyone because he asked me not to, but it's not fair for him to ask me to lie." I phrased it as a statement, when it was more of a question. "I can trust you."

His eyes widened. "Yeah, of course."

"When I caught him having sex," I sucked in a breath, "it was with a man."

There was no reaction from him. It was proof of what a great performer he could be. He schooled himself not to show any emotion. There wasn't unease, or pity for me, or suspicion about why my husband had turned toward men.

"I . . ." His shoulders lifted and his eyebrows pulled together. Then, he simply said, "Wow."

"Yeah," I agreed.

He was about to say something else when a song full of synthesizers began blaring from the lounge chair beside the pool where he'd dropped his stuff.

It cut through the heaviness, and my lips wanted to quirk in amusement. "Your ringtone's 'The Final Countdown?'"

He didn't join me in smiling. Instead, he looked worried. "It is when my mom's calling."

He was almost to his phone when the hairs on the back of my neck stood up, and I raced after him, although I wasn't sure why. It wasn't to stop him from answering. She could have been calling for any number of reasons, but Troy held the same trepidation as I did. My heart sputtered and climbed into my throat.

He tapped the screen and lifted the phone to his ear, his gaze fixed on me. "Hello?"

Jenna's voice was raised enough I could hear her. "Where are you? You turned your location off."

His face twisted. "I'm at Preston's."

This time she was so loud he held the phone away from his ear. "Don't you dare lie to me, Troy Edward Osbourne. I just got off the phone with Clark Graham."

Everything inside me vaporized.

Of course Clark had recognized Troy, and he'd rightly assumed Jenna wasn't aware of our relationship, because she wouldn't allow it if she were. So, he'd gone straight to her to punish me.

He'd never forgiven me for telling Derrick's wife, and I was sure he felt vindicated in exposing me. I could hear my ex's voice echoing in my head. *"Now we're even."*

My shoulders sank, and the utter turmoil I had was broadcast perfectly on Troy's handsome face.

"Fine. I'm at Erika's." His tone was empty. "We were going to tell you."

Whatever she said, it was too low for me to hear this time. He swallowed hard, making his Adam's apple bob in his throat while he lowered the phone. Tension held his shoulders tight as he stretched his hand toward me. "She, uh, wants to talk to you."

I exhaled sharply and took his offered phone. I closed

my eyes, centered myself, and brought it to my ear. "Jenna, I'm so sorry. We were—"

"You. Lying. Bitch." Venom dripped from every word. "He's half your age, *and my son*. You should be ashamed of yourself."

It was immediately followed by an electronic click as she disconnected the call, but I held his phone pressed to my cheek for several more seconds, as if my friendship with Jenna wasn't truly over until I lowered my hand.

He gently pulled the phone from me, dropped it on the chair, and circled his arms around my waist. I clung to his warmth because her words had invaded my mind and caused shivers to rack my body.

"I am ashamed," I whispered to him, "of how I lied to her."

He stroked a hand over the back of my head and hugged me closer. "She was going to be mad no matter what, and try to tell us we couldn't."

While he was right, "That doesn't make it okay."

"I know." His heartbeat was strong and steady, maintaining a perfectly calm tempo, and I envied him for it.

It was easier to focus my emotions into anger toward Clark instead of my own guilt, so I did that. It was so unfair. Troy and I had already decided to tell his parents. If we'd been caught in a compromising position a day later, we could have avoided Jenna learning it this way. Clark telling her was the freaking *worst* way possible for her to find out.

"Come on," Troy said softly. "Let's get dressed and we'll go talk to her."

I shot him a dubious look. I knew my friend and how

she'd react to her son showing up with me in tow. "She won't speak to me."

"Then I'll do the talking," he said, taking my hand in his.

Troy had a calming effect, which kept my level of anxiety down just enough so I didn't bail out of his Jeep when Jenna and Bill's house came into view.

But his calm demeanor came to a screeching halt when he spotted the stack of boxes at the curb. "What the fuck?"

I couldn't believe what I was seeing either. "Is that your stuff?"

Once we were in the driveway, he angrily shifted into park, shut off the engine, and climbed out of his seat. Jenna came through the gate carrying an open box with a computer keyboard sticking out the top.

"You're kicking me out?" he demanded.

She pulled to a stop, but when she spied me getting out of his Jeep, her eyes narrowed to slits and she moved to add the box to the pile. "You've lied to me enough times you've lost the privilege of living under my roof."

For added effect, she dropped the box and it landed with a hard, careless thud, making him wince.

"And you," she swung an angry finger toward me, "have some fucking nerve showing up here. Jesus, Erika, I thought you were my friend. *How could you*?"

My shoulders slumped and I swallowed the thick lump in my throat. "I'm sorry."

Troy was more focused on the immediate issue. "Where am I supposed to go?"

She shrugged. "I guess you should have thought about that before you went behind my back. I'm sure one of your friends has a couch you can sleep on."

He considered her statement for a long moment, then abruptly lunged for the box. His tone was forced indifference. "Yeah, sure." He tucked it under his arm and walked to the back of his SUV. "Or I could crash at my girlfriend's house."

I could hear the needle drag across the record playing in Jenna's head. "What?"

He carried on with loading the box into his Jeep while I stood dumbfounded. Maybe if I held perfectly still, they would forget I was here.

Fat chance.

She glared at me with so much accusation in her eyes, it was a miracle I stayed on my feet. This power struggle was classic Jenna. She was a storm. She'd get all worked up, only for her emotions to peter out, and then she'd be able to see reason. I just had no idea how long her category five hurricane was going to last.

"Don't be ridiculous. She can't be your girlfriend," she announced.

He didn't miss a beat. "You don't get a say in who I date. How many more times do I have to tell you that?"

She stared at her son like he'd lost his mind. "She's too old for you."

"Nope." He hauled another box up into his arms and shot me a grin. "I think she's just right."

Jenna made a sound of pure dissatisfaction, and her hands curled into fists. She was so upset she was shaking, and while I hated seeing my friend in distress, I couldn't help but wonder if this would be good for her long-term. She needed to give him a chance to be his own man. To be independent.

Didn't she understand her attempts to shield him had also prevented him from learning the lessons that failure could teach?

"Look," he said pointedly, "we're sorry we lied, and it's not a great excuse, but the way you're acting right now? It's exactly why we didn't want to tell you."

I pressed my fingertips to my forehead and massaged the wrinkle forming there. During the drive over, he'd reassured me he would handle it, so I'd tried to stay quiet. The last thing I wanted was to come between them more than I already had.

Yet, as I stood there, my irritation with Jenna began to grow. She had every right to be upset. I'd been a terrible friend. But him? "Are you throwing your son out . . . because you don't like who he's dating?"

Her face turned an ugly shade of red as it swung toward me. "*I'm not talking to you.*"

"That's fine. You can be as mad at me as you want. I deserve it." I cast a hand toward him. "But he doesn't. Let him be free to do what he wants. He's an adult, Jenna."

"Don't you dare lecture me! Adult or not, he's still *my* son. I know that doesn't mean shit to you, but I'm trying to stop him from making some truly awful decisions."

She didn't say it, but it was implied by her glare, and I sensed the heat rising in Troy. Which was ironic, since his tone was frosty. "Okay, so Erika's good enough to be your friend—your best friend—but still not good enough for me?"

His mother threw her hands up and looked around like she couldn't believe no one else was nearby to hear this ridiculousness. "No, she's not good enough and she's not my friend. Because if she were, she wouldn't have slept with you!" She couldn't seem to catch her breath. "Troy. This is unacceptable, and all I've ever wanted is what's best for you."

"No," he said. "All you've ever wanted is what's best for *you*." His posture was tense and confrontational. "You don't care about what I want."

She gasped. "Of course, I do."

"Really? Do I even like working for Bill's company?"

His question should have been rhetorical because even I knew the answer, and yet . . . she looked confused. As if she'd never even considered it.

His harsh tone left no doubt. "I told you—oh my God—so many times! But you only hear what you want. If you'd listened, you could have talked Bill out of offering his company to me. Instead, you pushed me into that situation and forced me to make everyone unhappy."

Unease seeped into the edge of her expression, because she knew there was some truth in what he'd said, and she worried she was losing control of the conversation. "I heard you, but it's such a good company. Steady and reliable—"

He sighed loudly and stared up at the sky. "You're

proving my point, Mom, that what I want doesn't matter."

Jenna stood in her driveway, struggling with the wild swing of emotions going through her. Rage at me battled with her guilt over controlling him, and it put her off-balance. "What you want matters, Troy."

"Yeah?" He was firm, but beneath it there was hope. He wanted to believe her. "Prove it. I want to try for a career in music, so you can start showing up and actually supporting me."

He turned, his chest lifted with pride and his eyes absolute as he pointed a sharp finger at me. His words brimmed with determination.

"And I want this woman. You need to get on board with that."

His defiant, sure claim on me made goosebumps burst down my legs as breath halted in my lungs.

Jenna was frozen awkwardly, becoming a statue whose only movement was the stunned blink of her eyes. After an eternity, her anger won out and her voice turned cold.

"No," she announced. "Never."

She slung down her ultimatum with defiance burning in her eyes. *It's her or me,* she silently screamed at him.

It didn't take Troy long to make his decision. He stacked one box on top of another and then picked them up.

"Fine. See you around," he said, and made his way to the Jeep.

Holy shit. I'd thought I couldn't possibly feel worse than I had when we'd arrived, but I'd been wrong. I'd not only destroyed my friendship, but his relationship with his mother.

It was hard not to break inside, and to distract, I focused on grabbing whatever I could so we could flee.

I had a grip on the handle of his suitcase when she abruptly spoke. Her voice was hollow and meant only for me. "He's making a huge mistake with you."

It wounded me deeply, but I pretended her words didn't reach me. "It's his to make."

TWENTY-TWO

Erika

It broke my heart when Troy asked if he could spend the night at my place, and then he broke it all over again when he was unsure which bedroom he'd be staying in. Like he was worried he was overstepping, and since we'd already had sex today, I'd need some distance.

It couldn't be further from the truth.

I want this woman, he'd declared.

It was too soon for me to be having all these feelings, but they existed regardless, and I needed him to know the same was true for me.

After dinner, I got out my guitar and played the song I'd started composing after our desperate kiss against the mirror when he'd found out he'd won the spot. He not only picked up the new song quickly, he suggested some tweaks and helped me improve it.

We didn't have sex that night when we went to bed together. Maybe it felt disrespectful to Jenna while she was still coming to grips with our relationship, but more than anything, I think we both wanted to connect in a new and different way. We kissed, and talked, and snuggled, and what had been a helluva day at least ended as a fantastic night.

Was this a glimpse of what could be? Because it didn't

feel like a mistake.

It felt right.

In the morning, I got ready for work and left him with a kiss and a spare key. I didn't know how long it'd take Jenna to become reasonable again toward her son, but I was sure she would and hoped it wouldn't be long. He said after his class today he'd make plans to start looking for his own place.

Which was important to him. Although I wanted to spend every spare moment together right now, I understood and supported the idea. The honeymoon phase for me was incredibly strong and deceptive.

My day at the office was challenging. A show promoter we'd contracted with wasn't responding to emails or phone calls, and the drummer of one of the bands I repped had gotten arrested for a DUI last night.

At lunch, I'd unblocked Clark's number and attempted to call him, but it rang once before going to voicemail, and I hung up, not knowing what kind of message I would leave. We needed to have a conversation. Obviously, he had something he wanted to say to me bad enough he'd decided to come by the house, and I wanted to give him a piece of my mind about that.

I thumbed out a message.

Me: We need to talk about yesterday.

As I was finishing up at the office, I checked my phone and he still hadn't read my message. I tried calling him again and got the same result.

Oh, how the tables had turned, he must have thought.

Now my ex was the one not taking any calls.

I'd just put my phone in my purse when it chirped with a text message.

Troy: Got a second to talk?

I punched his number, waved goodbye to Charlotte, and walked out the office door, my footsteps crunching on the leaves the wind had gathered on the front porch. "Hey. What's up?"

"So," he said, "I just got done putting my shit back."

I missed a step coming down the porch onto the sidewalk and nearly fell. "What? You're moving back in?"

"Temporarily, yeah." He sounded tired. "My mom called and asked me to come over so she could apologize."

"Oh." I pulled my eyebrows together, unsure how to feel about this. "I take it you went?"

He wasn't tired—he was emotionally drained. "Yeah. I was still pissed off, but she was in bad shape. When I got there, she looked like she'd been crying all morning."

His words cut through my heart. She'd been crying because of me. I'd known getting involved with Troy was going to carry huge consequences, and yet I'd still done it, her feelings be damned.

"Bill was there too," he said. "And I told them I was done. I needed to live my life and if they wanted to continue being a part of it, shit had to change. Like, right now."

I was tense just hearing it secondhand. "How did that go over?"

"It . . . went. I told them it'd mean a lot to me to have

them there on Saturday. But if she didn't believe in me and how I want to pursue music, then she shouldn't bother coming to my show." There was the sound of chair legs dragging across a hard floor, and I pictured him sitting down at his kitchen table. "So, she apologized and cried some more, and then Bill cried, and it was rough."

I pressed my hand to the center of my chest. "I'm sorry. Are you okay?"

"Yeah, and don't be sorry. It was good." He sounded cautiously optimistic. "I laid it all out there, said all the things I needed to about her smothering me, and I think she finally, really listened." He let out a long breath. "I'm still moving out, but I'm here until I get my own place, and they agreed to give me my space in the meantime."

I bit down on my lip. "Do you think they'll be able to?"

He paused. "She's still really upset about us, so yeah. I think she'd like to go back to not knowing, but since she can't . . ."

He didn't have to say it. She wanted to pretend I no longer existed.

"I tried telling her this isn't your fault," he said. "I was the one who went after you."

I raised an eyebrow. "I'm sure she liked hearing that."

There was no way she'd assign blame to her son over me.

"No, it didn't help," he admitted. "She just needs more time."

I wished that were true, but it was doubtful.

"So," he forced lightness into his voice, "I'm back to crashing at my place. Don't let me forget to give you back your key."

I'd reached my car and unlocked it but hesitated before opening the door. I'd loved last night.

I was greedy and wanted more nights like that.

My voice was breathless, excited to take the risk. He'd said he wanted me, and now I could make my own declaration for him. "You can hang on to it."

"Yeah?" I pictured him with a sexy smile on his face. "Cool."

I tugged open my door and slid into the driver's seat. "Do you want to get dinner together? It might be one of my last chances before you're a superstar."

While Stella's tour bus wouldn't arrive from Atlanta until Friday, she'd quietly slip into town tomorrow afternoon to try to avoid the paparazzi. She wanted a lowkey night out with her friends and team, which of course included Troy. It would be a fabulous opportunity, and I hoped he could find a moment to sweet talk Stella into mentoring him.

"I could do dinner," he said. "You want to pick me up? It might give you and my mom a chance to talk."

Was he kidding? "You just said she needs time. It doesn't sound like she's ready to talk."

"No," he said, "but . . . she'll come around. Trust me."

I hoped he was right.

Friday morning, Charlotte was surprisingly helpful,

offering to help me sift through contracts so I could find the information I was looking for, allowing me to go on to the next thing on my never-ending to-do list. Stella's concert was tomorrow, and I wanted all my ducks in a row so I didn't have to work tonight or tomorrow.

I could focus entirely on Troy.

He hadn't texted me yet to tell me how the evening with Stella had gone last night, but Ardy had looked haggard when he'd arrived at the office, mumbling about him being too old to be this tired.

Once he was tucked away in his office, I smiled at Charlotte. "Late night?"

She nodded. "I heard from Becca the bar stayed open an extra hour."

Meaning if Ardy and Troy had stayed to the end, it'd been three or four in the morning. I glanced at the clock on her computer screen, which read nine-forty, and sucked up the impatient urge to text my boyfriend and potentially wake him up. He had a huge day tomorrow and needed all the sleep he could get.

Charlotte scrolled through the contract she had pulled up, highlighting the clause I was looking for.

"Awesome, thanks." I straightened to go back to my office, but hesitated. "Hey, can I ask you something? Do you like working here?"

She looked up at me with confusion. "Sure."

My question had been too broad. "I guess what I'm asking is, if you could do whatever you wanted, would you be here working for your dad?"

Watching what Troy had gone through with his mother gave me new perspective. Maybe Charlotte disliked her job and I hadn't been fair to her. Ardy had a dominating presence, and it wasn't a stretch to assume he'd encouraged her to work at the business he'd built and ran.

She sat back in her chair and considered my question critically, and then her eyes turned sad. "No." She made a face. "I mean, maybe? It's like, when my dad said I was going to get to work at Warbler, I got all excited. I grew up surrounded by music, and I always expected it'd be a part of me."

I tilted my head in question.

She pivoted in her chair to better face me. "So, I thought I was going to get," she searched for the right word, "rock n' roll." She gestured to the contract on her computer screen. "Instead, I got this. This . . . is not rock n' roll."

My laugh was gentle. "No, it's not."

"I'm sure it's not news to you, but I suck at paperwork, and I don't like doing things I'm not good at."

There was a twinge inside me because I could absolutely relate. Who would enjoy doing something that made them feel inferior? "Have you told your dad this?"

Charlotte's pretty face skewed. "I don't think he's going to want me to keep working here if I say I don't like it."

"I don't know, your dad's a smart guy. He might have some ideas that are a better fit for you." Plus, he loved his daughter. He'd do all he could to make her happy.

Her expression was skeptical at first, but I watched the wheels turning behind her eyes as she began to consider what I'd said.

Her phone was lying face-up on her desk, so when the notification with Troy's name popped up on the lock screen, my eye went straight to it. "What's that?"

She picked up her phone and looked embarrassed. "I, um . . . set an alert on Troy's name."

Except for Ardy, no one at Warbler knew Troy and I were dating. We'd decided to hold off on revealing it until after Stella's tour was over. Our relationship had no bearing on him landing the show's opening spot, but this would keep any rumors of impropriety from circulating.

Charlotte's embarrassment was harmless. She worried she'd come off as a silly girl with a crush, but if she was, I couldn't fault her for it. I felt that way around him too.

"What's the notification?" I asked.

Was it more pictures from last night? He'd been in one Stella had posted to Instagram. But Charlotte's eyes widened as she stared at the screen, forcing me to step behind her and read over her shoulder.

"I guess that answers the question," she said flatly, "on whether or not he has a girlfriend."

My mouth went dry and my body cold as I processed what I was seeing. First, the red logo at the top of the screen caused dread. Nothing good for my clients had ever been posted on TMZ. Second, the headline made my stomach turn.

"Stella Auditions Her New Man!"

I didn't read the article because there was no point. The photo did all the storytelling.

The picture was grainy and angled from above, probably

taken by a drone and then zoomed in. It was the only way to get pictures of her property because the community was gated, and her fence was an impressively high wall, surrounding her estate on all sides. I'd been to her house once with Ardy, and we'd marveled at how far she'd come from the two-bedroom apartment she used to share with her parents and sister.

The image had been captured while Troy was mid-step in the circle drive, walking toward the open door of an SUV. It was likely Stella's personal car, preparing to take him home after their evening was over.

I didn't know the circumstances that led to the picture, but several facts were undeniable. He was wearing the same clothes he'd been in Stella's IG post from earlier in the night.

He'd gone over to her house afterward.

And the sun was up when the picture had been taken, meaning he'd spent the night.

It felt like I was back in that dark hallway, staring at Clark's office door, knowing everything was about to come apart and there was nothing I could do to stop it.

I straightened so abruptly, it caused alarm in Charlotte. "Are you okay?"

"Fine." Although the shake in my voice said otherwise. I put one foot in front of the other and forced myself to walk to my office.

It was fine, I told myself. I'd call him and there'd be a perfectly reasonable explanation. I tried not to think about how gorgeous Stella was, or how successful, or that she could catapult his career and make his dreams come true.

All I could think about was how young she was. Practically

his age. She was America's sweetheart, and maybe the only girl on this planet his mother would approve of.

My hands shook as I held my phone and tapped his contact name.

It rang.

And rang.

Somewhere 'Reckless' was playing because that was the ringtone he'd chosen for me. The fourth ring was interrupted by a click, and then his sleepy voice came through. "Hey."

"Hey!" I overcompensated, so it came out extra bright. "Sorry. Did I wake you?"

"Yeah, but that's okay. What's up?"

My pulse throbbed in the side of my neck. "How was your night?"

"It was great." He sounded marginally more alert. "She gave me all these tips and told me the stuff she wished she'd known starting out. I could have listened to her talk all night."

I'd told him to be a sponge. To do way more listening than talking, because people just starting out were weirdly overconfident and often came off as know-it-alls.

"All night?" I tried to sound nonchalant. "I heard y'all kept the place open late." I both did and didn't want to know the answer, so my voice was tight. "What time did you get home?

There was a fraction of a pause, but it was a fucking dagger to my heart. That microsecond was the time it took him to craft his lie.

He sounded distant. "A little after three." He tacked it on as if it were the perfect explanation. "We were doing shots."

"Three," I repeated.

"Yeah. Why?"

"I asked what time you got home," I maintained a cool veneer, "not what time you left the bar with her, Troy."

"What?" There was rustling on the other end. Had he bolted upright in bed? It sounded like the covers were shifting around him. "What are you talking about?"

"You spent the night at Stella's place." I'd naïvely hoped he'd tell me I was wrong, that it wasn't true.

But I was met with nothing but silence.

My tone was pure bitterness. "If you need help jogging your memory, go check TMZ."

He sounded desperate. "Okay, yeah. I went back to her place, but you need to believe me—nothing happened."

I wasn't Erika Graham anymore because I'd become a volcano of fury. "Are you fucking kidding me? You just lied, and now you're asking me to believe you?"

It hurt to breathe. He was supposed to be better than Clark. Troy had told me he didn't understand people who cheated, but . . . had it just been bullshit? I should have known better. He'd lied to his mom so many times, lying had to come easy for him now. And I hadn't just participated in lying with him, I'd actively *encouraged* it.

God, I was so stupid.

"Where are you?" There was louder rustling as he scurried out of bed. "Warbler? I'm coming over."

The agent side of me stepped in and took control. "No. We're not discussing this while I'm at work."

His tone was gruff. "See you in twenty minutes."

The call disconnected before I could protest. I dropped

my phone onto my desktop, clenched my fists, and paced my office. The image of him leaving Stella's house this morning was burned into my brain, but if I needed to reference it again, the notification from TMZ was right there on my lock screen.

I had no choice but to read the article, and then critically examine both his and Stella's posts on social media to glean all the facts I could. I needed to know in case he planned to feed me more lies.

As soon as I heard heavy footsteps marching up the front porch and the main door push open, I put on a stern expression and came out of my office.

Troy looked . . . disheveled. His t-shirt had wrinkles like he'd scooped it up off his bedroom floor and pulled it on, along with the khaki shorts he wore. His hair was wild—flattened on one side and sticking up in other places. Dark circles hung beneath his tired eyes.

Despite it, he still looked so damn good to me. This rumpled styling was caused by an urgent need to see me, and it was hard not to respond to it. But the business side of me had a very different reaction.

Charlotte lifted her head and blinked in surprise. "Oh, hey, Troy."

He didn't acknowledge her at all. His gaze swept the room, found me, and locked on.

I flung a finger at the door he'd just come through. "Outside with me."

It was overcast today, and there was electricity in the air. Rain would be coming at any second, and it gave me a good excuse to get him back in his car and out of sight.

"Erika—"

My voice was clipped and professional. "We'll talk in your Jeep."

Frustration etched his face, but he agreed to it by leading me down the sidewalk to where he'd parked. I said nothing when he held open the passenger door for me, I just climbed in. He closed the door with a loud thump, then rounded the backend of the SUV and got seated behind the wheel.

The moment his door was shut, speckles of rain dotted his windshield, like the storm had politely held off for us.

"I'm not your agent or manager anymore," I said, "but you cannot ever go out in public again looking like this, you understand? The tabloids will be all over you now because of this story. The last guy Stella dated—"

"Stop." He turned in his seat as much as he could to face me. "When the bar closed last night, the party was still going, so Stella invited us back to her place. That's all this was. We hung out in her studio, playing music and talking about the industry." His brow furrowed. "It got so late, she said it was cool if I wanted to crash in one of her guest rooms."

I had no idea what expression I was making, but the concern in his blue eyes deepened.

"I'll prove it. Her guest room has these huge fucking silver curtains and the bed's one of those memory foam ones where it's hard as a rock until you sink down in."

I blinked slowly, considering his story, but was skeptical. He'd said Stella had invited *us* and not *me*. The only photo published of someone leaving her house this morning was him, but that didn't necessarily mean it was the case. "Who else stayed over?"

When his eyes shifted away, the pain in my chest was back.

"Just me," he said quietly, "but seriously—nothing happened. You have to know that." The rain pattered against the windows and hurt welled in his voice. "How could you think I'd do that to you?"

Was he kidding?

"Oh, I don't know," bitterness filled my mouth, "maybe how I spent a year of my life fucking oblivious the man I loved was having an affair?" I lifted my gaze to the ceiling to stave off my emotions. "Christ, I can't believe I made the same mistake with you so fast."

I'd said it without thinking, and the meaning in my words filled every breathable inch of space inside his Jeep.

Troy went wooden. "Love?"

He'd latched onto that word, and I needed to put distance between it and us as quickly as possible. I couldn't love him. It wasn't possible for me to fall in love this quickly. This feeling of drowning in him was just the newness of our relationship.

"If nothing happened," I said, "then why lie about it?"

He was still dazed and struggled to pull himself back together. "I'm sorry I did that."

"I appreciate the apology, but that's not an explanation, Troy."

He frowned. "Okay, this is going to sound bad . . . but I did it because it made sense not to tell you. Because of your ex, I—"

"What the fuck?" My eyes widened. "You meant easier. It

was *easier* not telling me."

"So, we could avoid this?" He gestured between us. "You jumping to conclusions? Yeah. What your ex did to you was beyond shitty, but I am *not* him. I don't cheat. I've made it crystal fucking clear what I want, and it's not someone else, not Stella, and definitely not some other dude. I don't want anyone but you."

The rain was heavier now, pummeling the Jeep and the roar of it filled the silence between us. As it dragged on, I grew more upset.

And worried about what this meant for our future.

"It would be easier to believe you," I said, "if you hadn't just lied to me."

His expression was a mix of remorse and frustration. "I'm *sorry*. It was stupid and I wasn't completely awake when you—"

I lifted a hand, cutting him off. "I've been in the business a while. I know better than to take every story or picture at face value, because clicks matter more than the truth to a lot of people. There has to be trust between us, so I can believe you when you say nothing happened." I swallowed painfully. "But now that trust is gone."

"I know I fucked up." Worry etched his handsome face. "I'd take it back if I could, but I can't. All I can say is I promise it won't happen again." He hesitantly reached over and trailed his fingertips over my cheek, pushing my hair back behind my ear, and I wanted to soften at his touch. His voice fell to a whisper. "Can you at least believe that?"

The storm overhead beat down on the car in slashes of

rain, and I was grateful for the cover. Not just with how it prevented Charlotte from seeing us—because I was sure she was watching through the front window—but how secluded it felt.

For a brief time, it had created a bubble where my negative thoughts had a harder time penetrating my mind. But my devil's advocate spun up and told me all the reasons why he'd lie and leave me for someone else.

That what we had might not last.

And it would be better to cut my losses now.

Save myself from more pain down the road.

He searched my face, trying to figure out why I hadn't said anything, and his eyes widened in concern. "You're looking at me like you think we're doomed."

I didn't want to put it out in the universe, but the words came from me anyway. "Are we?" I whispered. "It's only going to get harder when you blow up."

Oh, he didn't like hearing that. "So . . . what are you saying? You want to give up? Just because I made a dumb mistake and things might get hard?"

Did I want to give up?

My thoughts were a mess, and when I didn't respond immediately, he withdrew like I'd slapped him. Surprise and hurt painted his expression, and the temperature in the car plummeted twenty degrees.

"You know what?" he snapped. "I'm tired and kind of hungover, so maybe you should go before I say something I don't mean."

"Look, I don't know what I'm feeling. Everything with us

happened so fast and it . . . scares me."

"I got it." His hands tightened on the steering wheel until his knuckles were white, and it was as if he hadn't heard a word I'd said. "There's an umbrella in the glove compartment if you want it."

He'd all but told me to get the hell out of his car. It was even more clear when he started his engine.

I wasn't one to overstay my welcome, so I shoved open the door and stepped out into the pouring rain. I'd never felt so lost as when I turned back to look at him.

He had to shout it over the storm. "She said you'd give up on me as soon as the going got tough. Like you always do."

Was he talking about his mother? My mouth hung open as the cold rain pelted down on me, making me numb.

"Don't prove her right, Erika."

Then he put his Jeep in gear, stepped on the gas, and as the car took off, the force of it pulled the door from my hand and slammed it shut.

TWENTY-THREE

Erika

The rest of my afternoon was spent with my emotions ping-ponging wildly. It was impossible to get any work done. One moment it would be rage at what Jenna had said about me, then unease she might have been right.

She tried so hard to shield Troy from failure, but wasn't that exactly what I was doing to my relationship with him?

I was able to get a grip when I focused on a goal. Clark's address was listed somewhere in our divorce papers, and once I found it, I drove over to his townhome after work. Thankfully, I spotted his car in the shared parking spaces, so it was likely he was home.

Anxiety twisted inside me as I pressed the doorbell. He'd become such a stranger to me over the last year. Would I recognize the man who opened the door? I sucked in a deep, preparing breath as it swung open.

Clark was still in his work clothes, a collared button-down shirt and slacks. His eyes went enormously wide as he peered at me. "Erika?"

It was rude, but since he'd come onto my property without an invitation, I did the same. It forced him to back up into his living room when I barged in. "We need to talk."

His shoulders slumped and his gaze fell to the floor.

"This is about me showing up at your house?"

"You're goddamn right, it—"

Something was off about his place. I'd been distracted when I'd charged in, but now as I glanced around, I realized how sparse it was. He'd taken some of the furniture in the divorce to populate his new place, but it didn't look like he'd bought anything new. There was the brown couch from our bonus room sitting in his living room, but no end tables or coffee table in front of it. Just a couch and TV stand, plus a stack of boxes against the back wall.

"Are you moving?" I asked.

"No."

"What's with the boxes?"

He hesitated. "I haven't gotten around to unpacking them all."

Awareness dawned on me. We'd separated a year ago, and he'd purchased this townhome almost immediately. "You live like this?"

He narrowed his eyes. "Yeah, I do."

It reminded me of his apartment in college, back when he'd been a bachelor. I'd forgotten he'd been kind of hopeless until I came along. His mother had done everything for him, even his laundry on the weekends. I'd had to teach him how to cook and clean, but I must have missed how to decorate.

There was nothing personable in this space, and it felt sad and temporary. "You should have asked Jenna for some interior design help when you spoke with her."

"You mean, when I called to tell her what I caught you doing with her son?"

If he wanted to get a rise out of me, it was wasted. I acted indifferent. "Yes, that's what I meant." I put my hands on my hips. "You want to tell me why you thought it was acceptable to come into my backyard without my permission?"

"Exactly how was I supposed to get your permission?" Irritation made his jaw set. "You hadn't answered my calls in months."

"You could have tried leaving a message."

"Right," he said sarcastically. "Because I had total confidence that you'd return it." It seemed like he was losing whatever battle was waging in his head. "I didn't have a fucking clue what to say, and it wasn't something I wanted to leave on a damn voicemail either."

The living area was open to the kitchen, and it was next to a stack of bills where I discovered the only framed picture he had on display. It was the two of us on our honeymoon in Greece, the Parthenon looming in the background. It was a great picture of our happiest time.

But we weren't those people anymore.

I gestured toward the frame. "I can't imagine Derrick likes that."

Clark's silence was painful and telling.

The animosity inside me waned. "You're not together?"

His eyes turned glassy. "A few months ago, he, uh . . . went back to his wife."

"Oh, Clark . . ." He'd told me he'd fallen in love, and despite everything, I hurt for him. I meant it genuinely. "I'm sorry."

"Why?" He wiped away a tear as if angry at it. "Don't you

think I got what I deserved?" He forced out a rueful smile. "I didn't have anyone to talk to about it. I pushed everyone away, and you were the only one who knew about us, so . . ."

"Was that why you called?" *Really?* He'd wanted relationship advice from me, his ex-wife? I shouldn't have been surprised. He'd always put the emotional labor on me. The divorce hadn't changed that.

"I understand why you didn't answer," he said quietly, "but before Derrick, you were my best friend." He swallowed a breath. "I'm sorry for how often I called. At first, I was going to try to apologize." He was terrified to admit it, but maybe he was tired of holding it in. "I was struggling with a lot of shit, and I didn't handle any of it well, but I found after a while, hearing your voice helped."

Oh, wow.

"You called . . . so you could hear my voicemail message?"

Color rose in his neck. It always happened when he was embarrassed. "I can't explain why, but whenever I was having a bad day or missed talking to you, I'd call. I figured you'd either eventually answer or block my number, and then I'd be able to move on."

I reeled from what he'd said, unable to find words.

"And when my calls started going straight to your voicemail, I still couldn't move forward." He sighed and pinched the bridge of his nose. "I was awful to you. I had so much guilt and shame I didn't know what to do with it, and so I let Derrick convince me it wasn't my fault. It was yours."

Oh, Lord, he began to cry. In twenty years of marriage, I'd only seen it once before, during the elevator ride down to the lobby on the worst birthday of my life. This unleashed emotion from him was just as unsettling as it'd been then, but it was also raw and real, and although he'd put me through hell, I couldn't help but pity him.

"I'm sorry," he said between ragged breaths. "I tried not to, but I loved him with everything I had. So much, I got lost in him."

And now that Derrick was gone, Clark was simply lost. It was undeniable the way he ached, and I was struck by how my ex and I had never spoken this way about each other when we'd dated or were married.

I'd never gotten lost in him.

"Please forgive me," he said.

"Part of me wants to," I confessed. "But you don't get to ask for that. No matter how shattered I felt, or how awful you were to me . . . I kept your secret. I didn't tell a soul—other than Derrick's wife—and she had *every* right to know." I put my hand on my hip. "You didn't tell Jenna about Troy and me because you thought she deserved to know. You did it to *hurt* me. I'm not ready to forgive that."

Bless his heart, that just made him cry harder. "I know. I'm sorry." He drew in a gulping breath. "I was upset. Everyone moved on except me." He sniffled. "You're a better person than I am."

"Yes," I said simply. "And hopefully I'll be able to forgive you someday, but that day is not today."

Eventually, Clark's crying subsided, and he straightened awkwardly. It wasn't the closure he hoped for, but I'd given him a year of unearned loyalty. I wasn't giving him anything else.

His eyes were red and his cheeks blotchy, and he cleared his throat as he wiped away his tears. It was an attempt to return to his normal state, but his voice was shaky. "Can I do anything to make it better?"

"Yes." The afternoon had me feeling like I was in freefall. "I'm going to ask you something and I need you to answer honestly."

Clark looked nervous. "What is it?"

"Do I give up too easily?"

His expression filled with relief and remorse. "There wasn't anything you could have done to save our marriage."

My laugh was humorless. "I meant like, more in general."

"Oh." He contemplated it for a long moment. "I don't know how to answer that."

"That kind of sounds like a yes," I said dryly.

"Well, it's really important to you to succeed. That's not news, right? But I think you get scared and let doubt hold you back. It's what sabotaged your music career." His tone was gentle, like a doctor revealing a bad diagnosis. "You weren't sure if you could make it, but you were sure you could succeed at failing. So, I think subconsciously that's what you did."

Holy shit, was that true?

"If you'd thrown yourself at it, gone all in . . . maybe it wouldn't have changed anything, but who knows? The last year you were making a run at it, you already believed it was never going to happen for you. So, it wasn't too surprising when that came true."

I wobbled on my shaky legs because it was a lot to take

in. Was my defeatist mentality self-fulfilling? If so, I'd been a hypocrite.

"Too scared of failing to really try," I said.

Clark nodded. He evaluated my unsteady state and shifted uneasily on his feet. "You all right?"

"Yes."

And no, because what Jenna had accused me of was right. I'd taken one look at the uncertainty of my future with Troy and let my fear of failure control me.

Could I break the cycle?

After I left Clark's, I drove home. I didn't eat dinner that night because my appetite was gone.

I put on my swimsuit, grabbed a glass of water, and got into my hot tub. My emotions were a disaster, and as I soaked, I tried to work through everything. What Clark revealed had done a number on me, and I hid from it for a little while beneath the steamy fog rising from my churning spa water.

Down the slope of my lawn, I heard Cassidy's playful scream, followed by a splash and Greg's laugh. They were in the deep end of his pool, and as she hurried to swim away from him, he chased after her. Her escape attempt was half-hearted, and as soon as he caught her, she grinned and kissed him, wrapping her arms around his shoulders.

Life is short, Dr. Lowe had said. *Do what makes*

you happy.

I knew what made me happy. It was the man who filled my head with music.

Troy was young and had made a mistake, but no one was perfect. Certainly not me, who'd let her fear of failure hold her back. And up until today, he'd been pretty damn perfect.

When I got out and toweled off, I saw the text messages he'd sent earlier.

> Troy: I'm sorry.

> Troy: I know you're scared, and you don't believe in us yet, but I can believe enough for the both of us.

When I hadn't responded, he'd sent another later.

> Troy: See you tomorrow.

I arrived at the Bridgestone Arena several hours before the concert, and as I put on my VIP lanyard badge, banging came from the stage. The stage techs were hard at work installing the light screens that would be the backdrop for Stella's show.

It was always strange to be in the space during load-in. The stadium lights were on, illuminating the folding chairs on the floor that were arranged in perfect rows around the engineering booth. Over the stage, the lighting rig was lowered and there were so many wires hooked up, it looked as if it were suspended by a net.

The black color of the stage wasn't as deep with the house lights on. There was no magic in the space . . . at least, not yet. But it whispered of tonight's transformation. It'd be a spectacular production for the twenty thousand screaming fans. Even if only half that crowd filed in to watch Troy's opening act, he'd perform for way more people than I ever had.

A fifteen second sample of Stella's music burst from the speakers, but then the soundcheck cut off. People hollered at others about tasks still needing to be done, and the arena was a symphony of controlled chaos.

Troy would be on that stage in a few hours, and I was so fucking thrilled for him.

I was walking on the outskirts of the floor seats when a golf cart with no roof rumbled by. Ardy was sitting up front with the driver, a guy wearing a black t-shirt with STAFF written in white across the back.

"Hey, kid," Ardy said. "Want a lift?"

I smiled and eagerly climbed into the rear-facing seat. It was going to be a long day, so I'd take every opportunity I could to get off my feet.

"To the bunker, my good man," Ardy said to the driver.

The cart took off, whizzing past the seats and up the banked aisle onto the concourse level. None of the concession stands were open yet, but tables were set up, and the merchandisers were clipping Stella t-shirts to wire displays.

The doors for ticketholders would be opening soon, and nervous energy buzzed in my bloodstream.

I turned sideways in my seat, so it'd be easier for Ardy to hear me. "How's he doing?"

He knew exactly who I was talking about. "Oh, you know. It comes in waves. He reminds me of how Stella was in the beginning. One second she'd be fine, and then the next, she'd have her arms wrapped around a trash can."

This afternoon Warbler had sent a car to pick up Troy, his parents, and his equipment, and I'd gotten notification they'd arrived not long ago. Ardy had been there to greet him and walk him back to the bunker suite where Troy could hang out until his soundchecks.

The cart slowed as it approached a set of double doors, which automatically slid open, and then we whirred down a quiet hall.

"How'd the thing go last night?" I asked. Troy had been invited to dinner with Stella and some of the executives at her record label.

Ardy turned his head so I could see his profile, but his expression was cryptic. "It went good."

I was hoping for more info, but the cart rounded a corner and pulled to a stop. The doors to the private suites lined the wall, and he pointed at the first one. "He's in there." He leaned down and pulled a radio out of the box at his feet and passed it to me. "Anything before six-thirty, text me. After that, we use the comm."

"You got it."

As the cart backed up, turned, and drove off, I clipped the battery pack of the radio to the waist of my pants and hooked the earpiece in. It was quiet now, but give it an hour,

I thought. There'd be a lot of chatter.

When I knocked on the door, Troy's rich voice came from behind it. "Come in."

The suite was called a bunker, and although it was windowless, it felt bright and airy and luxurious. The floors were oak, and the couch and two chairs opposite it were squared off and modern, covered in white leather. Over the bar, a huge television was mounted, and onscreen was a live feed of the stage.

Troy was at the back of the room, sitting at the high table, wearing jeans and a plain white t-shirt, an open can of Coke and his phone in front of him. He turned his head as I came in, and when he saw it was me, he pushed to his feet.

"Hi," he said softly.

I didn't use words. The smile that burst on my face was the biggest of my life.

I'd been happy before.

I'd been thrilled when Clark proposed. Ecstatic when I'd sold 'Reckless.' Elated after performing a huge show.

But this feeling now? It was something completely different.

Maybe you could only reach a certain level of happiness for yourself, but . . . happiness for someone else?

That was limitless. That was *joy*.

Oh, my God. I was going to watch his dream come true tonight, and the emotion I had couldn't be contained. It detonated like a bomb, flooding me with its power.

Troy's gorgeous face filled with worry, and his feet carried him swiftly toward me. "Oh no! Erika, don't cry."

"I'm sorry," I blubbered. I tilted my head back and hurriedly wiped under my eyes, before shaking out my hands like it could dispel my emotion.

His arms wrapped around my waist and his tone was desperate. "Whatever's wrong, it'll be okay."

I laughed softly through my tears because he thought I was upset. "No, I'm crying because I'm so damn happy for you."

He exhaled, and relief washed through his eyes. It continued down through him as I threw my arms around his shoulders, squeezing him tightly. Holding onto him anchored me. It settled my emotions and I sucked in a calming breath.

"Okay," embarrassment tinged my words, "sorry about that. When I saw you, it kind of hit me all at once."

Slowly, I relaxed my hold on him but he didn't let me go, making it so we could look in each other's eyes. His were so deep and beautiful. Next to his hands, they were quickly becoming my favorite part of him, because of the way he used them to look at me.

"I know you've got a million things on your mind," I said, "so let me clear one thing up." I slid my palm down over his shoulder and onto his chest, directly over his heart. "*This* is what I want."

Beneath my hand, the thump of his heart sped up.

My voice was unsteady, but my determination was strong. "I'm sorry I didn't say it before, but I won't give up. I wasn't just scared. After Clark, I was fucking terrified, but you didn't give up on me." I gained strength and power as I spoke. "You don't have to believe for both of us. I'm all in with this." I pressed my hand against his chest, wanting to possess the heart inside. "I'm all in with *you*."

Troy stared at me like he was on total overload, and— shit—had I broken him?

"If that's what you want," I breathed.

His focus drifted beyond me and he cleared his throat. "Mom? Bill? Can y'all give us a minute?"

Every muscle inside me went tense. As soon as I'd seen him, everything else had faded away, and then I'd been in a mad rush to get it all out. I hadn't paid any attention to the rest of the room, or the alcove beside the door where his parents had been sitting.

I stood as a statue in Troy's arms, unable to turn and look at Jenna, who'd basically overheard me tell her son I was in love with him. There was shuffling as they stood.

"We'll just . . . go take some pictures of the stage," Bill said.

I shut my eyes tightly, not opening them until the door clicked closed behind them.

My eyelids were only open for a fraction of a second before they fell closed under the power of Troy's kiss. It was so passionate, new tears stung at the corners of my eyes. He cupped the back of my head and adjusted the angle so he could part my lips with his and slip his tongue against mine.

A noise of satisfaction came from deep in my throat, and he increased the intensity of the kiss. I hadn't said I loved him using those exact words, but it was implied, and he was implying the same thing through this connection.

The world was spinning when his kiss ended. Our lips remained so close, they brushed over each other as we spoke, tasting and sampling like we couldn't get enough.

"In case that didn't make it clear," he whispered, "I want this."

"I thought you were in here alone." I smiled softly. "I might have waited to say all that if I'd known they were on the other side of the room."

"I made them because they were freaking me the fuck out."

The whiskers of his scruff bristled against my fingers as I touched his face. "Are you okay?"

He turned so he could drop a kiss in the center of my palm and gave me a sexy smirk. "I'm much better now." As if I were one hundred percent the reason for it. "You have this power over me. When I get nervous, I tell myself I'm singing only to you, and then I'm good."

Lord, he was killing me. "You can't just say stuff like that." My tone was teasing, even though I was serious. "You're going to make me cry again and my makeup is probably already a mess."

He brushed the pad of his thumb under my eye, probably wiping away a mascara darkened tear track. "Nope. Still the hottest thing I've ever seen."

His gaze skimmed down over my black blouse and black leather pants before landing on my hot pink heels.

"Your lucky shoes," he said.

"Yeah." I grinned. "I wore them for you."

"For us," he corrected.

TWENTY-FOUR

Troy

Black curtains hung across the stage, sectioning off what was already set for Stella's show. The stadium was buzzing with fans. We could hear the crowd from behind the wings, but also see some of them too. The stage was placed at one end of the bowl of the arena, meaning there were cheap seats that only had a view from the sides.

They could see Erika and me waiting together for the show to begin, as well as the stage manager, plus the guitar bay and other equipment. I had her hand wrapped in mine, and she hadn't let go of me since she'd grabbed on, so I figured it was all right. My nerves were getting to me, but I did my best to play it off like it was no big deal. Like I was totally cool with walking onstage and performing for thousands of people, and it wasn't giving me cold sweats.

It'd been a little over an hour since I'd completed my rehearsal walkthrough. I'd carried my guitar to my mark on center stage, strummed a few chords, and tested the beginning of my opening song. It was surreal. The seats were empty, but they'd spread out for miles in all directions, and I'd struggled to catch my breath.

There'd been hardly anyone around to listen to my soundcheck, and those few people who were in the arena had been too busy working to pay much attention to me.

Other than Erika.

She'd been out in the front row because she'd wanted to see what I'd look like up on the stage and give me some feedback. I was glad she'd done it, because it meant she was here in the wings with me now, right before I was set to go on. It also meant she'd be the first one to congratulate me when I was done.

Would she sugarcoat things and tell me I'd done a good job, even if I bombed? Hopefully, I wouldn't find out. The clock was ticking down to showtime, and my stomach was lined with lead. It was a strange fucking feeling to want something so bad, yet also dread it.

I reminded myself how she'd said she was all in with me. No matter what, I'd walk away from tonight with her, so wasn't everything else just a bonus? Didn't I already have exactly what I wanted?

The clock continued to tick.

"Where the hell did the last ninety minutes go?" I grumbled, mostly to myself as I stared at the vacant stage ahead of us.

I thought time had flown by, but Erika had an expression like it had dragged. It probably had for her. There were sections of 'hurry up and wait,' plus, after we'd returned from the soundcheck, my parents were in the suite, and it'd been fucking awkward.

My mom pretended not to notice the tension. She spent twenty minutes FaceTiming with my grandmother, the first five minutes of which made it clear Mimi had no clue how to use FaceTime.

I could tell Erika was still embarrassed my parents had overheard our conversation earlier, but she tried not to show it. She was nothing but a professional, ready to answer any question I had, and focus on helping me prepare. She'd seen both sides as a performer and a manager, and I couldn't imagine anyone being better than her.

Thirty minutes before the show, things got a little easier because there was more to do. She had me practice putting in and taking out my in-ear monitor while playing.

"In case it comes out," she said, "or the sound's too flat."

I pushed the earpiece in, which felt weird and unnatural, and went back to strumming. "Too flat?"

"It cancels everything out, so all you'll hear is your guitar. It might sound like you're performing in an empty room, and if you don't like that, then dump one side."

Even though it'd be dark and the stage lights would be bright, there was no way I'd feel like I was performing to an empty room when I was onstage—because no matter what, she was there. I'd picture Erika in front of me and everything would be okay.

She had me warm up my voice and then I put on the plaid shirt and leather cuff that was my signature look.

During all of this, my parents sat quietly off to the side.

They didn't approve of our relationship, but they understood she was my stand-in manager tonight because Ardy was with Stella, so my parents let Erika do her thing. Fifteen minutes ago, they'd hugged me and left the suite to go find their seats at the front of the house, giving Erika and me a few seconds alone.

If she'd planned to deliver a pep talk to me, I derailed it because I spent our final private moments together kissing her. It was what I wanted, and when I claimed it was the best way to distract me from my nerves, she allowed it.

It worked too.

As soon as I had my mouth on hers, she was all I could think about.

Then, we'd climbed aboard the cart, were transported down the tunnel, and unloaded into the backstage area.

Shit got real as I climbed the short staircase onto the side of the stage.

"Erika," my voice filled with panic, "I don't remember the lyrics."

She paused. "For which song?"

My heart was pounding. "Any of them."

But rather than look alarmed, she smiled. Her warm hands grabbed mine and she pulled me close enough to set her forehead against mine.

"I have climbed," she sang softly, *"the highest mountains."*

Hearing the opening line in her amazing voice was all I needed, and the rest of the lyrics flooded back in a wave of relief. "Okay," I whispered. "I got it."

The guy in charge of equipment appeared and handed me my acoustic guitar, but I kept one hand tangled with Erika's. I wasn't ready to let go of her just yet. The guy's gaze dropped to our linked hands, but his expression didn't change. He didn't care, and disappeared back to his seat beside the guitar bay.

We didn't have to wait long for the stage manager to show up. He was an older, grizzled-looking guy, and had been the one to explain where my marks were during my soundchecks.

He gave me a once-over and a smile. "You all set, man?"

"Yeah." Despite my warmup, my voice was tight, and I cleared my throat.

"Awesome." He pressed the button to his radio, and I heard his voice echo in Erika's earpiece. "We go in one minute."

"Oh, fucking shit," I muttered under my breath. I probably looked pale and clammy, but once I stepped on the stage, I'd be fine.

Erika's hand squeezed mine. "You're going to be incredible," she said. "I'm so happy for you."

It was hard to focus. Inside, I was being pulled in a million different directions, but at her voice, everything snapped into place. I didn't want her to be happy for me . . .

I wanted her to be happy for *us.*

I turned to stare at her. She looked so beautiful tonight. Sexy and powerful, and it wasn't lost on me that this woman was the entire reason I was here. "This is all because of you."

She laughed. "You are giving me way too much credit."

"I'm serious, Erika. I don't just mean the audition. The whole reason I learned to play was to impress you."

"House lights down," the stage manager announced.

My heart continued to beat furiously and blood roared through my ears, but I couldn't hear it. Only the excitement sweeping through the crowd when the arena suddenly darkened, signaling the concert was about to begin.

A smile grew on Erika's lips until she was grinning wildly.

"Well, then . . . go out there and impress me."

It was exactly what I needed to hear. "Yes, ma'am."

TWENTY-FIVE

Erika

Troy took a deep breath, and then he was moving forward in the darkness, carrying his guitar.

Did he know I was right there with him, breath hung painfully in my lungs? I'd done my best to be his strength, and now that he was on stage, the anxiety I'd held at bay ripped through me as an electrical current. It magnetized me in place. I wouldn't be able to move an inch for the next fifteen minutes.

In the low light, I saw his shadowy figure come to the microphone, put the guitar strap over his head, and settle into playing position. The swell of the crowd had faded, the initial excitement over the lights going down had dwindled nearly to a hush.

Troy struck the opening chord in the dark, and as it reverberated through the arena, the audience rose to their feet. The center spotlight burst onto him, bathing him in silvery light, and illuminated the enormous smile on his face. Gone was the boy who'd been nervous moments ago.

This man was a star.

And for the first time, it looked like he knew it.

His fingers moved deftly against the strings as he began the song that had started it all. His stripped-down version of

U2's 'Still Haven't Found What I'm Looking For,' and as soon as the crowd recognized the song, they roared their approval.

God, the *sound* of it.

The way his rich voice rang through the space, rebounding off the balcony level. He crooned into the microphone, singing and playing as if it were the sole purpose he'd been put on this earth to do. But I wasn't sure if that was true.

Maybe his purpose was to be the man I fell in love with.

It wasn't until he finished the last note that I came out of my trance. *One song down, two to go.*

But this was the part he'd confessed he was most nervous about. Warming up the crowd and showing off his personality.

"How y'all doing tonight, Nashville?" he said.

I'd snuck a peek at the crowd when we'd first gotten backstage. Most of the floor seats were full and the rest of the seats in the arena were dotted with people, and it sounded like every one of them answered his question with a scream of excitement.

"My name's Troy Osbourne, and I'm a local boy from right here in the Music City. For those of you who don't know, Stella gave me this amazing opportunity to come out and perform for y'all. Tonight's a special night, and not just for me. It's the last night of her tour, so I want make sure I do both her and our hometown proud." He had the pick in his hand, and it glinted as he used the back of his palm to wipe the sweat from his forehead. "So, what do you say we kick it up a notch? Sing along if you know it. This is 'Midnight Train to Memphis.'"

The song seized me in its grip like the first time I'd heard him preform. The gravel in his low notes was perfectly juxtaposed against the clear beauty on the high ones. His fingers flowed perfectly against the fretboard, and although I could only see a sliver of the audience, the people in it were moving to his music. He easily won them over.

When he finished the song, the crowd cheered much louder and longer.

"I love you, Pool Boy!" a female voice screamed from somewhere near the front.

The sound picked up Troy's nervous laugh, but it came off like he was bashful and not uncomfortable, which only added to his appeal. He put his hand around the microphone, and there was something surprisingly intimate about it. As if he wanted to invite the audience closer.

Only, he turned to look directly at me offstage.

"This final song was written by someone very special to me. I hope y'all enjoy it as much as I do."

Heat tingled across my skin, drawing goosebumps.

I'd written 'Power' for him, but also about us, so this was the moment I'd longed for, ever since telling him I was all in with our relationship. I couldn't wait for him to put our music out into the world.

When he played the opening chords, the key was wrong. The tempo was still slow, but faster than I'd intended it to be.

Wait a minute.

My anticipation had made my brain slow, and as I listened to the music, my mouth hung open in disbelief. Troy was playing a song I'd written all right . . . but it wasn't 'Power.'

"Only with you can I be reckless . . ." he sang.

I wrapped my arms around my body, holding in all my confusion and disappointment. Troy's set list had been confirmed soon after he'd gotten the opening spot. When had it been changed? And, *why*? Had Ardy decided it was better if Troy didn't perform an original and stuck to a song the audience would recognize?

Although this version of 'Reckless' was strikingly different from the one that had been a hit years ago. Alan's single had been upbeat and backed by a band, and he didn't have the vocal range Troy possessed.

Despite my surprise at the song change, my heart still warmed and fluttered at hearing Troy sing my lyrics and play the music I'd written. And his arrangement was so unique, so fresh, it felt like an entirely new song. The vocal runs he put at the end of his phrases gave me chills.

I couldn't tell if he had the rest of the crowd in the palm of his hand like he did me, but I had to assume. How could they witness this and not want to burst inside? It was like he'd boiled the song down to its essence, giving it ten times the power of the original.

Or maybe it sounded so incredible to me because he'd told me he imagined he was singing it just for me. As the song entered the final refrain, my body filled with so much emotion, it couldn't be contained, and tears welled in my eyes.

He stroked the strings one final time, like a musical exhale, and the crowd breathed right along with it, before breaking out into thunderous applause.

"Thank you so much," he said, sounding in awe. "I'm

Troy Osbourne, and it's been a pleasure. Stick around. The Red Door Band will be up here in a few minutes and they're going to keep y'all entertained."

The stage lights faded to black to more applause, and Troy's shadowy figure remained at the microphone until it was over, soaking it all in. Then he turned toward me, took off his guitar, and strode slowly in the dim light to the edge of the curtain. He handed off his guitar to an equipment tech, passing it with care, but also urgency.

It was because as soon as his hands were clear, he scooped me up into them, lifting and spinning me in a half-circle, making me squeak with delighted surprise. He was high from his performance, and he planted his lips over mine long before setting me back on my feet.

"I don't want to wake up from this dream," I whispered.

"Me neither." God, his smile. He kissed me again, threw his arm around my shoulder, and started walking us toward the stairs. "Did you like it?"

I laughed at his ridiculous question, and I wasn't sure if he meant his rendition of 'Reckless' or the performance in general, but the answer was the same for both. "It was incredible."

His chest rose as he took in a satisfied breath and the arm around me squeezed me closer.

When the cart delivered us back to the bunker hallway, Ardy stood in the open doorway to the suite at the other end, and waved at us to come in. As I walked toward the room that was undoubtedly Stella's dressing room, Troy wove his hand through mine.

Ardy watched this, but his expression didn't change, as if he wasn't bothered in the slightest. The stage manager hadn't been fazed by our hand holding earlier, either. Maybe it was because music folks had seen it all and generally were easy-going. It wasn't their business how the music got made; all that mattered was the show went on.

"Great job, kid," Ardy said, gesturing to the suite.

We stepped inside, and although the room was decorated the same as Troy's, the energy was wildly different. It was full of people, most of whom congregated by the table at the back, brimming with fancy appetizers and drinks. Stella sat in a chair in front of the large screen TV while a woman knelt beside her and applied bronzer. Behind her, a man had her long blonde locks rolled in a huge round brush and worked to blow dry it sleek and straight.

"Oh my God, Troy," she exclaimed in a bright voice as soon as she saw him, lifting a hand to signal to her hairstylist to give her a second. The hairdryer cut off. "You were amazing! I got chills." She turned to her makeup artist. "Remember, Lorraine? When I said I had goosebumps?"

The woman nodded in confirmation. "She did."

Troy shook his head as if he couldn't believe it. "Thank you." His tone was full of gratitude he struggled to adequately express. "I can't thank you enough for everything."

Stella scrunched her face in a warm smile. "You're welcome. I loved getting to do it." On screen, the crowd murmured in excitement. The lights had gone down, and the next act was preparing to start their set. She turned her gaze to the TV, but her attention was still with us. "Y'all are welcome to stay and hang out."

Troy wasn't really given a choice. Some of the music executives he'd dined with last night were here in Stella's suite, and they came over to offer their congratulations on the show.

"Do you need anything?" I asked him in the spare seconds we could grab between conversations. "Something to eat or drink?" I gestured to his monitor that was no longer hooked in his ear but hung by the cord around the back of his neck. "Want me to find someone to take that?"

"It's fine," he said quickly.

I smiled knowingly. He'd commented he felt legit when he'd first put it on, and he wasn't ready for that feeling to be over.

His expression suddenly went blank. "My parents."

I nodded. "I'll let them know you're here, and you'll see them after the show."

When I turned to go, he grabbed my wrist. "Wait, Erika . . . it's fine, I can do it."

It was clear he was torn. He wanted to see his folks and he worried this would be awkward for me, but I laughed. I was too happy for him to let anything bring me down.

Plus, today wasn't about me or Jenna or Bill anyway.

"No, you need to be in here. I've got this."

He was reluctant to let me go, but he did.

Outside of the suite, I could hear the frenetic, lively sound of The Red Door Band pumping through the arena. They had a fiddle player that was outstanding and always got the crowd on their feet. It meant I had to knock loudly when I gave a courtesy knock on the door to Troy's suite.

Inside I found Jenna and Bill sitting on the white leather couch, their anxious gazes turned to me.

"Hey there." I strode into the room and gave them a polite smile. "I just wanted to let y'all know Stella invited Troy to hang out with her for a bit, so he'll need to catch up later."

Jenna's disappointment rang through her expression and her shoulders slumped. "Oh."

I took a step closer, feeling the urge to comfort her. "This is a really good opportunity for him to network. Folks from Stella's record label are in there, and they want to chat him up." I gave her an understanding look. "He's eager to see you too."

Bill set his hand reassuringly on his wife's knee. "It's okay. We can see him after."

Jenna's gaze drifted from her husband over to me, and emotion teemed in her eyes. "I wanted to tell him how proud we are of him." She pressed her hand to her chest, her fingers toying absentmindedly with the lanyard to her VIP badge. "Will you tell him for us?"

The way she asked was hopeful and sweet, and it was as if she wouldn't trust hardly anyone else to deliver this important message . . . but she trusted *me*.

I swallowed a breath and nodded. "Of course." I cleared my throat, trying to disguise how affected I was. "Did you enjoy the show?"

I'd expected them to say yes, to gush about how amazing their son had been. Although I wouldn't have traded being backstage with him for anything, I was a little envious they'd gotten to experience his performance from the crowd.

What I hadn't expected was Jenna to leap from the couch, run at me, and crush me in a hug so powerful it was hard to breathe. The force of it made me stumble back a step.

"I'm sorry," she cried, squeezing me fiercely. "I didn't mean the awful things I said to you." When she relented and pulled back, she had to wipe away her tears. "I was so scared I was going to lose him."

I heard what she meant, the unspoken words she'd left off the end of her statement. She was scared she was going to lose Troy the way she'd lost his father. I'd never met Brett Osbourne, but he'd abandoned Jenna not long after their son had been born. He'd walked away, she'd said, because he wouldn't be tied down. He didn't care about anyone but himself.

My heart ached for my friend.

But didn't she know Troy would never walk away? That he was nothing like the man he shared DNA with? He was much more like his true father—the sweet man who was sitting silently on the couch, trying his damnedest not to get emotional. Seeing his wife upset got Bill *every* time.

"You're not going to lose him," I said.

"I don't want to lose you either," she said. "I handled it badly, but I'll try to do better, I promise. Please forgive me."

I blinked, stunned. She'd said hurtful things, but I wasn't blameless either. "And I'm sorry I lied to you. Can forgive me?"

She considered my statement thoughtfully. "I don't want to be kept in the dark anymore, Erika."

Hope sparked inside me that our friendship wasn't too

damaged to recover. "Yes, you got it."

"Are you in love with him?" she whispered.

I jolted. How the hell was I supposed to answer that? "Uh . . ."

"Because he's in love with you." She straightened and smoothed her hands down her pants, like she could wipe away the heavy emotion that easily. "I'm sorry, but you can't expect me to be happy about that. You're a lot older than him, and I'm going to need some time to be . . . less uncomfortable with the idea of you with my son."

"I understand."

Her shoulders lifted on a deep breath. "All I want is for him to be happy, and you've made his dream come true. Happier than anyone else. So . . . I can tell you I'll try. I can *try* to be okay with this. All right?"

I was too floored to say anything. I simply blinked in shock.

She nodded like I'd agreed with her. "Good." She'd said her piece, and her emotions turned on a dime. Excitement lurked in her eyes. "Let's go, Bill. I want to get back to our seats before Stella's show starts."

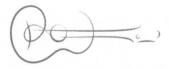

I found Troy sitting in the alcove of Stella's suite, deep in conversation with Ardy, but when I appeared, both men fell silent. It was odd, like they'd been talking about me. I took a seat on the bench beside Troy and gave them both a suspicious look.

Troy was oblivious. "Everything go okay with my folks?"

I nodded. "It went great. Like, really great." I couldn't wait to explain it to him later. "They're so proud of you."

There'd been tension in his shoulders, and it eased somewhat, but it didn't disappear altogether.

I tilted my head. "What are you two scheming about over here?"

Ardy chuckled. "No schemes. We were talking about his take on 'Reckless.' I wasn't sure about it, but the kid made a believer out of me."

My mouth went dry as I stared at Troy. I was terrified to ask it, because a big part of me didn't want to know the answer. "You wanted to sing 'Reckless' over 'Power?'"

But Ardy answered before Troy could, and his tone was dismissive. "'Power' wasn't the right choice for his set."

"What?" Heat flared inside me. Was this yet another decision that had been made on Troy's behalf without consulting him? Had he sung 'Reckless' because his new manager had ordered him to?

"Did you like the arrangement?" Ardy asked. "From what I heard, these two," he pointed to Stella, still in her makeup chair, and then Troy, "stayed up all night working on it. They wanted it to be a surprise for you."

I was grateful to be sitting down, because when the meaning of his statement hit me, I nearly fell over. *This* was what Troy had been doing over at Stella's place. He'd told me they'd hung out in her studio, playing music.

They'd been working on his rendition of 'Reckless.'

Was this why he'd lied? He'd wanted to keep it a surprise? It was a lot to process. When I peered at Troy, his eyes were cryptic. What was he thinking about?

"Yeah," I said between hurried breaths, "I loved it."

"Good." Ardy was pleased to have that settled. "He recorded it. I'm not his manager anymore, but I'd suggest putting it on his debut."

My head spun, making me dizzy. "Wait, *what*? You're quitting?"

"No," Troy said. "I, um . . ."

Ardy let out an actual giggle, finding it that hilarious. "He fired me."

I'd been upset with my boss, but it swung wildly toward my boyfriend. "What are you doing?"

"Apparently," Ardy said, stroking a hand over his beard, "the kid doesn't want me as a manager, he wants you. I'm inclined to give my artists what they want, because otherwise they get sad, and sad artists don't make as much money—which then makes me very sad."

My heart pounded in my ears, drowning out the rest of the room.

I had my hand closest to Troy resting on the bench, and he set his beside mine, our pinkie fingers touching. This simple gesture was somehow more powerful than anything else. He wanted to connect with me, but he also wanted to keep it professional.

Although I was beginning to doubt anyone would care. Romantic relationships between managers and artists weren't unheard of. If Ardy had no issue with us dating and working together, others would follow his lead.

Troy's eyes scoured my face, searching for my reaction, but I was too shocked to have one.

Ardy sensed the enormity of the conversation brewing and rose from his seat. "Excuse me, I'm going to check on Stella."

When he moved out of earshot, Troy's voice turned quiet, but it was still strong and powerful. "You said you're all in, so let's be all in together. I'm not doing it without you."

This handsome, talented man was willing to give up everything, once again, just for a chance with me.

"I want this," he continued. "Don't act like you don't too." His expression was so focused and determined, it made my pulse race. He leaned closer. "Yeah, it might not be easy, but I won't give up." He moved his hand, so it covered mine. "So, trust me, Erika, and say yes."

He was right. I wanted this. I wanted him personally and professionally, and the only thing holding me back was my fear. I wasn't going to let it stop me this time. My answer came quickly and sure. "Yes."

His grin lit up his entire face.

Once again, Troy and I stood in the wings, our hands laced together, only this time there was a lot more room since the backdrop curtain had been lifted. Nearby, Ardy was gathered with the rest of Stella's team, watching her final show.

The stage was bathed in bright strobing lights, and ahead of us, Stella strutted toward the crowd, flinging her hair over her shoulder as she sang into the sparkly mic in her hand. Her opening number had been one of her first crossover hits, and now she was performing the song 'Inferior' from her newest album, which was pure pop. The infectious tune was about a boyfriend who made her feel small to build himself up. It had a wicked hook, asking who was inferior now?

Not her, with a multi-platinum album and two Grammys to her name.

And she'd stayed grounded and gracious through it. It gave me so much hope for my boyfriend. He'd be a star like her someday, I just knew it.

Troy leaned over and had to shout it in my ear over the deafening music. "I have a question for you."

"What?"

"I have a question," he repeated, louder.

I shook my head. "No, I mean, what's your question?"

"Can I change some of the lyrics in 'Power?'"

He wanted to ask me this now? "Yeah," I shouted back. "It's your song, if you want to—"

"Cool," he announced. "I'll be right back."

He dropped my hand and strode forward, picking his earpiece up off his shoulder to wedge it back in his ear. The same equipment tech from before appeared with Troy's guitar, and after a quick exchange, Troy nodded and took it.

Onstage, Stella's song came to its end and while the

sold-out crowd of twenty thousand screamed, hyperaware-
ness rolled through me. What was going on?

"What's up, Nashville?" Stella asked, her voice flooding
the arena.

She barely sounded out of breath, even as she'd sung and
danced the hell out of her last number. The lighting changed
and softened from the harsh red to a subdued blue, and as
she spoke, the center section of the stage behind her began
to rise, stacking into a set of giant steps.

"This is such a bittersweet night for me," she continued,
"because this tour has been an amazing experience and now
that it's almost over, well, gosh . . . I wish it could last forever.
You know I have the greatest fans in the world, and I'm so
blessed and honored y'all are here." She clasped both of her
hands around the wireless microphone. "So, I want to make
tonight as special for y'all as it is for me, and debut something
original. You'll be the first to hear it. How does that sound?"

The crowd agreed, roaring so loud I felt it in my bones.

"I need some help though," she said. "Y'all remember
Troy Osbourne, don't you?" She cast her arm out to the side
of the stage, welcoming him to join her.

I lifted my hand, covering my gasp, not that anyone
would have been able to hear it. I stared in disbelief as he
strolled confidently onstage to cheers from the audience,
going directly to the microphone stand on the near side. It
must have risen with the stairs, which were graduated in
different hues of blue light now. As he readied his guitar,
she climbed the first few steps, and sat, her glittering skirt
draped around her.

With a subtle nod, she told him she was set.

There'd been maybe nine thousand people in the arena at the time he'd sang 'Reckless,' instead of the song I'd hoped for. Now, as he began playing the intro to 'Power,' it was for the entire sold-out concert and my knees went weak. Twenty thousand people would hear our song.

Dear God, everything was more intense when he began to sing. The opening verse was his alone, full of smoke and smolder, and when he hit the chorus, Stella joined him in harmony. It elevated the slow, sultry love song, and it was so beautiful, my bottom lip shook.

She sang the lead in the second verse while he played, and his carefully placed accompaniment was perfect. I hadn't thought of the song as a duet before, but now I didn't want it to be anything else.

He crooned to the audience about desire and being lured in to capture, and not wanting to break free. About the power his lover held over him. And when he came to the bridge, I discovered the lyrics he wanted to change.

"If I said how much I loved you, would you say you loved me too?"

If I wasn't already in love with him, I sure the hell was now.

Through the last note and the audience's cheering, an eagerness began to swell inside me, because I knew what was going to happen when he was done and I was desperate for it. He thanked the audience and Stella, said his goodbye, and then exited the stage.

My heart was in my throat as he stalked toward me, took out his in-ear monitor, and handed off his guitar to someone.

Anyone. It probably wasn't the right person, but it didn't matter. His focus was only on me, and mine was only on him.

"If I said how much I loved you," I repeated, "would you say you loved me too?"

The electricity crackled between us. He knew I wasn't reciting the lyric, and he was thrilled to answer my question. "Yes, ma'am."

"Then, I love you," I said.

He grinned, grabbed me by the waist, and pulled me tight against him. "These shoes you've got on really are lucky."

My mouth dropped open, but he laughed, and whispered it just before Stella's next song started.

"I love you too."

TWENTY-SIX

Troy

Erika glared at me, fire burning in her eyes. "I hate you."

"Sure you do, but you have twenty more seconds."

She was in a squat position and had a black battling rope in each hand, waving them in ripples against the mat. The loud, rhythmic pounding of them echoed through the empty high-intensity training room of the gym, and it matched the rock song streaming from her phone nearby.

I thought about making a comment about how much I liked her form, but I also wasn't stupid. She'd rage-quit our workout, and I didn't want this to end with her in a bad mood.

"Ten, nine, eight . . ." I counted down for her.

We'd discovered she liked bossing me around in bed, and I liked bossing her around in the gym. I'd quit my job as an instructor once my advance from the record label had cleared, but three times a week I met my girlfriend-slash-manager at the gym, and she let me do whatever I wanted to her.

Today was upper body with a side of cardio.

". . . three, two, one. Good job."

She tossed the ropes aside in a huff, put her hands on her hips, and paced a circle on the mat as she struggled to catch her breath. Did she have any idea how hot she looked right now? Her fitted tank top and sports bra beneath seemed designed to tease me with her cleavage, and her tight leggings flaunted her ass that, as I'd explained to her, was made for trouble.

"You suck," she growled, picking up her water bottle off the floor and unscrewing the cap.

I smirked.

Once she'd finished recovering, the endorphins would kick in and she'd be pumped about finishing such a challenging workout. Meanwhile, I considered the fastest way to peel her out of her clothes as she drank her water. It'd been four months since the best night of my life—when she'd said she loved me—and my desire for her had only gotten stronger over that time.

She'd written me six new songs too. More than half the album would be her words. The rest of the songwriting had been collaborations between us, or with Stella. I couldn't wait to release it.

"Did you finish packing?" she asked.

"I packed my guitar. Do I need anything else?"

I was joking, but she was not amused. We were on a flight this afternoon to L.A., where I'd meet up with Stella and shoot the music video for 'Power.' It'd be the first single, and the hope was Stella's accompaniment would launch my debut record.

Erika's voice turned seductive. "Well, as much as I like seeing you perform naked, you can't. That show's only for me."

She strolled to me and stroked a hand over my bare bicep. Just her touch made lust coil in my body, which was a problem. My gym shorts did fuck-all to conceal a boner.

"Yes, I'm packed," I said. It'd been easy because I'd barely finished moving into my new apartment and was sort of living out of a suitcase anyway. I spent a lot of nights at her place.

Last night, we'd fucked in her hot tub, the steam rising from our bodies into the cold winter air. Afterward, I'd tossed some shock into the water out of habit. She'd hired a new guy to take over maintaining her pool and spa, but he was married and in his late fifties, and she said she'd make sure she'd keep his schedule in mind whenever she got the urge to sunbathe topless.

"So, what you're saying is," she drawled, "you don't need to rush home."

Had my session not been enough for her? My tone was skeptical. "You want to work out some more?"

A sexy smile burned across her lips. "Kind of."

Oh.

Well, I was down. I was always down with her. Since no one else was in the HITT room, I put my hand on her ass and squeezed until her eyes lidded with desire. My voice was low. "What'd you have in mind?"

I was expecting her to invite me back to her place, but I wasn't thinking big enough. My girl was full of surprises.

"I'm thinking about the time you kissed me against the mirror." She pushed her hands up under my shirt, setting her warm palms against my chest. "How we both wanted to do more, but didn't have time."

My laugh was sinful and my voice full of sex. "We got time now."

"So," her fingertips trailed along my abdominals, tracing every inch, "if I asked you to fuck me in the dressing room, what would you say?"

I grinned. "I'd say yes, ma'am."

I'd always say yes to her.

MORE BY NIKKI SLOANE

THE BLINDFOLD CLUB SERIES
Three Simple Rules
Three Hard Lessons
Three Little Mistakes
Three Dirty Secrets
Three Sweet Nothings
Three Guilty Pleasures
One More Rule

THE SORDID SERIES
Sordid
Torrid
Destroy

SPORTS ROMANCE
The Rivalry

THE NASHVILLE NEIGHBORHOOD
The Doctor
The Pool Boy
The Architect

FILTHY RICH AMERICANS
The Initiation | The Obsession | The Deception
The Redemption
The Temptation

THANK YOUs AND FUCK YOUs

My husband is all the things. He's my rock of support, the glue holding our family together, and the love of my life. Thank you for lifting me up when I was down and helping me get this book over the finish line.

Thank you to Nina Grinstead, Aubrey Bondurant, Rebecca Nebel, and Veronica Larsen for listening when I was struggling.

Thank you to my team of editors, Andrea Lefkowitz, Becky Barney, and Toni Rakestraw (and Lori Whitwam for her help connecting us) for working miracles under an impossible deadline and garbage drafts.

Thank you to all my readers, bloggers, and fellow authors. You are the bright spot in my day, which is desperately needed these days! Thanks for reminding me just how lucky I am I get to chase my dreams.

And lastly, fuck you to COVID-19 and the year 2020. Writing a book when the world was on fire really freaking sucked.

ABOUT THE AUTHOR

USA Today bestselling author Nikki Sloane landed in graphic design after her careers as a waitress, a screenwriter, and a ballroom dance instructor fell through. Now she writes full-time and lives in Kentucky with her husband, two sons, and a pug who is more slug than dog.

She is a three-time Romance Writers of America RITA© Finalist, a Passionate Plume winner, a Goodreads Choice Awards semifinalist, and couldn't be any happier that people enjoy reading her sexy words.

www.NikkiSloane.com

www.twitter.com/AuthorNSloane

www.facebook.com/NikkiSloaneAuthor

www.instagram.com/nikkisloane

CPSIA information can be obtained
at www.ICGtesting.com
Printed in the USA
BVHW031751220123
656847BV00016B/210